Welcome to Puddling-on-the-Wold, where the sons and daughters of Victorian nobility come for a little rest, recuperation, and "rehab," in this brand-new series of rebellious romance from Maggie Robinson.

After a harrowing tour of duty abroad, Captain Lord Henry Challoner fought to keep his memories at bay with two of his preferred vices: liquor and ladies. But the gin did more harm than good—as did Henry's romantic entanglements, since he was supposed to be finding a suitable bride. Next stop: The tiny village in Gloucestershire, where Henry can finally sober up without distraction or temptation. Or so he thinks…

A simple country schoolteacher, Rachel Everett was never meant to cross paths with a gentleman such as Henry. What could such a worldly man ever see in her? As it turns out, everything. Beautiful, fiercely intelligent Rachel is Henry's dream woman—and wife. Such a match would be scandalous for his family of course, and Rachel has no business meddling with a resident at the famed, rather draconian, Puddling Rehabilitation Foundation. All the better, for two lost souls with nothing to lose—and oh so very much to gain.

Books by Maggie Robinson

Cotswold Confidential Series

Schooling the Viscount

The London List Series

Lord Gray's List
Captain Durant's Countess
Lady Anne's Lover

The Courtesan Court Series

Mistress by Mistake
"Not Quite a Courtesan" in *Lords of Passion*
Mistress by Midnight
Mistress by Marriage
Master of Sin

Novellas

"To Match a Thief" in *Improper Gentleman*

Published by Kensington Publishing Corporation

Schooling the Viscount

Cotswold Confidential

Maggie Robinson

LYRICAL PRESS
Kensington Publishing Corp.
www.kensingtonbooks.com

Chapter 1

It was a cosmic joke. Exiled to a Cotswold village, the most candy-box, utterly banal sort of burgh one could ever hope to find, with a name fit for a nursery rhyme. Rolling hills, sun-kissed stone, front gardens and window boxes bursting with the kind of vegetation which would have kept the maddest gardener up all night in delight.

There had been other exiles, he knew. Apparently this Puddling-place was some sort of a secret reformation spot. A health spa without the filthy-tasting mineral water. A Bath without Bath chairs and Roman ruins.

Despite his infirmities, he was plenty healthy, thank you very much. He'd spent his first week marching up and down the streets—all five of them—staring into the faces of passers-by, wondering who else was subject to his current indignity. Visiting each shop—all five of *them*. Peering into cottage windows that overlooked the cobbled road—you couldn't help but look in. He saw polite, bland inhabitants, seemingly happy to be living in a place time forgot.

One hardly knew that this was the late nineteenth century, for God's sake. Newspapers always were sold out when he came around to the combination Post Office and grocery on Market Street. There was not a modern invention to be found—no local train, no telegraph towers. Or burlesque girls. He was completely cut off from the world as he knew it, except for his daily afternoon tea with the vicar.

Tea. Vicar. Two words usually not in his vocabulary.

All of the Puddling people looked innocent. Jolly and clean. Untouched by any kind of debauchery or depravity. Well, that's what fresh air and an excess of sheep and sleep did for one, he supposed. Any kind of conversation with the local specimens had resulted in a boredom so profound he was tempted to stick a fork in his working eardrum.

He wasn't going to let Puddling-on-the-Wold change him one iota. This petunia-scented imprisonment couldn't last forever. The pater would eventually relent and allow him back to Town. All he had to do was steer clear of trouble and look sufficiently saved in front of the vicar. Born again. Slayer of his demons and ready to do battle as one of Britain's young hopes.

Faugh. He'd tried that in South Africa, and where had that led? Ten short brutal weeks of war, his disfigurement and a dependency on drink and the occasional opium pipe.

And women. Lovely, curvy, wanton women, none of them candidates to follow in his late mother's footsteps as the next Marchioness of Harland, not that he wanted his pater the marquess to pop off any time soon, no matter how draconian his father had been sentencing him to live in this blasted storybook village.

Captain Lord Henry Challoner had some heart, after all.

Henry wasn't really a captain any more, although the paperwork hadn't quite caught up to him. He shouldn't have been one in the first place. Hadn't done much to deserve it. Men he'd commanded had died, and he himself had wound up captured with those who lived in a barn not fit for a flea-bitten jackass. There were no jackasses in the veld as far as Henry knew.

Besides himself.

He was on his required damned daily walk this bloody beautiful spring afternoon, equipped with a stout staff that wasn't purely decorative. He'd been shot in the foot—thankfully, he hadn't done it to himself or that really would have been *the* cosmic joke—and would probably limp for the rest of his life.

Henry supposed he was lucky he still had a foot; the Boer farmers who'd briefly held him prisoner after the ambush had not been surgically adept. Now, if he'd been about to calve—

The absurdity of his train of thought made him laugh out loud. He hadn't laughed in a week, and the sound startled him. A bird trilled loudly enough for him to hear it from the clipped hedgerow, a temperate sun shone serenely overhead in the cloudless sky, and Henry wanted to raise his stick in revolt.

Puddling-in-the-Wold was just too perfect. Each stone cottage was snug, each little shop stocked with exactly what one would want, providing one had taken a temperance pledge. There were no alcoholic spirits on offer—Henry had inquired everywhere. His bribes and blandishments had been useless. The entire town was teetotal.

Even the Communion wine in the little Norman church appeared to be grape juice, and watered down at that. Moderation was all very well, but abstention? Henry shuddered.

Perhaps there were some berries in a bush he could ferment somehow. Wine was made with dandelion weeds, wasn't it? Being a viscount, he knew nothing about cookery, but knew better than to ask Mrs. Grace, his current housekeeper. She'd come with the cottage he'd been assigned, and was implacable in regards to his health and diet. It was as if he was back in the nursery again with Nanny, with wholesome soups and scrambled eggs and stewed fruit.

At five and twenty, he was too old to be treated like a child, no matter how childish he'd been. He'd been in his African garrison for years keeping the Zulus and the Boers at bay. Bad enough Chelmsford had invaded the Zulu territory without the authorization of the British government, resulting in the bloodiest battles imaginable, but then the idiots at Whitehall decided to annex the Transvaal Republic to stir up the Boers. Henry had done his duty on both fronts, and he wanted a roast, by God, and horseradish sauce. New potatoes larded with butter and parsley. Sponge cake filled with jam. Apricots in brandy. Something rich and delicious he could sink his teeth into, since he was no longer nibbling on any slender necks. In the week he'd been here, he'd not seen one woman in the village under fifty, and he'd looked.

Hard.

But hold on. He heard children singing up ahead as he stumbled down the ever-narrowing lane that looked like it led to freedom from the Puddling Valley. Beyond was a perfect green hill and perfect white sheep, wide open spaces without a cottage in sight.

If there were children, there had to be mothers, right? Women of childbearing age were youngish, and perhaps one of them was a lonely widow. Henry made an effort to trot a little faster, gritting his teeth at the grinding pain in his foot.

He hadn't come this way before. He was, in fact, breaking a rule. There was a fixed itinerary for his walk, and he wasn't on it. Take that, Puddling prison guards!

Rounding a corner, there was before him a gated stone wall, and beyond it a stone schoolhouse, with perhaps a dozen urchins dancing about in a circle in the grassy field. Henry's own dancing days were finished, but he could appreciate the enthusiasm and joy before him, and he leaned on his stick to watch.

He was spotted immediately by a towheaded girl of about six, who pointed and screamed. Even with his hearing loss, he was impressed with the infant's lung power. He hadn't had a reception like that since his father Arthur Challoner, the Marquess of Harland, discovered Lysette LaRue and Francie Jones in his bedroom at Harland House a week ago.

Henry should not have brought the girls home. He'd still be carousing in London, smoking and drinking and dining and trying to forget if he'd only kept his pants buttoned. Sneaking Lysette and Francie in had been the last straw, and the pater had had enough. Hero or not —and Henry really wasn't— Something Had To Be Done.

Hence Puddling and rehabilitation. That same morning, Henry had been bundled up without his valet and incarcerated in the ancient Harland travel coach, his father blistering him verbally the many miles it took to reach this godforsaken place. Henry was almost grateful for the partial deafness in his right ear—he'd been a little too close to a jammed cannon, and when it unjammed, the damn thing let him down in the most audible way.

He had been much better off with his Martini-Henry singleshot rifle, although in his opinion, the British army had been damn poorly outfitted all the way around. Much of the weaponry was obsolete, and it wasn't very strategic to pop up on the dusty plain in bright red uniforms. The filthy, khaki-covered farmers they'd fought against for a short but hideous two months had been expert marksmen, bruising riders, and determined to maintain their independence by any means necessary.

So now Henry was half-deaf *and* half-lame. Delightful.

He knew there must be train service to this part of the world, but then his father would have been deprived of his limitless lecture if he'd purchased two tickets. Upon arrival, the pater had met with the vicar in the Rifle and Roses—whoever heard of a pub that sold no ale? Or, for that matter, a vicar who did business in a pub?—while Henry was confined to the carriage, practically in handcuffs. His head had been too sore to object to his treatment, and he knew he deserved it on some level. Almost welcomed it.

He was a disappointment, and he was tired of himself beyond belief.

It seemed he was some sort of devil as well. The shrieking child before him acted as if he had horns. Henry ran a hand through his hatless blond hair to make sure none had sprouted up.

Someone stepped out the schoolhouse door at the commotion. A female someone, who was not over fifty. Henry felt his heart leap.

She was dark-haired and rosy-cheeked, built along sturdy country lines, ample of hip and bosom and the most luscious thing he'd seen since he'd arrived. Henry grinned.

The screaming continued. Did he have a spinach leaf from his nutritious but dull lunch stuck in his teeth?

"Now, Mary Ann, be quiet. It's just one of our Guests," the young woman murmured in a low, soothing voice. She knelt in front of the little girl as the rest of the students gave Henry the stink-eye.

"Good afternoon." His voice was rusty, unused except when falsely complimenting Mrs. Grace on her culinary skills or inquiring everywhere about alcohol, although he'd given that up after the third day. Henry's conversations with the vicar every afternoon were mostly one-sided, and the side wasn't his.

The children stared back at him, silent. Had they been warned about him? As far as he knew, he'd never hurt a child. Hurt men, yes, but that was his job. He'd been in the army for six years, much to his father's displeasure, and he'd killed a lot of people one way or another.

"I'm relatively harmless. You don't have to be afraid." *Harmless Henry.* There was a certain ring to it, even if it was untrue.

The young woman rose and took Mary Ann by the hand. "Say good afternoon, sweetheart. We must be polite to our Guests."

What was this guest business? If Henry was being entertained in any way by the Puddling populace, they were doing a piss-poor job of it.

Chapter 2

Drat. Rachel Everett bit her lip. Lord Challoner was not supposed to see her. Up until today, he'd been methodical in his afternoon perambulation, following his prescribed schedule, turning left at his gate and wandering about the steep, twisting village streets aimlessly for an hour just as he was supposed to. Reports were that he looked cross and uncomfortable, which was the normal course of events for Puddling-on-the-Wold's special Guests.

Things were always hard in the beginning. There was resentment, and, very occasionally, some violence. The poor vicar and those before him had survived many a tossed teacup— and worse.

The school was difficult to find, tucked away in a field near the bottom end of the hilly village, and not on Lord Challoner's map. Rachel knew he had been strictly forbidden to leave the area—he hadn't much money, and the nearest train station was five miles away. A walk of that distance was not impossible, but a man with his injury would find it unpleasant.

Likely he would have a hard time getting back up the lane to his cottage today and might even need assistance. Everyone in Greater Puddling-on-the-Wold had been informed of his residence and would be on the lookout for any difficulty or irregularity.

Like escape. It *had* happened. In 1807, a duke's daughter smuggled herself out of town in a laundry hamper. The Sykes family, with whom she had lodged, were still living down the breach in security, although Lady Maribel had married Sir Colin Sykes so that had turned out all right in the end. And in 1854, an unfortunate Guest had climbed the church's bell tower in a poorly-planned attempt to fly. Umbrellas had not been designed for such a purpose, even if he'd sported two of them. The young man had been coaxed down carefully and sent to Bethlem Hospital, which was better equipped to deal with his avian ambitions.

Or so the people of Puddling-on-the-Wold hoped. Treatment methods had evolved over the decades, and there had not been an Incident in quite a while. The vicar kept a full accounting of the many success stories achieved in the last seventy-odd years by his predecessors. Their Guests had grown up, gotten married, become fathers and mothers. Most were respectably settled. Pillars of society. Their youthful follies were behind them, their families forever grateful. The coffers of Puddling-on-the-Wold were full, and each resident received a generous bonus every year just for living within the village's boundary lines, whether they were instrumental in a Guest's recovery or not.

And that was crucial to the well-being of the town. The North had siphoned off the wool trade, and crop prices had been depressed—like some of their Guests—since before Rachel was born. There was no industry hereabouts but a small group of mad potters and furniture makers who were trying to redesign the art world. They contributed nothing to the economy of Puddling save for misshaped mugs and uncomfortable chairs for the church fete. Puddlingites bought them out of pity.

Each Guest required an individual program, and Rachel Everett was *not* on Lord Challoner's. He was meant to avoid female companionship, which had been somewhat awkward to arrange. Eventually the younger women of Puddling would be allowed out of their houses and back into the church and shops, but for the first two weeks of his stay Henry Challoner was to remain unaware of their existence during his walks until his carnal appetites were cooled and under control.

The poor man was a sexual deviant. Addicted to spirits and drugs too. Rachel imagined his war experiences had left him shattered, and had some sympathy. She'd heard her own father had spent far too many hours in the Rifle and Roses after the Crimean War.

The entire town was anxious to see the back of young Lord Challoner so the pub could open its taps again. It didn't seem quite fair to some of the residents that they should have to suffer right along with their Guests, but sacrifices had to be made. Excessive drinking was a very common problem among the beau monde.

At least they were not still hosting poor Greta Holmes-Hamilton, who had been sent to Puddling on a slimming regimen before her wedding. Rachel had missed the bake shop very much during the three months it had closed during Greta's visit. It was much more convenient to buy treats than to bake for herself and her father, but Rachel had sealed up the windows of their cottage with dish towels so Greta wouldn't smell the cinnamon rolls as she happened to pass by on *her* daily walk.

Greta had been a vision in her bridal gown. The vicar had clipped the photograph out of *The Times* for the villagers to see, although she was not smiling in it. The poor girl was probably forbidden to eat her own wedding cake. From the conversations Rachel had with Greta, Mrs. Holmes-Hamilton was something of a martinet when it came to organizing Greta's life.

But Greta was gone now, hopefully to domestic bliss, and here was someone else in her place.

"Tom, you may ring the bell. Children, you are dismissed."

It was only ten or so minutes before the usual time. The children reentered the schoolhouse for their lunch pails and belongings, then skipped away through the gate in the wall, scattering uphill through the village. A few glanced backward at the Guest and their teacher, who faced each other over the golden Cotswold stone.

"Allow me to introduce myself," he began.

"I know who you are," Rachel said, making him sound like Dr. William Palmer, the Prince of Poisoners. It was imperative that she freeze him out and send him back where he came from. In another week she might nod coldly if she encountered him, but not yet.

"Then you have an advantage. Everyone's in on this caper, yes?"

Rachel tried to make her eyebrows ripple into one dark caterpillar. "I don't understand what you mean."

"All of you Puddling persons are in this together. It's like one charming, open-air jail, with each of you acting as coppers. I finally read my so-called Welcome Packet. I thought at first it was just the vicar chap and Mrs. Grace, but I'm beginning to see the error of my ways."

If only he were. But it was much too soon. Guests stayed a minimum of twenty-eight days, and some took much longer to take the Cure and perform their Service.

"I'm sorry, Lord Challoner, but I must get back to grading papers. Good day." Rachel turned to go, but as she did, Lord Challoner, using his stick for leverage, leaped over the low stone wall. He stumbled upon landing and fell in a well-tailored heap at her feet.

"Damn," he muttered, spitting out a blade of grass, "I should have used the gate."

"You should have gone home!" Rachel said with asperity. She reached a hand down to help him up.

And promptly found herself pulled down into his lap.

"If anyone sees us—" she hissed, punching his shoulder. Her blows were ineffective. He seemed to be made of marble and just grinned at her like one of her naughtier students. Only they would never dream of cuddling her in such a shocking way!

"No chance of that, unless there are Puddling pigeons flying over us, and the sheep over there don't care, I'm sure. You are lovely when you are angry. Forgive me, I just couldn't help myself. There you were, above me like a solemn angel, offering succor. What could I do but reach for perfection? I simply forgot myself."

He took a great gulp of air. "By Jove, you smell like an angel too. Wisteria. Cloves. Pencil shavings. Ah, ambrosia."

The man was ridiculous.

"When was the last time you encountered an angel, Lord Challoner? In some music hall? I am not that sort of woman."

"No, more's the pity. I suppose you want to get up." He sighed, the breath tickling her ear in the oddest way. "I've never held a woman against her will before."

Rachel could see why not—he was too handsome for his own good, not that *she* was moved in the least. Women of weaker virtue were bound to be quivering masses of feminine jelly after one smile. "Well, you're doing so now. Unhand me."

"But of course. You didn't get hurt when you fell, did you? Perhaps I should examine you for broken bones." One fingertip touched her cheek.

"I'm not the one who fell, you…you…"

"Rascal?" he asked hopefully. "I have been called worse."

Rachel never cursed, but she was very close to that now. And the more she struggled to regain her footing, the odder Lord Challoner's expression became.

"I'm so sorry," he said. Then he kissed her.

Rachel had been kissed before. When she was sixteen, she'd been terribly in love with Sir Bertram Sykes's younger son Wallace, grandson of the wicked duke's daughter Maribel, who had tested Puddling's resolve more than Napoleon ever did. Wallace had kissed her—clumsily—behind the dunking booth at the St. Jude church fete before he went off to university.

She never saw him again. The poor boy had died of influenza during Michaelmas term.

There was not a surplus of young men in Puddling-on-the-Wold. Young women, either. Most did not want to stay and restrict themselves to the village's peculiar customs of closed pubs, closed bakeshops and closed minds. They went off to school, to war, to London. Rachel couldn't blame them—if she didn't have her ancient father to care for, she would go too.

So she was here. Being kissed. She didn't have much to compare it to. Lord Challoner's lips were firm and dry. He smelled good, not of wisteria and pencil shavings, but of some expensive, manly cologne she was unfamiliar with. Then he did something at the seam of her lips with his tongue—his tongue!—and she was so surprised she opened her eyes and mouth to yell.

That was ill-conceived. His tongue was now touching hers in the most unsettling way, warm and swooping. Rachel had to shut her eyes so she wouldn't go cross-eyed. But before she closed them, she noted Lord Challoner had very blond, very long eyelashes, which flicked every time his tongue did that twisty thing inside her mouth.

Oh dear. This went against all his treatment plans. Why, she was probably setting him back in his recovery and his father the Marquess of Harland would ask for a refund.

Rachel was becoming an enabler of an Incident. So she did what she had to do and slapped poor Henry Challoner's face even if she didn't want to.

At all.

Chapter 3

Sweet God, but she was lovely. Delicious. She tasted of spearmint and was soft as a cloud on his lap.

Not that she was at all wispy. Her bottom was plump and every time she wiggled, his cock jolted to attention. It had taken Francie and Lysette a great deal of anxious maneuvering to jolt his cock, and Henry was reasonably surprised at Miss Whosit's ability to arouse him so easily.

He'd been a trifle worried about his prowess lately, truth be told. Perhaps it had been the excess alcohol that had depressed his ardor most nights. Or the lack of sleep, or the irregular beating of his heart.

Sometimes he imagined the damned thing would fragment in his chest like a mortar shell and he'd be put out of his misery.

Henry had not been a coward when it counted, but he felt like a coward now in supposed peacetime. The armistice was signed just last month, too late to do him any good. How could he pretend everything was all right?

Well, of course it was all right this very minute. He had a fresh-scented young woman in his lap, whose skin, what he could feel of it, was satin-soft. She was kissing him open-mouthed, her tongue tangling with his. He really had absolutely no complaints. This Puddling place was improving by the lick.

Until the slap. Henry's head snapped back against the stone wall with a sickening *thunk*, and for a moment he saw stars. Or perhaps swirling bullets—it was hard to tell. Then the young woman's dismayed face came into focus.

Lord, he didn't even know her name, but she looked concerned, and so she should. He hadn't been walloped like that since his school days. She might have even done him permanent damage, cracked his skull or some such. He was already physically impaired. Damn if he was going to wind up shuffling about not even knowing his own name.

"Oh! I'm so sorry!" Miss Whosit tried to scramble off his lap, but Henry held her fast. "Are you hurt? Bleeding? I didn't mean for you to hit your head."

Was he bleeding? Henry didn't care for the sight of blood. He'd seen far too much of it recently. He refrained from trying to touch the back of his throbbing head—he'd have to release Miss Whosit to do so, and he had no intention whatsoever of doing that. She fit so nicely into his lap. Was so warm and cuddly and pretty. He felt...complete.

Henry stared into the cloudless heavens. The sky was bright blue, and he fancied it matched his eyes. Would she make the comparison herself? He batted his eyelashes.

"Who—who are you? Where am I?" he groaned.

Was he laying it on too thick? Nothing ventured, nothing gained.

"Oh my God. You *are* injured." Her cool hand stroked his brow, and it was all Henry could do not to get up and do cartwheels.

"Head. Hurts. So very badly." He squinched his eyes shut as if the sun pained him.

"I'll fetch the doctor." There was more wiggling. "Please let me go so I can get help," Miss Whosit pleaded.

"So cold. Alone. Don't leave me." He drew her closer. Her breasts were...simply amazing.

The famous actor Charles Kemble had nothing on Henry Challoner, though of course Kemble was dead, so it wasn't that hard to surpass him. If his post-army career as a ne'er-do-well ever palled, he knew after this display he could always tread the boards.

"I *must* leave you, Lord Challoner," Miss Whosit said desperately.

Her lips were close. Henry could feel her breath on his cheek, and the hairs on the back of his neck rose along with that other inconvenient thing. Exactly when would Miss Whosit notice?

Ah. The elbow to his gut. Right about now, he reckoned.

"Release me this instant or I shall scream and scream!"

Just like little Mary Ann. There might be a positive aspect to being somewhat deaf at this close range.

"Wha—who?" Henry began, trying to postpone the inevitable. He shook his head as if he was trying to clear it.

"You, Lord Challoner, are a disgrace! I wasn't born yesterday, you know. You're trying to take advantage of my soft heart, and I admit you almost had me fooled. The only thing wrong with you is that you are a libertine! Get that—get that *thing* away from my bottom!"

"Quite a natural reaction, you know," Henry said soothingly, grabbing her pummeling fists. "A man can't help himself. Even if you weren't so awfully attractive, I imagine the results would be just the same. It's biological. You're an educated woman, I presume. A teacher and all that."

"I teach *children*, and such biological subjects have not arisen," Miss Whosit spat.

"Well, it's risen now, and I'm afraid I have no control over it. I don't mean to insult you. In fact, I like you quite a lot. You have spirit. Beauty. I'd like to get to know you better." Henry gave her his best crooked smile.

He couldn't be faulted for trying. It wasn't every day pretty women fell in his lap. Well, technically she didn't precisely fall. But she was here now, in a state of absolute fury.

She had odd eyes. Like slate or storm clouds. Blackish silver or silvery black. He could feel them boring holes into his head, possibly his soul.

"Let go of me *now*, or I shall go to Reverend Walker at the first opportunity."

That did it. Henry loosened his grip and Miss Whosit sprang up, beating her dark, dull skirt as if it were on fire.

Henry was not really afraid of Reverend Walker. The fellow was not much older than he was, and had a boring earnestness that was dead stultifying. But Vincent Walker was in communication with the pater. If Henry didn't behave here, who knows where else the old man would send him to teach him the lessons of self-denial which seemed to be so necessary to continue the Harland line. The Arctic Circle? Back to Africa? Henry shivered thinking of them both, and Africa was hotter than Hell.

"All right, all right. You win. But I have been starved for company, and there you were," Henry said, feeling a trifle mulish.

"You are not permitted female com—" Miss Whosit bit off the rest of her sentence.

"Ha! I knew it! It's a grand conspiracy and you're all in it, monitoring my every move. Where are all the young women hidden, eh? The cellars and attics? You're the first non-crone I've seen since I arrived."

Miss Whosit's eyes shifted. "Never mind. It's all part of your treatment for your addiction."

"My addiction! I'll have you know Lysette and Francie were just an aberration. I was at loose ends and not entirely in my right mind. I don't usually make it a practice to go to bed with two women at the same time."

Lately, it had been hard enough to go to bed with one, precisely since he couldn't get hard at all.

Until Miss Whosit. She was his good-luck charm. A talisman. Henry wasn't a lost cause after all. Now all he had to do was persuade her to have an affair while he was cooped up here killing time.

She didn't look interested at present. Her arms were clutched over her magnificent bosom, and her luscious mouth was pinched in disapproval. No doubt gentlemen didn't discuss such things with young unmarried ladies. Henry had been out of society and at war too long, but supposed that was no excuse. He *had* been raised a gentleman, though the best tutors and schools had bored him witless. As soon as he was sent down from Oxford he enlisted, buying his commission with his own money over his father's vociferous objection.

He'd seen some of the world. Too much of it. All he wanted now was some fun. What was wrong with that? He'd faced battle and siege, torment and starvation. No one seemed to understand. Was he was meant to forget everything that happened just because his father thought he should?

He reminded himself that the recent Boer war had lasted barely ten weeks. His part in it had ceased as soon as his foot was done for and he was in hospital after being exchanged for some poor blokes with pitchforks the English had captured.

He wished he could cooperate, he truly did. It was no picnic having the dreams he did. Sometimes he was even awake when they happened. A branch snapping, an actress's shriek—who knew what would bring on the next episode? Henry was losing his mind one dimmed sound at a time, and was anxious to get the process over with.

He knew he wasn't the only fellow with bad memories, but his old army friends didn't seem to want to talk about theirs. Instead they threw themselves into gay society just like he did, hoping that revelry might dull the dread.

But the dread was always there, even in this schoolyard. Henry's temporary return to masculine normalcy abated, and he felt equal to standing without embarrassing either one of them further.

The wind had definitely gone out of his sails. What had he been thinking to assault a blameless young schoolteacher? God forbid his thoughtless actions brought more time to his Puddling prison sentence. The kiss had been a revelation, but probably only because it had been a week since he'd kissed anyone. Or two anyones.

His father had always drilled into him that he should think before he acted, and true to form, Henry had once again resisted doing the sensible thing. Now he'd imperiled his release from this reformation place.

Rustication place.

Rehabilitation place.

Renewal place.

Where did that last word come from? Henry couldn't make himself new again. He was as jaded as they came. He tried to think back when he'd felt simple joy aside from five minutes ago.

And failed.

He straightened up and cleared the worrying lump in his throat. He was not about to cry, was he? That would put the icing on the loony cake. "I do most sincerely apologize, Miss..."

"Everett," she said with reluctance.

He doffed an imaginary hat. "Viscount Challoner at your service. It's just a courtesy title. Forgive my presumption. If we can keep this little incident between us and the sheep, I'd appreciate it. Reverend Walker might misinterpret it."

"I think Mr. Walker would understand your motivations completely. He may seem naïve, but he was picked for his position with great care. Not everyone is suitable to shepherd this parish. It's...unusual."

"Comes along with a pack of temporary reprobates and lunatics, does it? Is there anyone else here like me?"

"There is no one like you, Lord Challoner. Each of us is a responsible individual with our own blessings and burdens given us by God."

"I see Walker's gotten to you," he muttered. "I mean, another Guest, as you so quaintly call me?"

"We try to provide services for one Guest at a time. Occasionally there are overlaps, but not at the moment."

Not that he could have gone carousing anywhere with a like-minded irresponsible individual. The graveyard? The bake shop? They had their charms, Henry was sure, but there was nothing like a smoky pub or music hall to get his blood flowing.

"These services. Just what exactly do they consist of, besides the daily lecture over the tea table?"

"You'll see," Miss Everett said primly. "Now, I really have to go. Will you be able to manage the hill?"

It had been all he could do not to hurtle downwards this afternoon and fall flat on his pretty face. It was damned steep—no wonder he hadn't attempted it before. But the green beyond had beckoned. As far as Henry could tell though, the track ended at the schoolyard gate. Unless he wanted to wade through a stream and climb up another hill and commune with the sheep, he was doomed.

"I was a soldier. I'm used to marching in unideal conditions. I don't suppose I could persuade you to keep me company?" he asked, already knowing the answer.

Miss Everett shook her head. "I'd get in as much trouble as you would."

"Well, then. It was…lovely to meet you. I don't expect I'll ever see you again, will I?"

Another head shake.

Damn, this place was brutal.

"In that case…" Henry took a step toward her. She was so startled she didn't have time to shrink back or dash for help with the school bell.

He was going to kiss her again. Make the kiss last for as long as he was interred in this bloody place with its blasted hill and invisible beautiful women. Kiss her until she fainted or begged for more. Kiss her until he forgot who he was and why he was here. Kiss her—

And that was his last thought until she snatched his stick and knocked him to the ground.

Chapter 4

It was his own fault. She'd only meant to shake the stick at him, but somehow he'd lost his balance again and hit his head. Again. This time there was no "Where am I? Who am I?" business. Lord Challoner lay inert in the grass. Cotswold stone walls were lovely yet sharpish on top, with a row of triangles meant to deter any intelligent animal. Unintelligent Lord Challoner had pitched sideways on the schoolyard wall and the amount of blood at his temple was rather gruesome.

Rachel had gathered her skirts and run to the cottage closest to the school, where her father's best friend Ham Ross lived. Thank heavens he was home and his wheel barrow mostly empty of manure. Between the two of them they stuffed the unconscious man in it and rolled him up the hill into the center of the village, huffing and puffing all the way.

Puddlingites had lined the cobblestone street or looked out their windows at the grisly procession. The doctor had been called for, and Rachel knew she was in deep trouble.

The worst bit was hauling him through the iron gate and up the staggered stone steps that led to his cottage. Fortunately some of the observers pitched in to help and pushed the wheel barrow up the long path to the front door. Rachel couldn't help but notice Stonecrop Cottage's garden was quite beautiful, as nice as her own, and the view over the village and hills was spectacular. St. Jude's spire was visible over the hawthorn hedges, a vigilant reminder of why the man was here.

St. Jude was the patron saint of hope and impossible causes. Nothing but the best for their Guests.

Now she had to explain what happened to Mrs. Grace, and the vicar was due any second for tea. Rachel was certain they'd take one look at her and know she'd been kissed, and kissed well. Lord Challoner had been about to try again, the bounder, and she'd reacted swiftly with little thought of the possible consequences.

She'd never meant to injure him, just scare some sense into him. But he'd tripped as she'd raised the stick, and somehow he and the stones had collided him into unconsciousness.

He couldn't go around kissing her, or anyone else. It was totally against the Rehabilitation Rules that had been so painstakingly negotiated between the vicar and Lord Challoner's father, the Marquess of Harland. The rules changed depending on the Guest. In Rachel's opinion, Lord Challoner was not apt to follow them no matter who they were written for. She was afraid he was not destined to be a Puddling success.

There had been failures, but never on Mr. Walker's watch. Of course, he'd only been in Puddling four years.

Lord Challoner was carried into the small glass conservatory and laid on a wicker chaise, Mrs. Grace determining that he should not bleed on the good sofa and carpet in the front parlor. Stonecrop was one of three cottages reserved for Guests, and the nicest of the lot. It had been built within the past three years in Mrs. Taylor's back garden at exorbitant expense, since previous guests had complained bitterly about the primitive accommodations of the ancient crumbling cottages that regular Puddlingites lived in. There were two spacious bedrooms and a proper bathing chamber with a flushing toilet upstairs, and a large kitchen and reception room on the ground floor.

A few years ago, the town fathers received a gift of a conservatory to be added on from the son of a baron who'd had a worrisome habit of talking to plants. The greenery in the walled garden had flourished during his three-month stay, and he'd left clutching his journals to prove to his papa that he was not, in fact, crazy. Much to his father's chagrin, the young man had secured a position at an agricultural college. He might never make a proper baron, but he was certainly amongst friends in his laboratory.

Nothing grew in the conservatory right now except a spindly brown fern on a plant stand. The room was furnished with wicker, and had an excellent view of the private garden. Rachel sat down on one of the chairs, admired the pelargoniums outside and waited for the interrogation to begin.

Mrs. Grace fixed her with a grim gray stare. Her eyes looked like chips of ice, and Rachel knew if she had any sense, she'd be afraid.

"What did you do?"

"I? Nothing! The man tried to jump over the schoolyard wall and fell."

"Tried to jump? Why would he do that when there's a perfectly good gate and he's a cripple?"

He wasn't precisely crippled; he just limped a little. "I have no idea." That, at least, was the truth. Rachel could not begin to fathom what was in Lord Challoner's mind, or even if he had one.

"Did you speak to him?"

"N-not really."

"Rachel Elizabeth Everett," Mrs. Grace said, "I know a fib when I hear it."

"Well, I mean, I said good day. I was just dismissing the children when he came by. It would have been rude to ignore him."

"You are supposed to be rude!" The housekeeper brushed Lord Challoner's long fair hair back from his wound. It was saturated with blood. "He'll need stitches, I think." She took a sniff. "And his clothes— fit for the burn pile. I had misgivings when he left today. I don't trust this man at all. He's much too charming. Used to getting everything he wants. Spoiled, that's what he is."

Mrs. Grace didn't get to be a Guest housekeeper-cum-jailor for nothing. She was a very astute woman, but Rachel found some fault with her conclusions.

"He was in the army. He can't have had it easy there."

"Faugh! Those officers just send out the enlisted men to be slaughtered. He probably just sat in a silk tent with all the comforts of home and a cigar and brandy."

Rachel had read the reports in the newspapers, and doubted very much that Captain Lord Challoner's war had been a picnic, but she kept her thoughts to herself.

"Perhaps you should fetch water and towels for when the doctor comes," Rachel suggested.

"I can't leave you here alone with him!"

"Oh, for heaven's sake. He's in no shape to attack me. My virtue is safe."

Mrs. Grace sniffed again but left. Rachel examined her hands. The wheelbarrow's handles had been rough and blisters were forming.

"Is the dragon lady gone?"

Rachel jumped. Lord Challoner had one eye open and a rueful grin on his face.

"How long have you been awake?"

"Oh, I'd say when you lot nearly tipped that wheelbarrow into the ditch at the bottom of the hill. Couldn't you have found me better transportation? I smell like shit."

He did, too. Rachel felt her face grow hot. "You ungrateful beast! Awake all that time, yet you made us push you up the hill? Ham Ross is seventy-seven years old!"

"Well, I thought it was safer to pretend I was knocked out. You might have murdered me else. You are a violent woman, Miss Everett. I don't think I've ever encountered such ferocity, not even when I was luxuriously camped out with my cigars and brandy on the African plain."

"You fell. It was an accident," Rachel said, thoroughly mortified. He'd heard every word.

"You took my cane. My lifeline."

"Oh, pooh. You do very well without it." All of his movements had been recorded, and most days he managed to cruise around Puddling unaided.

"You raised it at me!"

"And *you* hit yourself on it." As he fell sideways onto the jagged edges of the wall. It had happened so fast Rachel hadn't even had time to blink.

"Yes," he said dryly, "I can see now the entire incident was all my fault. And now my favorite jacket is ruined. What the devil is this?" He put his hand in a pocket and drew out a deformed carrot. "Mr. Ross's, I presume? I hope he wasn't counting on it for his dinner."

Where was Dr. Oakley? Or Mrs. Grace? Rachel plucked at her skirt nervously.

"You owe me, Miss Whosit, I mean Miss Everett. You've probably set back my recovery by eons. I will not spend more than the next twenty-one days here if I have to cover myself with that sheepskin rug over there on the floor and crawl up the hill on all fours and baa. Just what exactly can I do to repent and get out of here?"

Rachel knew the marquess's demands by heart. Every Puddlingite did. "Your father wants you to settle down and become respectable. Find a proper vocation for one of your status. Get married."

"Very well. Will you marry me, Miss Everett, so I can get the hell out of here?"

Chapter 5

Ha. That rendered her speechless. Served her right, after attacking him. Twice.

To be fair, the last time wasn't exactly her fault. He'd lost his balance and tripped. Henry used to be so light on his feet, too. Dashing in his regimentals on a ballroom floor, a much sought-after partner on a girl's dance card, don't you know. The hole in his foot seemed to put a period to that phase of his life, which was a pity. It had been great fun snuggling up against various female forms as he spun them around the room no matter what continent he'd been on.

Miss Everett's female form was sublime, but Henry didn't expect to get anywhere near it again. Sparks were shooting from the young woman's mercury-like eyes and he felt rebuked. Singed. Not to mention that a river of blood was working its way down his face. Where was the water and toweling? Mrs. Grace was surprisingly inefficient.

"M-m-m..." Miss Everett was still robbed of coherence.

"Marry? Why not? We are both healthy young adults. That's if I recover. I suppose I could get an infection and die before the vows, but let's not borrow trouble. If I didn't die in Africa, why should I die in this Puddling paradise? I should warn you—but you probably know this—in fact you probably know my hat size—that I'm slightly deaf in one ear. You may have to shout your "I do" to make yourself heard. Having a deaf husband is an advantage, you know. You might scream at me like a veritable fishwife with few if any consequences. Whisper your dressmaker's bills and I'll be unable to take exception."

Miss Everett sat in a block of sunshine gaping like a landed mackerel. No, that was unfair. She really wasn't very fishy, more like a mermaid than anything. Henry imagined tangling himself in the long dark hair that had fallen out of her bun during her exertions up the almost-mountain to the heart of the village. He might be caught for days and never mind her net.

Wouldn't the pater spit bullets if he brought home a Puddling bride? The idea was so preposterous it had a great deal of merit.

He heard the rap of the knocker at the front door and closed his eyes again. Mrs. Grace's grumble and a man's low voice wafted into the sunroom. The doctor or the vicar, most likely, here to save the day or his soul, depending.

Henry noted Miss Everett had covered up their amorous encounter, which was all to the good. Apparently he was to be denied association with any females younger than his grandmothers here, and they, the poor women, were dead. And then he was somehow going to be cured of drink and his very natural desire for a warm woman—or two—and go home and marry some frigid girl of his father's choosing. There were so many things wrong with this plan, Henry didn't have enough fingers and toes to count.

He wondered how long he should pretend to be unconscious. If he refused to wake up, would they ship him off to some sanitarium? Escape might be possible. He could jump out of the carriage and roll under a hedgerow, steal a horse and ride to—

"I believe he's just coming around, Dr. Oakley. He spoke just a minute ago."

Thwarted. Was the little witch a mind reader? Henry fluttered his lashes.

"Well, lad, I see you've made a proper mess of your head. Millie, is that hot water you have there? Excellent. Now, this will smart, and it's a pity I can't give you a wee nip to get through it, but that's against your Plan. You've been stitched up before, aye, being a soldier and all?" The doctor applied a scalding hot towel to his forehead and Henry flinched, then nodded. He was sure he could withstand anything this country sawbones could mete out.

Until the man poked the giant needle into his brain.

"Yow!"

"Stay still or it will hurt worse. Don't want to be scarred for life, do you, a handsome young man such as yourself? You may have to part your hair in a different direction for a while."

Henry was sure he heard Miss Everett snicker. It was all her fault, being there in that grassy schoolyard, her curves blinding, her voice the sort of thing that washed sailors up on rocks. Yes, she was a mermaid, about to fillet him and discard his bones.

Did mermaids eat fish? The thought was rather cannibalistic.

"Now then," the doctor said patiently as he pierced Henry's skin with a hundred pricks, "what were you doing so far afield? You're meant to be walking in the village center. Lured by the green, green hills? There's no way out for you, my boy. The road ends. Best get used to it."

"I wanted a change," Henry said stiffly, when he stopped biting his tongue to prevent screaming.

"Aye, you young people are all alike. Don't appreciate what's in front of your face. Puddling has lost its share of youth, but not one of our Guests in a long time. Stick to the main streets, that's my advice."

"All five of them?"

"And what's wrong with that? Would six make a difference?"

"I don't know if you noticed, sir, but there's nothing to *do* here," Henry ground out.

"Precisely. Puddling is a very soothing place. You'll get used to it, as I said."

Henry doubted that, no matter how many times the doctor repeated it. He sat up and tried to touch the bandage on his head.

"Leave it! You don't want to ruin my handiwork, do you? I'll let the vicar know you're indisposed. I advise rest and quiet. No tea today."

Thank the Lord for small mercies. No lecture over the sugar lumps.

"Rachel, are you still here? You'd better come with me. Millie, thank you for your assistance." The doctor packed up his bag and disappeared, pushing Miss Everett ahead of him. Henry was deprived of a last look at Miss Everett's bottom.

Rachel. It was all rather biblical. Henry had forgotten what Rachel had been up to in the Old Testament but was determined to find out.

"I say, Mrs. Grace, do we have a Bible in the cottage?"

His housekeeper looked at him as if he'd grown another head. "Yes, my lord. In the parlor."

"Fetch it for me, please. I'm not sure I'm steady enough to get it right now, being a *cripple*."

Mrs. Grace had the grace to blush and hurried out of the conservatory.

It was devilish hot in the room and Henry loosened his necktie. Such pointless things, neckties. Who had thought it was a good idea to strangle oneself every day? In a fit of pique, he ripped it off, only to discover it was blood-stained anyhow.

Mrs. Grace returned with an enormous leather-bound Bible that appeared virtually untouched. No doubt the other Guests had avoided it and their own many sins. After reading a very depressing account in

Genesis of poor Rachel, Henry wondered why anyone would curse a girl child with such a name.

The whole story was scandalous—trickery, disguised brides, theft, affairs with servants, death in childbirth. Counting up all the sons and daughters by numerous wives and mistresses, old Jacob certainly had not walked the straight and narrow. And Henry's father had been so testy about Lysette and Francie. Had the man not read his Bible?

He would discuss this very issue with Reverend Walker when he came to visit tomorrow. Henry could barely wait to see the expression on the young vicar's face. Just explain all *that*, if you please. Such carrying on defied strict Victorian society's every edict.

Feeling one hundred percent better, Henry rose from the wicker chaise and went out into the lush little garden. He could see the church spire and its new weathercock over the chimneypots. Mr. Walker had confided that not long ago, some Puddlingite was fined for putting thirty bullet holes in the old one, preventing it from spinning correctly.

That was the extent of excitement here—one was forced to shoot copper roosters out of sheer boredom, and then wonder which way the wind was blowing. No wonder the young people left.

Henry wondered why Rachel was still here. She was very pretty, and should be married by now. He estimated she was around his own age, give or take a year or two. Why hadn't some local farmer swept her up? It was difficult to believe she'd never received a proposal besides his.

His lips twitched. He wondered if a clandestine courtship was possible under the prying Puddling eyes. Even now a lace curtain twitched from the upper story in the neighboring house. Henry had half a mind to unbutton his trousers and water the garden.

No. Surely that would be against the rules. They'd really think him a pervert then.

He threw himself down on the iron bench and stared at the little fish pond, wondering if anything could survive the green scum on the top. A giant bumblebee whizzed over his head, and birds chirped remorselessly from the flowering trees. It was all very pastoral, a far cry from the noise and dirt of London.

Or the vast sunbaked plains of the veld.

Twenty-one more days. If he behaved himself. It behooved him to do so, thus wooing Rachel Everett was out of the question. She was probably a virgin anyway, and not likely to succumb to the usually fatal Challoner charm. Henry had always been successful with the ladies. It was only since his injury and return home that he'd had difficulty spurring enthusiasm for the conquest.

By God, he was only twenty-five years old, not some pensioner like Ham Ross, who moved pretty spryly uphill for a man his age. Henry wasn't spry at all. He couldn't even jump over a low stone wall.

He was feeling sorry for himself again, a pointless endeavor. The good reverend kept telling him he had a lot to be grateful for, and Henry reckoned the man was right. He might be under his father's thumb at the moment, which was never a good place to be, but it was all in the name of "helping" him.

Henry didn't feel helped, however. His dreams were still unpleasant, despite waking up to the bleating of sheep rather than breech-loading rifles. His foot ached and his mind was foggy.

And he was *thirsty*.

Mrs. Grace appeared at the conservatory door. "Would you like your tea in the garden today, my lord?"

Tea. Bah. It wasn't as if he was *addicted* to drink, despite what everyone here seemed to think. Certainly, he liked a good time, and wine or whiskey often facilitated his pleasure. He'd been a gentleman about it all—he didn't roll under the table in a coma or sing on the street or lose his luncheon. One would hardly know he'd tippled.

Or so he told himself. Perhaps it was true that lately he'd gotten a trifle carried away. Lysette and Francie might be considered proof of that.

"That would be lovely, Mrs. Grace," Henry said with little enthusiasm. At least there would be no vicar to harp on his numerous blessings. Henry was aware he was lucky he hadn't been born in a slum. He was a viscount with all the hereditary privileges. One day the pater would pop off and Henry might even find himself in Parliament doing something about all those slum dwellers he'd seen when he returned. Somehow he'd never noticed before when he was a young man kicking up his heels in London.

But why should he wait? He might do something right now and earn his way out of this hell. Were there any poor people in Puddling? He couldn't offer them money—he had none himself, just enough for the odd bun at the bake shop every other day. Perhaps Walker would know who was in need. Henry might read to the blind or play checkers with a sick non-contagious child. Not Mary Ann.

How low he had fallen when he looked forward to such tame activities.

Chapter 6

Rachel had evaded Dr. Oakley's searching looks and had gone back to the schoolhouse. Dust motes swirled in the afternoon sun, and she sat at her desk staring at their glittery brilliance. Perhaps it would have been better if she got up and dusted them away, but somehow she didn't trust her knees.

That blasted man had proposed to her. Of course, to him it was all a lark. He didn't mean a word of it. But Rachel had, like most girls, dreamed about a proposal from a handsome swain someday, and had quite looked forward to it, even if the possibility was becoming more remote by the year.

Lord Challoner had the handsome part down pat—he had curling golden hair and sky blue eyes, was tall and fit and, well, somewhat fabulous. Unlike many fashionable young men, he was clean-shaven. He must have looked a treat in his uniform, and had probably broken hearts anywhere his booted foot stepped. His limp didn't bother her at all—it was barely noticeable unless one looked for it.

He did have brackets about his mouth and eyes, showing his years in the sun and the cost of what it took to disguise his pain. She didn't think they were from his dissipation alone. In fact, she was beginning to wonder whether the man was as bad as he was supposed to be.

He was a dreadful flirt, true. But there was something in his eyes—

Rachel shook her head of such nonsense. She had ever brought home wounded hedgehogs and half-drowned kittens. Right now, the ugliest dog in the world had a place of honor in front of the hearth because no one else had wanted him. She was too sympathetic by half, even with her pupils. The parish school committee had spoken to her twice about her lax disciplinary standards. One more time and she'd be removed as Puddling's primary school teacher.

She gave the dust motes a stern look. They continued to tumble down from the rafters.

Ah, she was hopeless. Rachel believed children flourished with soft words of praise rather than canings and humiliation. She wasn't mean by nature, and didn't much want to be.

She'd had no training to teach—the job had fallen into her lap more by way of last resort than anything. There were few children here in Puddling, and fewer teacher candidates. What with the yearly bonus every Puddlingite family received, they could afford to send their children away to school to better themselves. Most didn't come back to the restrictive village. Who wanted to live in a place where the pub was closed more than half the year? Many of the Guests had problems knowing when to lower their elbows. It was a shame moderation seemed to be such a difficult concept for the *bon ton*.

Rachel was a moderate sort of woman herself—moderately tall, moderately smart, moderately pretty. She was nothing special. It was only because she was the only woman under fifty Lord Challoner had seen that he'd latched onto her, as it were. The latching had been amazing, but it was not to be repeated.

Noting the time, she shoved papers to be graded in her canvas satchel, locked up the school house and made her way back up the hill to the small attached cottage on New Street she shared with her father. New Street had been new in 1483, and its houses were built for shorter, less privacy-seeking people. The rooms were miniscule, the stairs terrifyingly vertical, and her father had taken over the front parlor as his bedroom accordingly as he'd aged.

He spent most of his time outdoors when the weather was good. She found him in the postage stamp-sized back garden, sitting on a chair and puffing on his pipe. The remains of his tea tray were propped on a barrel, and Rachel noted the extra cup. Ham had wasted no time.

"You're very late today," Pete Everett said. Rufus, the ugliest dog in the world, wagged his tail but didn't even bother to get up from his flagstone square. Ungrateful beast.

"Don't worry, Dad. Supper will be on the table in no time." It would be leftover stew, soft enough for the old man to chew with the few teeth he had left. Rachel had been a late-in-life child for her parents, a rather stunning surprise considering their ages of forty-five and sixty.

Despite being much younger than her husband, Rachel's mother had died three years ago. Rachel felt honor-bound to remain in Puddling to care for her father until he joined his wife. Though she thanked God her father was in excellent health, every now and again she wondered what she was missing in the outside world. Puddling's pleasures were deliberately rather finite in deference to its pleasure-abusing Guests, and reading novels and newspapers after supper could only get one so far.

Rachel had never been to London. Had never really been anywhere except nearby Stroud on Market Day and a church field trip to the Roman ruins at Cirencester. Though her father had been born right here in this seventeenth-century weaver's house eighty-four years ago, he'd traveled far afield, serving in the army in India and the Crimea for decades. Their home was crammed with souvenirs from those places, lovingly dusted and polished daily by her father. His eyesight was still good enough to tell when she didn't clean the brass bells thoroughly, though he'd never work the loom in the upstairs room again.

"Never mind about dinner. Aren't you going to tell me?" Pete Everett asked.

"Tell you what?" Rachel replied, stalling for time.

"Ham came over to see me. Didn't want to waste the climb into the village. At our age, he might not make it up Honeywell Lane again except in a coffin to the churchyard. What's our new Guest like?"

Rachel had never been able to fib to her father, or really anybody. It was a curse.

"I only spoke to him for a moment. He came by the school."

Pete blew a smoke ring over a raspberry bush. The little garden was his pride and joy and he took care of it all by himself, with Rufus obligingly digging alongside him on occasion. "Ham says he's a good-looking fellow."

Rachel pretended to pull up a weed that wasn't there. "I suppose."

"Army man, I understand."

Lord Challoner's particulars had been passed around the village so that Puddlingites would know how to deal with him. "I read that, too."

"Wounded in Africa. War is a dreadful thing, Rachel. Don't let any of your sons go for soldiers." He'd been full of hair-raising tales when she was a little girl.

"I'd have to get married to have sons, Dad."

"That might happen yet. I worry about you. I won't be around forever, you know."

"Yes, you will. And don't worry. I'm perfectly fine just as I am."

It was almost true. Or it had been until she'd been kissed by Lord Henry Challoner and felt bumblebees buzzing inside her head. "So, did you have a good visit with Ham? I don't know what I would have done without him."

"Ham likes to play the hero. Always has, ever since he was a little nipper, and so I told him. He hasn't had this much fun is years. Center of attention."

It was true they'd formed quite the wheelbarrow parade. "Nevertheless. The exertion wasn't too much for him?"

"Ham's strong as an ox. I envy him. Rachel, you're avoiding the subject. What was Lord Challoner doing at the school?"

"I think he meant to explore." Escape was more like it. The school lane ended, Puddling Stream began, and enticing steep green hills rose up all around it. The center of Puddling was on a tricky hill itself, and most days Rachel was breathless by the time she walked home.

Her father set his pipe down on the barrel. "Do you think he'll bother you again?"

"I shouldn't think so. Dr. Oakley was very firm with him. He's to stick to his usual walk from now on."

"What if he doesn't? He knows where you are now, Rachel." He looked grim.

"For heaven's sake! He just went right instead of left. The man has no interest in me whatsoever. I'm not like his fancy London ladies."

Maybe he went around asking them to marry him too.

"No. You're better. Young reprobate like that—there's no telling what mischief he's used to getting into. You watch yourself, my girl. Ham says he's willing to sit outside the school with his blunderbuss when he's done collecting eggs. He invited me to join him. I still have my sword."

It only needed that. A septuagenarian and an octogenarian guarding her from the predations of a Guest. "Your concern is very flattering, Dad, but you're worrying over nothing. Lord Challoner is a gentleman, for all the trouble he's been in lately. I think he's just had difficulty adjusting to civilian life."

"Pah. He should be grateful he's not in some foreign place getting his brains blown out." He tapped the ashes out of his pipe, and they fell on the stone path and Rufus sneezed. "You won't do anything silly, will you?"

"Silly? What do you mean?"

"You're so soft-hearted, always thinking the best of everyone. That man wouldn't be here if he didn't have real problems. We're the resort of last resort, you know. His father must be desperate."

Or difficult. Uninformed. Controlling. Rachel had seen Guests come and go, and often thought their families contributed a great deal to their problems.

Rachel had been lucky. Her parents doted on her, yet provided the discipline for her to grow up unspoiled. She may not have traveled anywhere, but if she ever did she was sure she could hold her own. She was sensible. Clear-headed.

Usually.

She grinned at her father. "I promise I'll behave. Now sit right there and enjoy the sun. I'll just go in and see about supper."

She hurried into the warm kitchen and took her apron off its hook. Her father was every bit as capable as she was to reheat the stew, but she liked doing what she could for him. He was determined not to be a burden, and he wasn't. His mind was sharper than hers at times, and it was obvious he'd enjoyed his visit with his old friend Ham. He'd cut into the fruitcake and forgot to close the tin. The two of them had eaten almost all of it in a very short period of time.

Rachel set the pine table and looked out the window over the sink. Her father's eyes were closed. Ham must have interrupted his afternoon nap, and the excitement of the day had gotten to him.

It wouldn't do for Rachel to feel excited. So what if she'd received her second (and almost third) kiss? It meant nothing to a fellow like Lord Challoner, who practically kissed women for a living.

Rachel wondered what *he* was having for supper. Probably not leftovers. Mrs. Grace was a good, plain cook and had a new range to work on. Shockingly, his cottage was even electrified with a generator, and there was a boiler to heat the tap water. All the modern conveniences. Only the Sykes estate on the other side of the village could rival Stonecrop Cottage for being up-to-date.

But, according to Lord Challoner, there was "nothing to do." How would he like to heat up water to wash the dishes, or pour lime down the privy hole? Trip on uneven stones on the floor and listen to the wind rattle the old window panes? That would keep him busy enough.

Rachel knew she was being unfair. The man must have sacrificed his comfort being in the army for six years. He'd done his share of sleeping rough and eating muck. The Boer farmers had humiliated the greatest power on earth, besieging their forts and ambushing convoys. Commissions were being formed this very minute to look into it. How did the great British Empire lose face so badly?

No wonder he drank and wenched to try to forget. And there were his injuries, too. But, she reminded herself, he was not a wounded or ugly puppy, but a proud, powerful lord who still had bark and bite to him.

He was To Be Avoided.

Chapter 7

"Fu—" He bit off the expletive and steadied himself. Henry had hit his head on the bedroom doorway *again*. Had the cottage been built for midgets? He knew it was newer—there was even a plaque over the front door with the builder's initials and the date, barely three years ago. People weren't as short as they used to be, but of course, Henry was taller than most. He would have to remember to "Duck or Grouse," as those clever signs in old inns said.

He turned on the lamp and caught sight of himself in the mirror. His bandage had migrated south, and the whack to his head had caused his wound to leak. Bloody hell. Mrs. Grace had left for the day, not that he wanted her help. She would just screw up her lips and go all prune-faced on him, as though he'd been tiddly on his way to bed.

As if he could get inebriated on tea—he'd had pots and pots of it today to keep him awake in case he was suffering from a concussion. The result was he was feeling a little wild, blood racing, and sorely wished for a bit of poppy to put him to sleep.

Definitely forbidden, and likely unavailable in purest Puddling. He'd have to count imaginary sheep, though Lord knows there were plenty of real ones about. They were probably right out there on the hill outside his window jumping fences.

Henry had a magnificent view from the cottage, but it was dark now. The village, save from the earlier ringing of the church bells, was dead quiet. The incessant bells had given him a headache—it must have been bell ringers' practice, since they went on forever in various intonations and made no note whatsoever of the time. He'd only come upstairs because his watch told him it was ten o'clock, not because he was tired.

Henry was buckling under to his schedule, and he hated himself for it. Until a few months ago, he'd been the one giving the orders. After his capture, he'd spent a few miserable days bleeding until he was exchanged for a flock of Boer prisoners. His Majesty's Army had not done it out of the goodness of its heart, but through the bullying of his father, whose contacts were of the very highest, right up to the queen herself.

And then Henry—still in his hospital bed—had faced a formal inquiry alleging that he *allowed* himself to be captured—that he'd failed his rank and country and class. The whole process had infuriated him. Try retreating when your boot's been shot off and your foot is on fire, he'd wanted to say. But he lay unbowed—as if you can lie down and still be unbowed—for the hearing, biting his tongue. What was the point of telling these stupid old men off? They knew nothing about ordinary soldiers and were never likely to. The recent wars had been debacles, and Henry was glad he was shot of his army life, even if he'd had to have been shot to get out. Getting a damned tin of tobacco from Queen Victoria at Christmas was not enough to make up for even a minute of it.

He didn't even smoke, one bad habit he was *not* guilty of.

But he'd wanted a career in the army, and he'd gotten it. The pater was right to tell him he'd made a mistake, and he'd been too stubborn at nineteen to listen. His father should have locked him in his room to prevent the inevitable consequences. Sent him to Puddling *then.*

Instead, he was locked away now in this dwarf's cottage minus Snow White. Oh, Henry supposed it was all right—the conservatory was a pleasant space, the garden well-planted, most of the furniture in the rest of the house very plush. A pretty padded Puddling prison. He was becoming quite alliterative in his latest captivity now, wasn't he?

And if only he followed the damned rules, he'd be sprung in three weeks, possibly less, if he could convince that Walker fellow that he was totally reformed.

Henry supposed that meant no more kissing schoolteachers, which was a damned shame.

He'd forgotten the Service business. Apparently Henry had to do something to prove to the Puddling Powers That Be that he knew the errors of his ways, would think of others and was prepared to forsake all pleasure forever. Henry wondered if his reading to orphans scheme would fit the bill.

He punched his pillow down, still fully dressed. Damn, he wasn't tired at all. The air in the cottage felt close, and suddenly he couldn't bear it.

He would walk. Look at the stars. Breathe in some sheep-scented air. The wool trade may have collapsed hereabouts, but there were still plenty of the little buggers around, their taunting bleats reminding Henry they were free but he was not.

He lit a small lantern from the dresser in the kitchen, grabbed his cane from the front hall and opened the door. A long narrow pebbled path led down to the street, with a few deep steps at the end to reach the gate and cobbled Honeywell Lane.

He'd seen the well on his walk to the schoolhouse, a pretty stone thing that still seemed to be in use. There were precious few signs of modernity here, which, Henry supposed, was the point of Puddling. How could you sin when there was no opportunity?

The house windows were mostly dark, the only sound his footfall and the slap of his stick. Henry hissed a bit at the uneven pavement and its effect on his foot, but he was determined to walk himself into sleep. He knew his way by now, up St. Jude's Street toward the towering church, right on Vicarage Lane, around Market Street to New Street, back to St. Jude's, the holy quadrumvirate. His own lane made five, and he knew where it led now: to a dead-end at a stream. He'd been a fool to stumble down it this afternoon—if he hadn't been driven up in his first-class wheelbarrow, he'd probably still be navigating the hill.

Henry's foot yearned for a straightaway, something smooth and paved and flat, but wasn't going to get it here. The starry skies above twinkled, but he focused on the lane under his feet, minding the dips and divots. All he needed now was a twisted ankle as well as a sore head.

He wasn't even sure if he was allowed out at night. Probably not. He was meant to get a solid eight hours' sleep. Breakfast was at eight sharp, after he shaved, bathed and dressed. Mrs. Grace had refused to feed him in his scruff and dressing gown.

Henry passed the public baths on the corner. How lucky he was not to share his ablutions with strangers. Although army life had robbed him of the kind of privacy he'd previously enjoyed, and his brief experience as a prisoner of war made him all the more grateful he was demobilized. Stonecrop Cottage was totally up-to-date in the bathing department with hot and cold running water, though he understood the rest of the town was very much behind the times. Since he had his very own dynamo in the shed, he didn't need to read by candlelight, as a few cottagers seemed to be doing.

Henry wondered what they were reading. Racy novels? Unlikely. There was a tiny lending library on Vicarage Lane, but Henry had resolutely passed it by each day without stepping inside. He was sure every book would be of an 'improving' sort, or chock-full of sermons. No thank you. He was sermonized sufficiently by Mr. Walker every afternoon.

He turned onto New Street, which was crammed with old buildings. New Street had not been new in a very long time. According to Mr. Walker, who seemed very proud of his parish, a couple of hundred years ago all the cottages had weaving rooms on the top floors, when Puddling had been known far and wide for its cloth. Now it was a secret spot to sequester scandalous scions of society.

Good God, this alliteration had to stop!

He was saved from chastising himself further by a small growling dog who sped out of an alley between houses, hackles raised. Henry thought it was best to stop and shine his lantern on the creature in hopes it would be temporarily blinded so he could go on his way. The dog—if that was indeed what it was—Henry had never seen such a misshapen mongrel—was not deterred. Its growl changed to a near-rabid bark which would wake up everyone on the street.

"Sh. Good doggie. Um, bad doggie." It was hard to know what tack to take. If anything, the dog barked louder with each syllable.

A light spilled from the upper story window, and a head popped out. "Rufus! Be quiet! Come!"

Henry knew that voice. The soothing angel-mermaid voice that led to terrible trouble. Would she drop a flower pot on his head when she discovered who had riled her dog?

So this is where his schoolteacher lived, a modest attached stone cottage right on the road. Presumably the little alleyway the dog raced out of led to the back garden, where, judging from a frayed rope at his neck, he might have been tethered.

Rufus had an inordinate interest in Henry's cane, which he now shook so vigorously between bared teeth that Henry had difficulty holding on to it. What was it with the Everetts and his walking stick? At least the animal hadn't noticed his trouser cuff. Yet.

"Who's down there? Bother. It's *you*."

"Yes, that sums it up rather nicely. Would you mind very much coming down and unfastening your dog from my person?"

"Oh, God! Is he biting you?"

"Not just yet. But I'm sure he can smell the potential delectability of my ankle, even with a pushed-in snout like that."

"I knew all that fruitcake would unsettle him," she said. Whatever fruitcake had to do with Henry's predicament he wasn't sure, but Miss

Everett disappeared from her window. He held on for dear life as the mongrel attempted to play tug-of-war with his unwilling victim.

Henry was determined not to topple down in Miss Everett's presence again if he could help it and held steady. He could always clout Rufus on the head with his lantern if worse came to worst, but he knew instinctively that Miss Everett wouldn't like it. One didn't keep a dog like this for its good looks—she must have great affection for him, since Rufus looked put together by a blind man at the dog parts factory. Small head, dangling ears, squashed face, and a body that looked like a sausage on stumps.

"Down, Rufus," Henry said tentatively. Rufus turned his bug-eyes on him and glared, not giving up his grip on the cane one inch. Henry diverted his attention to the front door of the cottage, so was startled when Miss Everett appeared from the alley in her dressing gown, her hair a river of black silk down her back.

"Shh! My father's sleeping," she hissed.

"I doubt that," Henry whispered back. "Your dog barked his head off." Even being partially deaf, Henry's ears were still ringing.

Miss Everett cocked her head. "He's just in the front room."

"Well, then we should continue our conversation in the back. If your dog will stop attacking my stick."

"We do not need to continue anything. Rufus, come."

Rufus growled and held fast. Miss Everett tugged on the bit of rope, the dog tugged back, and Henry found himself on his arse.

Again.

Would the humiliation ever end? The lantern extinguished itself and clattered away down the road, and they were left in the dark.

"Oh, dear." Henry thought he heard a snicker. "Can you get up, or should I fetch a wheelbarrow?"

Impertinent minx. "I'm fine." Only his consequence was bruised. Henry sprung up from the gutter, his trousers only slightly damp.

"What are you doing out?" Miss Everett asked waspishly, handing him back his now dogless stick.

"I didn't realize I was confined to quarters. It's a lovely night, and I wanted some fresh country air. Is that a crime hereabouts?"

"If it isn't, it should be. The town isn't safe for strangers to walk around in the dark."

It was true there was not a lick of light, or a helpful night watchman with a working lantern. "I'm hardly a stranger. I've walked up this road every day now for a week. I could do it blindfolded."

"Stop bragging—it's a very unattractive quality in a man. Good evening, then." She turned to go, somewhat hunched over as she still held the hideous Rufus by the shortened rope.

"Wait."

Miss Everett paused. "What now, Lord Challoner?"

Henry really didn't know what to say, except that he was reluctant to leave the woman frowning at him in the dark. He was even more wide awake now than he'd been to start with, and going home to stew alone was not appealing in the least.

"I—I think your dog may have bitten me."

"You *think*? I thought you said—"

"I was confused. Trying to be brave. Everything happened so quickly."

"Where?"

"Where what?"

"Where did Rufus bite you, my lord?"

"Um. My leg. It hurts like the devil," Henry lied. He reached down as if he were rubbing it, found the small knife he kept in his boot and stealthily stabbed though tweed and stocking and skin.

Clearly, he was mad.

"I'm not sure where Mrs. Grace might keep bandages and such," Henry continued, straightening and slipping the knife in his pocket.

"You'd better come in then." She sounded doubtful, as she should. There were two curs on the street now. "Around the back way."

Henry followed her down the narrow alley and through a wooden gate. The night air was perfumed with flowers from the back garden. It must be lovely and lush in the daylight; Henry could barely get through the bushes. Miss Everett tied Rufus back up to a stake, and Henry observed in the dim starlight there was rather large doghouse for such an unprepossessing animal.

They entered by way of the kitchen door and Miss Everett lit a lamp on the dresser. The room was small but scrupulously clean. Warm, too. The range was probably the only steady source of heat in the cottage. She put the kettle on and faced him squarely. "Remove your pants, my lord."

This was more like it. Henry hoped slashing himself had been worth something, and this exceeded his expectations. But he was still a gentleman deep down. Miss Everett needed to be saved from herself.

"Did I hear you correctly?"

"Unless you think you can roll them up over your calf. I shouldn't like you to lose any circulation while I treat the wound."

Blood was flowing to a part of him best left undiscovered. Henry hoped his shirttail would cover it and Miss Everett wouldn't notice. "Very wise. All right. Do you have nursing experience?"

Miss Everett sighed. "I teach school, and half the students in my class are little boys." She picked up a bottle and cloths from a shelf and waved them at him. "Always prepared. Does that answer your question?"

"Indeed it does," Henry said, working his buttons free with one hand. The other propped him up on the scrubbed pine table. His leg *did* hurt in fact. The walk might have been too much for him in his present condition, injured from tip to toe. He wondered if the bandage around his head was on straight.

Miss Everett's back was turned as she rummaged through a cupboard. "Sit down, and put this over your lap." She handed him what appeared to be a tablecloth. Henry could smell starch and sunshine, and had a vision of this young woman hanging laundry in her little back garden. His pants puddled around his ankles, and suddenly he felt venal and stupid.

"I hope we don't wake your father," Henry said truthfully. He felt at a distinct disadvantage wearing table linen.

"He's a sound sleeper. Now, this may hurt...."

Chapter 8

Rachel examined what could only be called a scratch. She'd seen dog bites, and she doubted very much if Rufus had bitten this man. There was very little blood, and the cut was remarkably straight, almost as if nicked by a knife. What was Lord Challoner playing at?

He was so full of charm and excuses. Well, she was not about to be charmed.

"Holy Mother of God!" he cried.

"The sting will stop soon. You don't wish your leg to become infected, do you? Dog bites are notorious."

"You could hack my leg off and it would be preferable! What is on that cloth?"

"Just a home remedy. Very effective." Lord Challoner was gulping manfully, trying to repress the tears in his eyes, and she enjoyed every second. "I wonder if you need stitches."

"Of course I don't need stitches! It's just the merest injury. Not worth bothering about, really."

"You were in an awful hurry to remove your trousers," Rachel said, slapping a sticking plaster on his calf with considerable vehemence.

"At your suggestion! I assure you doing so was the furthest thing from my mind!"

"Hm." She thought she saw a blush to his cheek in the dim lamplight.

"What's all this then?"

Drat. Her father stood in the doorway in his nightshirt and nightcap. They'd converted their front room to his bedroom when the stairs had become too much for him to mount. That last squeeze and Lord Challoner's reaction must have roused him.

"Dad, I'm so sorry we woke you up. Lord Challoner met with an accident on the street and I brought him in."

"Lord Challoner, eh? Our newest Guest. Ham told me you were knocked unconscious. I see you've recovered."

Lord Challoner stood, clutching her mother's best tablecloth in front of him like a warrior's shield. "More or less, sir. Thanks to the kind offices of your daughter. She has come to my rescue twice today."

"You're not here in Puddling to get yourself into more trouble, my lad," Rachel's father said sternly. He wasn't one bit cowed by their Guest's rank. "Rachel, go upstairs to bed. You're not decent."

She glanced down at her thick wool wrapper, which covered her up to her chin. If Lord Challoner had thought to catch a glimpse of anything untoward, he had been doomed.

On the other hand, *she* had seen the man's thighs, knees and calves. He was beautifully muscled, and remarkably brown, as if this area of his body had been exposed to the sun. Were British troops in Africa parading about half-naked like the natives? It was an intriguing thought.

It was reputed to be so hot there. Infernal. Rachel would like to ask Lord Challoner questions about his experiences, but she wasn't supposed to be speaking to him.

Ever.

Well, she supposed she might read a book. Soldiers liked to come home and write memoirs. Glorify war and their part in it. Somehow, she wasn't convinced by their words.

"Dad, Lord Challoner is a gentleman." Except for the kissing and proposing part.. "You needn't worry," Rachel fibbed.

"So you say. But I've read his dossier, as have you."

"Then you have me at a disadvantage, Mr. Everett. Everyone here knows my peccadilloes, or think they do. My reputation is really not as black as my father made out."

Her father raised his eyebrows. "Nobody incarcerates their relatives here at the rate they pay for the fun of it. You've let your family down."

Rachel drew a shocked breath. Her father was known for his bluntness, but he might be overstepping.

The room was very still. Lord Challoner grew white about the mouth, and was clearly struggling with his temper.

"You don't know me. I have been to war, sir."

Pete Everett snorted. "So have I. I saw my share of uprisings in India. And I was in the Crimea. Not an officer like you, of course. You young bucks think you're the only ones to ever have suffered. The stories I could tell you would make your hair curl. Worse than that damned poem written about it. I'll admit I spent a few hours in the pub when I came home, but I saw the error of my ways soon enough."

"Bully for you."

Oh, dear. "I'm sure my father doesn't mean to insult you," Rachel said.

"Doesn't he? He's implying that I'm weak. Self-indulgent. I'm just supposed to pull myself together and carry on, aren't I? As if nothing ever happened. As if I saw nothing. Did nothing. I never took part in any butchery, did I? I'm not as bad as the savages we were meant to conquer. You have a lot in common with my superiors, Mr. Everett. I wish I shared your optimism that life is hunky-dory."

Lord Challoner's bleak expression said even more than his words did. They were supposed to be helping him here in Puddling, not drive him further into despair and more debauchery.

"It's very late," Rachel said hurriedly. "You need your rest."

"Do I? If only I could sleep without dreaming, Miss Everett. But I'm denied any diversion here—no sleeping aid, for example. So I'll just go home and wait for dawn and another fascinating day in Puddling-on-the-Wold to enfold. Who knows what tomorrow may bring? A stray lamb? A cloudless sky? Do tell Mr. Walker I await him with eagerness."

Somehow he managed to pull up his trousers without dropping the cloth and exited the cottage with dignity. Rufus barked as he passed through the garden.

Rachel refolded the tablecloth and returned it to its shelf. "Dad, was that necessary? You seemed...cruel."

"Cruel to be kind. I saw the way the man was looking at you."

"Don't be silly! Lord Challoner's just bored. And sad, too." For all his alleged wild ways, she'd seen the melancholy streak in him. And her father's eyesight wasn't what it was.

"Don't tell me you've got a soft spot for that bounder. He'd not a bird with a broken wing."

Wasn't he? Rachel shrugged. "I do feel a bit sorry for him. He feels isolated."

"He's supposed to be isolated! No loose women, no alcohol, no opium. How can he be cured of his addictions, unless his father puts him in a sanitarium? That will be next if he doesn't improve here, and much worse. If he's unhappy here, just imagine how he'll feel there."

"I'm sure you're right." It was unusual for her father to be so grumpy, but his sleep had been disturbed.

At least he *could* sleep. Poor Lord Challoner seemed to have difficulty doing so, wandering around Puddling at midnight.

"Let's go back to bed," she said with a brightness she didn't feel. Her father shuffled down the dark hall to the parlor, and she climbed the steep stairs to her bedroom. Pulling the window curtain back, she looked for Lord Challoner on the street, but he'd disappeared. Not even the tap of his cane was audible in the spring night.

Rachel took a deep breath. Even though he'd tried to trick her, Rachel couldn't fault the man. He'd been lonely and wanted a few more minutes of her company. Rufus had been more interested in his stick than his flesh, and if given the chance, would have licked him to death.

She thought of the dog, naughty little imp. Her father and Ham had been so busy discussing the excitement of the day that Rufus had eaten the first round of fruitcake they'd cut for their tea. He'd been put outside since his digestion was always a tricky thing—he was not only an unattractive dog, but somewhat sickly. Ordinarily he'd have been curled up next to Rachel, snoring the night away, his misshapen head on her pillow.

If Rufus was the closest thing she'd ever come to a husband, Rachel's life was in a sorry state.

She'd been proposed to today. Yesterday, now. True, it was in jest. But what if she took Captain Lord Henry Challoner up on it?

Rufus wasn't the only imp around. How ridiculous she was being, imagining she could be the wife of a viscount, whether he was deranged or not. One day he'd come to his senses, look over at his frumpy schoolteacher wife, and commit himself to Bedlam.

But still. To leave Puddling and its limitations behind was a very tempting thought. Most every other young person had done it, despite the lure of the annual Puddling pounds. Farm and wool prices were low, and there had never been manufacturing in the area. There was simply no way for a young man to earn his way here.

Of course, there was her father to think of. He'd have to come too. Surely a viscount's house had a spare room? But he wouldn't like London much. Rachel wondered where the Harland family's country seat was.

Good grief. She needed to go to sleep and stop daydreaming such nonsense. Or nightdreaming. She'd be exhausted tomorrow, and the challenges of dealing with ten mischievous children were not inconsequential.

She was a planner, though, and had lessons ready for tomorrow and beyond. Much like the Puddling Rehabilitation Method, there was a sequence to everything, although sometimes Rachel broke her own rules.

Like Lord Challoner, who'd turned right instead of left. She could have hidden in the schoolhouse until Mary Ann stopped screaming. Eventually Lord Challoner would have become bored or deafer and turned around. There had been nothing to see but children running in circles.

But Rachel, fatefully, had stepped outside, and now Lord Challoner knew of her presence, even where she lived. She had altered his treatment schedule and didn't know how to fix it.

Didn't want to fix it. God help her, she wanted to see the man again.

Chapter 9

Henry had arrived home last night in what could only be called a snit. He considered himself an even-tempered, jolly fellow—as did Francie and Lysette and all the rest of those fluffy girls he'd met recently—but that night-capped old man had ruffled Henry's feathers almost as badly as the pater did.

Everyone was so self-righteous. So bloody perfect. It all amounted to "Do your duty and shut up about it." Well, Henry had, and he couldn't seem to. Not that he was whiny and feeling sorry for himself. But he simply could not stop the jerky images of carnage in his head when he closed his eyes.

So much suffering, and for what? Diamonds? Gold? Oh, Henry knew there were other reasons for the war, but his bitterness made him disgusted with the whole thing. Ordinary farmers had nearly handed the United Kingdom its honor on a platter.

The most inglorious aspect? Facing his superiors to determine if he'd be charged because he'd been captured. He knew the pater had interfered there too. He was not the man his father wanted him to be. Trouble was, Henry didn't know what man *he* wanted to be.

He was twenty-five, his careless youth behind him. He'd discovered the army wasn't a lark of dressing up in braided uniform and dancing with pretty girls. He was half-deaf and, as Mrs. Grace said so succinctly, crippled. It was time for him to…do something. But what?

The idea of going home to slide under his father's thumb didn't appeal. The marquess would probably live forever out of spite, so Henry felt disobliged to learn all the ropes of estate management just quite yet. His father was only forty-eight, and Harlands usually lived to a ripe old age when they weren't tempting fate on the South African plain.

His father wanted him to marry. Just because *he'd* done so at an early age and had a son before he was Henry's age didn't mean that was a suitable course for his heir. But one couldn't argue with the pater. When one did, one wound up in Puddling-on-the-Wold.

Henry adjusted his necktie in the mirror, noting the blue circles under his blue eyes. Well, at least his skin matched his irises. Dr. Oakley's bandage was still mostly in place, giving him a linen halo, the closest he'd ever get to one. According to his father, hell was in his future if he didn't reform. Henry tore it off and replaced it with a much smaller sticking plaster. The stitches were black and ugly but would be removed soon enough.

He'd heard Mrs. Grace let herself in half an hour ago, so odds were his breakfast was awaiting him in the conservatory. Henry relished the bright heat of it in the morning, even if he sometimes felt exposed behind the glass windows. But so far his neighbors had not climbed up the stone walls to get a look at him as he tucked into his eggs and bacon. He felt like a bug under a microscope anyhow—the entire village knew of his embarrassing lack of control.

Drink. Drugs. Too many women. But never the right one.

Except…No. Henry shook his head. No point to letting his mind wander. He was just in a desperate case letting his imagination run away with him.

Rachel Everett. Thick dark hair, cool silvery eyes, a lush figure that would tempt a saint to fall from grace. Lord knows, Henry wasn't a saint, and couldn't afford the temptation if he was to ever break out of here.

And there was her sharp tongue too. Henry didn't relish being flayed alive.

He decided to whistle his way down the stairs, remembering to duck on the low crossbeam. Already this morning he'd achieved a modicum of success. He was one day closer to leaving Puddling and his inadequacies.

"Good morning, Mrs. Grace," he said with a brio he wasn't quite feeling.

"My lord." The woman made the words sound like a pejorative. She disapproved of Henry thoroughly, and no matter how he tried to charm her, he met an implacable wall.

"What's for breakfast today? Steak and ale? Apple pie and warm custard?" Henry asked, knowing the absurdity of his wishes.

"The usual, Lord Challoner. You will find your breakfast in the conservatory. Ring if you require anything else."

Oh, Henry required, but was not going to acquire—he knew that much by now. Meekly nodding, he entered the bright room and sat at the wicker table on his wicker chair. A dish of gray porridge, steam rising, awaited him. There was no sugar or cream for it. A sullen dish of prunes was beside it, along with a single cup of black coffee and a silver-plated rack filled with cold dry toast. No butter, no jam. All that was missing was a foul-tasting restorative tonic, no doubt because its contents would be ninety percent alcohol. God forbid Henry had too much stimulation—the prunes would have to be the pinnacle.

He passed the bake shop on his daily walk. Perhaps he could stop in later and buy something with his very limited funds. He'd never had much of a sweet tooth before, but now he could have eaten an entire Victoria sponge in one sitting and yearn for another.

There was, of course, no newspaper. The intention was to cut him off from the world to reflect upon his sins. Forty days in the desert, or in his case, twenty-eight. A week had already gone by. Surely Henry could manage three more.

It wasn't as if he missed his friends. Hell, those closest to him the last six years were all over the world now, if they had survived. The old school chums he'd bumped into in London seemed rather callow and had little in common with him, except for the pursuit of dubious pleasure. When Henry got back—

But would he be allowed to go back, or be buried on his father's estate learning the latest farming techniques? Henry shuddered. Kings Harland was not all that far from Puddling actually, maybe fifteen miles away. Nestled in a valley, its aspect was one of tranquility on the surface. Beneath, it was an entirely different story. It took a great deal of effort to achieve such perfection. Henry had even caught his father with hedge clippers trying to prune the yew trees himself.

Puddling had yew trees—one hundred uniform pyramids in the churchyard, guaranteed to make his father jealous. It was a very restful place, with ancient table tombs whose inscriptions had been lost to the elements. Maybe Henry would sit in the churchyard with his shop-bought bun later, admiring the order and greenery, listening to the church bells.

Faugh. How his life had devolved. All that was missing from the scenario was a book of sermons in his bun-less hand. Life couldn't be that flat, could it?

Apparently, it could. Henry swallowed his breakfast manfully and watched birds fly over the cottage. He didn't know what kind of birds they were, and refused to find out.

He usually took his walk after lunch, but there was no reason why he shouldn't alter his routine. Mrs. Grace would be happy to be rid of him— she was a demon at dusting and Henry often felt in her way. The usual master-servant relationship was not established at Stonecrop Cottage; if anything, Henry obeyed *her* dictates.

He carried his breakfast tray into the kitchen, something he never would have done at either of his houses. Correction: his father's houses. Henry owned no property of his own. After spending some of his inheritance from his grandmothers on his commission, there was still plenty of money left for his future. Enough to purchase a small estate far from the pater's, if he had the inclination to manage one. Technically, he was still in the army, but the orders would be completed any day now to release him. His injuries precluded him from further service, for which Henry was heartily grateful.

"I'm going out, Mrs. Grace," he said, setting the tray on the table.

She gave him her usual disapproving frown. "Is that wise, after your injury? Dr. Oakley recommended quiet."

So, she hadn't heard about his midnight ramble. That was a bit of a miracle. Henry imagined Puddlingites semaphoring his exploration with their morning wash.

"You can't get much more quiet than Puddling-on-the-Wold. I thought I'd look in at St. Jude's."

Mrs. Grace's nostrils flared in disbelief. "Suit yourself. Don't be late to lunch."

Ah, lunch. Clear broth. A gristled mutton chop if he was lucky. Rice pudding. What was that? A raisin and a speck of cinnamon? Nirvana!

His warden was not impressed with his birthright that was for sure. And why should she be? Being born into the peerage was sheer luck, though some might find it anything but. If Henry had been an ordinary soldier, he might be limping up Bond Street right now instead of visiting a graveyard.

Or begging. To his shame, Henry had passed veterans on his wild nights out. The few coins he'd tossed did nothing to alleviate their suffering.

And then, Henry knew what he must do. *How* to do it was the question. He would talk to Mr. Walker. Surely this would count toward his mysterious Service.

Theirs not to make reply,
Theirs not to reason why,
Theirs but to do and die.

The army's incompetence had been going on forty years or more. The history books were full of glory, but Henry knew otherwise.

Mr. Everett. Henry would talk to him, too. Find out how he'd come back from the Crimea and soldiered on in civilian life. There was a key here somewhere. A purpose. He'd been too shallow and obsessed with his own misery to find it before, but things were *almost* clear in the bright morning light.

He turned left at his gate, as he was meant to do, even though he felt the distinct pull of the schoolhouse. He'd save Mr. Walker for later—the man would come for tea, the only meal for which Mrs. Grace seemed to make an effort. Of course, Henry was forbidden the treats on Mr. Walker's plate. Just bread and butter for him. By the time he left Puddling, he'd be a wraith.

Curtains twitched as he walked by, swinging his stick in a faux jaunty manner. There were bites on it from that wretched beast, and for a moment Henry wondered about the wisdom of his course. But he'd faced worse than a bedamned dog, and perhaps the thing was still tied outside out of harm's way.

Up Honeywell to St. Jude's, right on Vicarage, around Market to New. Henry hadn't noticed cottage names in the dark, and wondered which house the Everetts lived in. That dog had come barreling out of a narrow alley, but there were several interspersing the cottages. It wasn't until Henry heard that unique frenzied bark that he knew where he was.

He knocked on the ancient studded front door with no result. Well, there was nothing for it but to traverse the alley to the back yard as he'd done last night. Perhaps the old gentleman was in the kitchen having his breakfast, a feast far better than Henry's own, he was sure.

Rufus erupted, heralding Henry's arrival. The animal was loose behind the wooden gate, and wasn't the only creature in the garden. There, in a calico apron, her hair covered by a kerchief, was Miss Rachel Everett herself.

Chapter 10

Lord Challoner was the very last man she expected to see approach the back gate. Her father had properly repelled him last night. Blistered him, really. Yet here he was, resplendent in finely tailored clothes meant for the country, his boots polished and his longish golden hair curling at his starched collar.

"This is beginning to become a habit. No school today?" he asked, tipping his cap. The bandage at his temple had been reduced in size and was nearly covered by his tousled hair.

"Down, Rufus! Right this minute!" Amazingly, the dog slunk off from his post at the fence to the doghouse, growling only a little. "My father isn't well. Mr. Walker is taking over for me today." Vincent was good about substituting for her. Good with the children, too, even though he would much rather be reading Scripture or writing a sermon.

Rachel knew he was her champion when it came to school matters, and was excellent at soothing the occasional ire of the three members of the parish school committee. They thought Rachel was too "modern." Too lax. She couldn't in all conscience cane little children when they were naughty, even if doing so meant she'd keep her job.

It was Lord Challoner's fault that her father and she had had such a difficult night. Dad had been terribly agitated after the viscount was patched up for his nonexistent dog bite, and had tossed and turned, crying out so often in his sleep that Rachel sat with him until he quieted. Sitting in the dark at his bedside had given Rachel ample time—too much time—to think.

"I'm sorry to hear it. Has Dr. Oakley been to see him?"

"He isn't really ill—that is to say, my father didn't sleep well and isn't feeling like himself. I didn't want to leave him alone." When her father was overtired, he became somewhat absent-minded. Rachel didn't think he'd actually burn the house down, but one never knew.

"That's too bad. I was hoping to speak to him."

Rachel felt the ground slip beneath her feet. "You were? I thought after last night...." Truthfully she'd thought Lord Challoner so offended she'd never lay eyes upon him again except in a clipping in Vincent's scrapbook.

"Yes. Well, we didn't get off on the best footing, but I got an idea I wished to explore with him."

An idea? To explore with her father? Lord Challoner really did hit his head yesterday.

"I'll just see if he's awake." Rachel left Lord Challoner at the gate, with a glare at Rufus to behave. She knew she wasn't being hospitable, but she was nervous. If the neighbors saw him here hanging about, there would be trouble for them all. Rachel's father depended on their yearly supplement for being Puddling citizens. If they broke the terms of the Puddling Rehabilitation Rules, the allotment could be withheld.

They wouldn't starve. Her father had his army pension. Rachel's salary was very modest, but then they had modest needs. The garden was productive, and they usually bartered for meat or other staples. There were some savings, too, although her father never quoted an exact figure. Enough to get them through the coming year, she hoped, until all memories of Captain Lord Henry Challoner had passed.

That's what Puddling did, serve as a temporary retreat with no strings attached and no friendships formed. Except for that baron's son who'd given the town a conservatory in thanks for his humane treatment, there was no trace of previous Guests to be found anywhere but the scrapbooks, carefully hidden away in the parish records. Puddlingites were generally kind, but businesslike. And right now, Rachel knew her little family risked censure.

She stepped through the kitchen and down the hall to the front room. Her father was sitting up in bed, his spectacles sliding down his nose, a worn book between his gnarled hands. All those years of weaving as a boy and after he left the army had left him arthritic. It was almost a mercy when the local wool trade collapsed and his hands could be still.

"What are you reading, Dad?"

"A history book. They got it all wrong, of course."

"We—we have a visitor. The Guest. Lord Challoner."

Her father closed the book with a snap. "What does that young jackanapes want with us? Doesn't he have the sense God gave him? He's not wanted here."

"You may not want him, but he wants you. He's asking to talk to you. He says he has an idea."

Pete Everett snorted. "I'd be very surprised if that idler's brain could support one."

"Dad, you're being unfair. He was an officer."

"Exactly. Don't get me started on officers."

"They can't all be alike," Rachel reasoned. "He's in the garden. The alley, actually. Should I ask him to come inside?" Truth to tell, Rachel was a little embarrassed about the state of the front room. It still sported a couple of chairs, but her father's bed and dresser took up most of the space.

"I'm not dressed, damn it. The man wrecked my night and now my day. Can't a fellow relax in his own home?" her father grumbled. "I'll see him in the garden in five minutes. You'd best make yourself scarce before there's any talk."

Rachel kissed her father's cheek. "I'll go to the bakery. Is there anything you'd like?"

"Gingerbread. I haven't had any since Christmas."

That would be Rachel's fault. It was hard to bake regularly and write lesson plans and grade papers at the same time, plus keep the house tidy. And sing in the choir and do the altar flowers and sew her own clothes as well as items for charity in the women's sewing circle and meet with her book club every week. Rachel was as busy as she could be, to fill up all the empty corners that sometimes bedeviled her. Her friends had left Puddling, her schoolgirl crush had died, and though she loved her father dearly, he didn't always understand.

She scooped out some coins from a cracked teacup on the kitchen shelf and took off her apron and kerchief. A quick look in the mirror by the door told her she looked as tired as she felt. Her hair had been flattened by the scarf, and her gray work dress did her no favors.

If Wallace Sykes had lived, would she be his wife by now, pampered and cosseted? Highly unlikely. A baronet's son would have looked higher than an old weaver's daughter, no matter how much he'd wanted to kiss her behind the dunking booth.

And his father, Sir Bertram Sykes, was barely civil when they spoke after church. He sat on the school committee that threatened to oust her. Accepted as his daughter-in-law? Never. Wallace had been his favorite son, and a young woman of greater consequence would have been necessary for the Sykes line.

Rachel imagined she only had her job because no one else in the village wanted to do it. Puddling was unwilling to advertise the position, since whoever moved here would qualify for the annual compensation. Puddlingites kept to themselves, and kept their pocketbooks closer.

Lord Challoner, brave soul that he was, had let himself into the garden and sat on a weathered bench. Rufus lay at his feet, the man's walking stick between his jaws.

"Oh, no! Rufus, bad dog!"

Lord Challoner smiled at her. Rachel's breath caught. He really had a lovely smile, enhanced by a dimple on the left side. "Don't worry. I have several more. A few chunks out of this one won't do any harm. Is your father up to seeing me?"

She nodded and sat down beside him. "He's just making himself presentable."

"I don't mean to disturb him. I can come back at another time."

"No. I think it's best you get this…over with." Rachel paused. "You should know, he doesn't have much respect for people in authority."

"Is he a revolutionary? Should I be worried about keeping my head from the Puddling guillotine? I warn you, between the low beams at Stonecrop and your drystone walls, it won't take much for me to lose it."

Rachel chuckled. "He's not dangerous, only opinionated."

"And he doesn't have a high opinion of me. He made that clear last night." The light had gone out of Lord Challoner's blue, blue eyes. Rachel felt her pity for the man return.

"It's not you in particular. He's not very fond of generals. Politicians. The rich."

"Well, I'm none of those things at the moment, certainly not a general. The pater has me on a very short leash here, as I'm sure you all know. My biggest monetary extravagance will be in the bake shop later, and then I'll be skint. I've been absolutely dying for something sweet to eat."

"I'm going there right now. Can I bring you back something?"

His handsome face flushed. "I cannot take charity from you. It wouldn't be right."

"It wouldn't be charity!" Rachel protested. "Just Puddling hospitality. I'll fix tea, too."

"I haven't had elevenses since I was a boy. Mrs. Grace will accuse me of ruining my appetite for lunch."

"We won't tell her."

He lifted a golden eyebrow. "Come now. She'll know as soon as I lick the crumbs from my lips. She's frightening."

"I'll make sure you return crumbless. My father has asked for gingerbread. Will that do?"

"It will." Lord Challoner cleared his throat. "I want to thank you for not calling the authorities on me, Miss Everett."

"Why would I do that?"

"Oh, surely you know. I haven't been entirely truthful with you. And I—I've taken advantage. Overstepped my bounds. I can't tell you how happy I was to see you in the garden when I got here so I could apologize."

"You've done nothing to apologize for," Rachel said. Her lips still felt a bit tingly if she allowed herself to remember yesterday.

"You know I have. But I'm determined to be a better man. Good God, that sounds like a cliché. But I do mean it. And not just because I want to go home."

Rachel felt her own blushes coming on. "That sounds very admirable, my lord."

"You'll help me, won't you?" he asked, sounding anxious.

"I—I don't know that I can. It's not allowed." He wasn't supposed to have contact with any young woman in Puddling, not that there were many of them to begin with.

"I'll speak to Mr. Walker. I'd like to see more of you." He placed his gloved hand upon hers, and Rachel felt a frisson of…something.

"Oh? Do you, young man? What kind of rigmarole are you babbling about now?"

Her father had come out of the house, and neither of them had noticed. Rachel rose, and after a few awkward seconds, so did Lord Challoner. Rufus was no help; the cane was still firmly in his mouth.

"Sir, this isn't what it looks like."

"My eyes still work. In fact, every part of me works. How I'd like to knock you down and teach you a lesson."

"Dad!" Rachel cried, horrified.

"Don't you see what he's doing? Talking you up sweet. Before you know it, his hand will be up your skirt and you'll be ruined. What will he care? He'll be gone."

Rachel felt lightheaded. Her father was never so crude. "You don't understand—"

"I've seen men like him before here. Young and full of themselves. No limits. All the money in the world. Spoiled rotten. He thinks he can get anything he wants. Well, not my daughter. Never. Rachel, go in the house."

Rachel was in agony. She hated to defy her father. He was usually reasonable. But he was quaking with anger now, standing up to Lord Challoner who had at least half a foot and three stone on him. She had to stop this before he got hurt.

Lord Challoner touched her elbow ever so gently. "It's all right, Miss Everett. I can take care of myself. Why don't you go get the gingerbread? I'll be here when you get back."

Was he mad? Rachel's father was about to punch him!

"I don't think that's wise," she whispered.

"I haven't been wise in years," he whispered back. "It will be all right. I promise."

For some reason, she believed him, and closed the gate.

She was just as mad as he.

Chapter 11

"Good-for-nothing dog. Sic him, Rufus!"

Rufus wagged his tail and ignored Mr. Everett, far too busy destroying Henry's Malacca cane.

"If we can just discuss this like gentlemen," Henry said in a conciliatory tone, "I can allay your fears over my intentions toward your daughter."

"Gentleman! Pah!" Mr. Everett spit but was thankfully off the mark.

Henry gestured toward a garden chair. Everything in this pocket patch was like a mini-Eden, neat and lush. "Please sit down, sir. Miss Everett said you weren't feeling up to snuff."

"I feel fine. I'll feel better when you go away," the old man grumbled.

"I came today to thank you. Your words woke me up, as it were."

"And robbed *me* of my sleep."

"I'm sorry to hear that. I have difficulty sleeping myself. Did you never have bad dreams when you returned home after the army?"

Mr. Everett's gaze slid to a rather spectacular ruby-pink peony bush. "I can't recall. It was so long ago."

"I've only been home a few months. Perhaps in twenty-five years' time, I will have forgotten the incompetence and its resulting bloodshed."

Mr. Everett raised both eyebrows, but only said, "Perhaps I will sit down after all."

"I want to do something for soldiers like me who come home and can't sleep. We're made to feel ashamed, you know, even by others who served."

"Like me."

Henry nodded. "Civilians don't understand—I don't expect them to. But to be dismissed by people who know what it's like is very hard to bear."

"You can't dwell—"

"I'm not *dwelling*, Mr. Everett. Believe me, I'd like to think of other things. I tried to distract myself, hence the wine, women and excesses. It didn't work, and now I'm here."

"You officers have clubs."

"And no one wants to talk about anything serious. We're all afraid we'll be called cowards. Be accused of being less than the manly ideal. It's all surface chatter, while I know there are those who are suffering. They can't sleep. Drink too much. Beat their wives, for all I know. Do you think Puddling could take some, just for a week or two? I could pay when I get access to my funds. A quiet stay in the country where no one will judge you. Well, except for you and Mrs. Grace."

"That's not fair!"

"No, it isn't. How is it that people can feel sorry about my foot but not about my brain? Quite frankly, I think it's more injured than the rest of me. It just doesn't show."

Would Everett report him to the Puddling powers? Was Henry asking to be put in some mental hospital by being so frank? It was a risk to speak like this to a perfect stranger, but somehow Henry knew this man understood what he was talking about.

"I drank too."

The words were so low Henry could barely hear them. He leaned forward. "Go ahead."

"When I came back. Before I was married. But I met Rachel's mother and wanted to stop." Everett chuckled. "The truth is, she wouldn't have me otherwise. She was much younger, a skilled weaver. Had a house of her own. She didn't need a sot for a husband, or any husband, for that matter. Very independent, she was. Had her part of the allotment, too. Made me wait a good long time before she said yes."

The man examined his crooked hands, worn from weaving and gardening. "We thought we'd left it too late to have children. But then we had Rachel. Quite a surprise to us, she was. I won't stand to see her hurt."

"I would never hurt her," Henry said.

"You've already turned her head. Nothing can come of it."

Henry bit his tongue. Everett was right. Rachel was far beneath him according to society's obdurate rules. Henry's father might have a stroke if he brought her home. Although she was pretty and well-spoken, Henry would be expected to do better.

He couldn't possibly. *Hell.* He was half in love with her already, and he didn't even believe in love.

He changed the subject. "So you met a good woman and simply stopped."

"There was nothing simple about it."

"Not everyone can find a good woman to help them change their ways," Henry said. "I think it might be useful for men to talk about things they worry about, without shame. Be honest. To know they're not alone." He thought of his one-way conversations with Vincent Walker. Maybe he would talk back later this afternoon.

"We're all alone when it comes down to it, lad. We make our own way. Our own choices."

"You are right, of course." The choices Henry had made led him straight to Puddling, perhaps not so very bad a thing. He was thinking more clearly this morning than he had in an age.

"Well, Mr. Everett, do you think Puddling could host a few more fellows like me? Enlisted men as well as officers."

Rachel's father shrugged. "You know we only deal with the Quality here. It's part of the original agreement."

Henry felt deflated. "Very well. I'll just have to look for a different place when I'm free. What do you think of my idea, Mr. Everett?"

"It has some merit, I suppose. But it probably won't make your bad dreams go away."

The old man was speaking from experience. He'd reformed, but still the Cossacks came when you least expected them.

Henry pushed up from the bench, and Everett rose with him. The dog had been busy making mincemeat of his cane and it was a lost cause. Henry would have to do without it on the walk home. He extended a hand. "Thank you for your time, sir."

"You're not leaving! I've got the gingerbread!"

Henry turned to see Rachel, her cheeks pink and her hair a bit flyaway. She must have run both ways.

"Now, Rachel," her father cautioned, "Lord Challoner has things to do. He has to keep to his routine." It was a warning if Henry ever heard one.

"Nonsense, Dad. A bit of gingerbread and a cup of tea won't take any time at all. I'll go put the kettle on. You two sit outside and enjoy this beautiful morning. I'll bring out a tray."

"Fuck." The old man sat back down, unrepentant over his language.

Henry remained standing. "I don't want to get you both in trouble. You've been very kind."

"Oh, sit down. I'll deal with the governors. They won't be best pleased."

"The governors?"

"Those that administer the Puddling Rehabilitation Foundation. They determine the appropriate program for each Guest—we have a variety to choose from, you know. And they distribute the funds to the townspeople annually. Make and enforce the rules."

Henry sat and tried to smile. "I take it we're breaking them now."

Everett sighed. "Oh, yes. It's not so bad you met me, but Rachel is completely off-limits."

"Who are these governors?"

"Sir Bertram Sykes is chairman. Has his fingers in a lot of the village's pies, being the richest man about. Pretty odd when his own mother was one of the early Guests. Quite a handful, she was. If you ask me, she never really settled down—I remember her from when I was a lad. Charlie Oakley, Vincent Walker—whoever the current doctor and vicar are automatically get on the board. Miss Violet Churchill. Frank Stanchfield, the grocer. Two others...I'm sorry, I forget. My memory isn't what it was. It's always seven, though. Since the very beginning in 1806."

"Three-quarters of a century," Henry marveled. "How does it work, exactly?"

Everett scratched behind an ear and settled in to talk. "In the beginning, the better—and I'm using that word loosely, now—families of England put money in, as a sort of insurance program. Knew that if they needed a place to stash their difficult relatives, they'd have something better than their attics or a lunatic asylum. Puddlingites shared the pot. After a bit, one of the Sykes decided to invest the proceeds, and the pot got bigger. Now there are individual fees from the Guests' families as well, people who weren't part of the original agreement, like your pa. Word spreads amongst your class. Everyone knows about Puddling-on-the-Wold."

"I didn't," Henry said.

"But your father did. Hustled you right here when the trouble came, didn't he?"

Henry nodded. He'd been thrown into the carriage most precipitously, having barely enough time to pull his pants up or kiss the girls goodbye.

"It's been a gold mine for the village," Everett continued. "You may not know it to look at me, but I've plenty in the bank. Even Rachel doesn't know how much." He named a figure that raised Henry's eyebrows.

The girl was virtually an heiress!

The Everett cottage was modest, but appearances could be deceiving, as Henry well knew. "So, your daughter has a dowry." An understatement.

"Now don't go and get any ideas! My Rachel's not for the likes of you."

Henry decided not to take offense. "You'd object to a viscount for a son-in-law?"

"I object to *you*, young man. Moderation in all things, that's my motto."

"It wasn't always," Henry reminded him gently.

"That's neither here nor there," Everett mumbled. "We're not talking about me."

"What if..." Henry stopped himself. A minute ago he was thinking clearly; suddenly, he felt muddled. He wasn't fit to be anyone's husband, and he barely knew Rachel Everett. It was just that in her presence he felt a bit...calmer, but stimulated, too.

That made no sense. No wonder he was stuck here in Puddling with a daily lecture and gallons of tea.

Speaking of which. He leaped up to help Rachel as she came into the garden with a large tray, forgetting completely that one foot was more or less uncooperative. His knee buckled, but he was saved from making a fool of himself by Rufus, who chose that moment to jump up at him. His jerky movement only looked like he was bending to pet the dog, and he sat back down promptly, Rufus climbing into his lap as if they were the best of friends.

"I would have come to your assistance, but your dog had other ideas," Henry said, giving the dog an affectionate scratch behind its ear.

"Down, Rufus! Bad dog!" Rachel set the tray on an overturned barrel that seemed to serve as a table. "I do apologize for his bad manners, my lord. He seems quite taken with you."

"And I with him," Henry lied. "What sort of a dog is he?"

Rachel blushed. "We are not sure of his parentage. A neighbor's bitch had puppies, and he was the only one who hadn't found a home."

"Lucky little fellow." Henry turned his face as the dog attempted to lick him. Rachel picked Rufus up from his lap and set him back on the ground.

"It'll be the dog house for you next," Everett said, pouring his own cup of tea. Henry wasn't sure if he meant the dog or him.

"Dad! I'll do that. Lord Challoner will think us savages."

They probably didn't use the pretty china on the tray every day. Rachel had fussed, and Henry was absurdly flattered. She passed him a cup of tea and a flower-sprigged plate with a slice of iced gingerbread on it. Henry placed the dishes on top of the bench. It was a far cry from the tea parties of his youth, with linen clothes and lashings of silver—and a disapproving butler hovering nearby—but somehow the fresh air made everything taste better.

"Rachel's gingerbread beats this when she makes it," Everett said. Henry wondered if the man remembered he was supposed to be discouraging Henry's attentions.

"It's very good." And it was. For a homely brown rectangle, it disappeared quickly.

"Would you like more, my lord?"

No. Henry didn't want to waste time chewing when he longed to get Rachel Everett behind a raspberry bush. But, he behaved himself. Said the right things to both his hosts until Mr. Everett yawned.

"It's time I face my housekeeper." Henry reluctantly got to his feet, slower this time so he wouldn't disgrace himself. "This was...the nicest time I've had in Puddling yet. Thank you both for your hospitality. I hope I see you again."

Mr. Everett frowned. But Henry was used to out-maneuvering the enemy and his superiors, and one old man and seven governors were not going to get in his way.

Chapter 12

Rachel slipped out the back door of the cottage. Her father was sleeping soundly; had, in fact, napped in the afternoon and had gone to bed early. He hadn't said much about their visitor or what he'd come for, and Rachel was grateful. She wasn't sure she could make him believe that she was not the least bit interested in Lord Challoner, that he was just another routine Guest who didn't make her heart and eyelashes flutter.

She knew she was being foolish. She wasn't a silly schoolgirl anymore, but a twenty-three year old woman who should know that handsome is as handsome does. Rachel had seen good-looking men before—well, all right, not so very many—and she'd never been susceptible. Vincent Walker had been right here this afternoon to report on the school day and he was certainly handsome enough, but she didn't feel a hint of breathlessness. She made total sense when she talked to him. Spoke in complete sentences. Her wits didn't ramble and she didn't wonder how he looked without his trousers on. Vincent was a friend of sorts, and destined to stay one.

Rachel was not going to become Mrs. Walker, no matter how many times interfering Puddlingites threw the two of them together.

It wasn't as if Rachel objected to being a clergyman's wife. She was as charitably inclined as the next person, and took the Commandments seriously. She felt God's encompassing love every time she stepped out her door and gazed at the green hills beyond the village, or comforted a crying child. There was beauty and innocence all around her, and she worked to combat the ugly and venal when she came across them.

But to marry without love, even if there was some affection, would not be in her future if she could help it. She would go to her grave a virgin, as wasteful as that seemed.

Perhaps not. What if...

She shook her head in the cool night air. She was missing sleep, that was all. Her mind was wandering where it really shouldn't go, and she needed to circle it back. Where was her inner border collie? Fast asleep under a tree, letting the sheep frolic and trample his paws with no consequences.

Rachel could see why a woman would like to dally with Captain Lord Henry Challoner. He was beautiful, if that could be said for a man. He had a wicked, mischievous streak, but some vulnerability too. He certainly wouldn't want anyone to feel sorry for him, but would he turn down some comfort?

He would. He must, if he was ever to leave this place. His father would be furious if he didn't, and probably try to ruin Puddling's reputation. If Guests were not safe from their follies here, why would anyone ever be sent here again? Rachel's rash desire could ruin seventy-five years of success, not to mention bankrupt the village, if she was discovered in Lord Challoner's arms.

Rufus jumped into her lap after she sat down on the bench. Just a few hours ago, Lord Challoner's elegant bottom was right here, encased in fine tweed cloth, a bolt of which probably equaled her yearly salary. Rachel closed her eyes to the stars overhead and imagined she was sitting on his warm lap. Cozy. He might whisper something she didn't quite catch into her ear, then pepper her throat with kisses. His hand would cup her aching breast, skim a nipple—

Oh, really. She was writing her own salacious mental novel and must stop at once. But her traitorous body was tingling and her mind turning to mush, thinking how an experienced man like Henry Challoner could bring her to ecstasy with one finger smoothing over her clavicle.

Well, that was probably impossible. The clavicle was not a sensual spot, was it? Yet Rachel imagined his manicured finger tracing the bones of her jaw and chest until she begged him to go lower. Much lower.

She dumped Rufus off her lap and he gave a startled yip. "Go in your doghouse," Rachel ordered, her voice sounding far from commanding.

Rufus looked ungainly, but he was a very smart dog. With a snort, he frisked away and she soon heard him attack the bone he'd hidden inside in a private dark corner. The gnawing sound was the only thing audible in the night—there was a palpable hush over Puddling, just as it should be, all good people abed. Scattered stars above winked but couldn't see, and Rachel shifted and lifted her nightgown.

She had touched herself a very few times before, but always with a faceless fantasy. Tonight, she had Henry Challoner, who loomed over her, his fair hair begging to be swept back over his noble brow.

It *was* noble, too, although a little dinged at the moment. Rachel removed the bandage and healed him with one blink. Her fingers became lost in his soft curls. His lips quirked and came closer.

They were full but not feminine. Designed to smile and tease. They touched hers with the slightest pressure, and she opened to him.

Opened everywhere. Her legs parted and he found the sweet secret swelling of flesh. She was wet just from thinking of him, and his smile widened over hers. His stroke was sure, and not gentle. His thumb circled and spun her to the brink in hardly any time at all, his tongue doing the same inside her mouth. Round and round, until every inch of her body felt loose but poised to knot up any second. She leaned back against the bench, gasping, whispering forbidden words, words she shouldn't even know and would never say aloud to any man. Fever shot through her. The climb began as she arched up, her muscles taut, releasing to liquid heat, flaming and dying, then flickering up again. Higher and higher still. Rachel mustn't make a sound, but oh how she wanted to, grateful for this moment of pure joy.

She was wicked, doing such a thing outdoors beneath heaven. But God must see into her heart, take pity on her, know she just needed—

The gate creaked. Rufus came running from the doghouse growling like a dog three times his size.

"Down."

There was no mistaking the voice, rough though it sounded. Rachel removed her hand and frantically pulled down her nightgown.

How long had he been standing there? What had he heard?

He must have seen.

She felt hot and cold all over. Nauseous. She wanted to die, although dying seemed too easy an out. The shovel was just right over there by the shed. Perhaps he could help her bury herself alive and end her mortification.

"I couldn't sleep. I'm not sure why I came this way and up the alley. Tempting fate, I suppose, and Rufus. I'm glad I did."

His voice was pitched low, the words thick. He was truly looming over her now. Rachel licked her lips, opened her mouth and croaked. Rufus was gathered up in the crook of his arm, his belly being rubbed, tongue lolling sideways. Could she be jealous of the dog?

Yes.

"That was...beautiful. You were beautiful. I wish there was more than a half-moon."

Rachel hadn't even noticed the moon rising. It sat low and bright, and she felt naked under his hot gaze.

"I—you should go," she whispered. She was mortified. Horrified. Embarrassed. There needed to be a stronger word for her current emotions.

"Not yet. I'm not sure I can walk." Henry—Lord Challoner—gestured towards his trousers. Even in the dark, Rachel could see the tenting evidence of his arousal.

"This isn't right, you sneaking about," she hissed.

"I know," he said simply. He put the dog down and sat on the bench uninvited. "I can smell you. Oh, God." He drew a hand over his face. "I don't think I can last."

"This is completely improper. Go away!" Rufus scurried off to the doghouse. If only Lord Challoner would do the same.

"Don't want to. Rachel Everett, you are ruining me." He sounded as if he were in pain.

"That's exactly right! What if you are discovered here? We'd both be in disgrace. You can't be cured if you're engaged in...whatever it's called."

"Voyeurism. I must say nothing I've ever seen before tops the last ten minutes. I've never been so hard in my life."

He'd *watched* people?

"Shut up!" The neighbors would wake, and know what she'd set in motion. She'd be punished, and so would the village in the end.

"You're the one making all the noise. I had no idea a prim schoolteacher could have such a colorful vocabulary."

Rachel was going to expire of shame or apoplexy, whatever came first. "You are a scoundrel! In fact, you are absolutely horrible!"

"Guilty as charged. But you're not precisely innocent, are you?"

Rachel's face grew hotter. He was right. She'd committed some sort of sin tonight, and a few other nights, too. Her vivid desires had been mostly suppressed until Lord Henry Challoner jumped over the wall and into her head. There he'd been with his cocky smile. That adorable dimple. His rumpled curls and aristocratic nose. Whatever tragedies he'd suffered were absent as imaginary Henry had brought her to completion.

But her own hand was responsible, and she couldn't really blame him for being so insidiously attractive.

"I'll have you know I am a virgin!"

Henry clucked. "That's too bad. I could use some help here."

Rachel shut her eyes, willing him away.

She could feel him lean nearer. "That won't work, you know. I'm not going to disappear just because you can't see me."

Her eyes flew open, and she pushed him away. "Please, *please* go. We're both in dreadful danger. I'll lose my job, and you'll be stuck here another month."

"That wouldn't be so bad if I had your company." Such gallant words, even if he didn't mean them.

"But you wouldn't have my company. They'll send me away and dose you with saltpeter."

Lord Challoner shook his head. "Not if we were married."

She had never met such an exasperating man. "Not that again! Are you never serious?"

"Rachel, I *am* serious. I heard you call my name when you came. You want me, and I want you. Marriages have begun on shakier footings."

"But your father—"

"To hell with my father!" He was angry now, no trace of that crease in his cheek. "The man doesn't control my purse strings. I'm of age, and I have some money of my own. I only came because he was so sure Puddling would help my—my condition. I'd gotten quite desperate, you know. Sometimes I felt like I was on a spinning merry-go-round that picked up speed and was impossible to get off. But I see things more clearly now."

She opened her mouth, but he set a finger across her lips. "I *do*, Rachel. After a little more than a week, Puddling has worked its miracle. I even have an idea to help other poor fools like me. You could help. You're very soothing to be around when you're not frigging yourself."

She was truly speechless now. He *was* mad.

"I'd better go. It's late, and the last thing I want to do is get you in trouble. If I can smuggle a letter out, I'll see about getting a special license. We can be married in a few days. Walker can do the honors."

He would destroy everything that Puddling stood for—his father the marquess would see to that.

She couldn't, wouldn't let that happen.

Chapter 13

Henry's blood sang. He knew it would be all right somehow. In a few days he'd be settled. Have a purpose. His wild ways would be behind him. He'd have a wife who was filled with passion, not some desiccated society girl of his father's choosing who would lie like a dead thing under him.

The pater might object to Miss Rachel Elizabeth Everett on the basis of her modest birth and upbringing, but she stood to inherit a small fortune. And she was beyond comely, with her cascading dark hair and unusual eyes. Her plump thighs and even plumper breasts. But his erection would never go away unless he stopped admiring her under the moonlight.

By God, she'd been magnificent, head thrown back and writhing on the bench, her hand hidden in her curls. Her legs were so long and white, and he had imagined them wrapped around him the longer he stood stunned at the garden gate.

At first, he had thought he was hallucinating again, this time without the benefit of opiates, but his eyes weren't deceiving him. In his most scattered thoughts, he'd never expected to see Rachel in the throes of passion, half-naked and crying out his name in her crisis. And all the enticingly filthy things she'd whispered before—and he'd heard every bit of it, even with his faulty hearing. It was a bloody miracle, and he was the luckiest man in the world.

"No. I will never marry you. Now go home."

His castle in the air crumpled. "What?"

"I knew you were standing there at the gate. I just said what I did to trick you and to amuse myself. To see how far you'd go. You might say it was all a performance to an audience of one. Good to know it worked."

She was lying. He knew it, and told her so.

"God, Henry, you're so predictable. So needy. There's a reason you're here. You aren't every maiden's dream. More like their nightmare. Who wants to be saddled for life with a fellow like you? Get yourself under control, would you? You're far too impulsive—it says so right in your dossier."

His impulsiveness had saved his life more times than he could count. Sometimes it was better to act than think.

But apparently not tonight.

Her words were designed to hurt, and they would have—if he believed them. She'd gone all stiff and bristly. Gone was the sinuous girl who arched and stretched and trembled. Who had cried out for him in her greatest need. Those were her real words, not these cold things that now fell from her scornful lips.

"You don't mean it."

"I don't? You don't know what I mean, or who I am, Henry. We are strangers, and will stay that way. We have nothing in common. If you weren't so...disturbed, you'd recognize that. I'm not your port in the storm. You're just bored, and I'm handy."

"That's not true." It may have been at first, when she'd dazzled him in the schoolyard. But from the little bit of time he'd spent with her since, he'd grown to like her quite a lot. She had wit, kindness and couldn't be bullied. The pater would have a hard time bringing her to heel.

"You think if you marry me, it will be the ultimate poke in the eye to your father. Well, I'm not playing that game, let me tell you."

"No!" *Could she read his mind?* Those smoky gray eyes of hers saw everything, even in the darkness.

"Spare me. You chafe at his rules, and how better to break them than by bringing home an unsuitable woman? I'm not an experiment, Henry. You'll grow tired of me once the novelty wears off, and then we'll both be miserable. And besides," she said, taking a breath, "I am already engaged."

Impossible! "You never said so. Your father never mentioned it, either." Why wasn't she screaming this other lover's name when her fingers were so busy?

Unless there was another Henry. Another "my lord."

Henry had been good at maths, and the chances of that were pretty much nil.

"My father doesn't know yet. It's a secret."

"Who is it?" Henry demanded. He would give any local yokel a run for his money. He was a bloody viscount, heir to a marquessate! Perhaps a bit...disturbed, as she said, but not entirely deranged. Henry had prospects. Plans. A future.

"It's Vincent. Vincent Walker."

"The *vicar*?"

This was most unwelcome news. Walker was a nice-looking fellow. One might even call him handsome in a bland, parson-like way, even if he had a bit of a receding hairline. He was well-spoken and had been well-educated.

But a damned *vicar*. She couldn't throw herself away on a man like that, visiting the poor and the sick and making calf's foot jelly for the rest of her life. Rolling bandages. Knitting hats for chilly babies. Singing in the choir. Presiding over the cake table at the annual church fete. Filling up the vicarage on Vicarage Lane with pious little Walkers.

It was unthinkable, although he'd managed to think quite a few sentences.

"Yes. We have an understanding." She stood, her nightgown swirling around her shapely ankles. "I am tired, and going to bed. I strongly advise you to do the same."

"I'm not sleepy." That had been the trouble an hour ago, and was definitely the case now. Henry's brain was in revolt.

She couldn't be in love with Walker. She had kissed him—he, Henry—with desire and innocence. Henry would bet his sorry life she'd never even kissed the other man. Or *any* man.

She folded her arms over her lovely bosom. "Perhaps you should be getting more fresh air and exercise. Those are part of your daily requirements."

"As well as a talk and tea with your fiancé. Do you have any intimate message for him for me to convey tomorrow? He's never said a word to me about you as he's talked my ear off about Puddling's perfections. I long to assist in young love, since it seems I am to have no happiness of my own."

She put her arm out and tugged at his sleeve. "No! That is to say, he would be distressed to know I've revealed our arrangement. It's early days yet. Please don't say anything to him." Her voice had risen, and there was a touch of hysteria to it.

"What? I can't congratulate the old boy? Ask him for pointers on how to woo the second-prettiest girl in the village? Who would that be, anyway?"

Rachel grabbed his hand and squeezed it. "You mustn't say a word to him! Promise me!"

"I can," said Henry, hoping the circulation would return. "But promises were made to be broken, especially by such an unreliable person as I am.

One never knows what I might say or do. I'll need incentive to keep my mouth shut."

"I have nothing I can give you," Rachel said, releasing his hand, clearly furious. "No true gentleman would ask for bribe money."

"Who said anything about money? Perhaps a slice of gingerbread would do. Or a kiss. And you must know by now, I'm no gentleman." He took a wobbly step forward. His foot was killing him.

"I will not kiss you! I'm an engaged woman!"

"Walker will never know. It's not as if you're already married. When's the big day?"

"We haven't set a date. He hasn't spoken to my father yet to ask for my hand."

"And what a lovely hand it is." Henry had captured one as she'd waved both around to repel him. She tried to pull away, but he could hold fast too.

Slow and steady wins the race, Henry, he reminded himself, as he gazed into her eyes, or what he could see of them in the hushed darkness. He did that circling the palm thing; it was always a sure-fire success. Just the slightest touch from his thumb, and women were putty. It was not to Henry's benefit to question why tickling and kissing places like palms and back of knees and earlobes made women a little crazy. He raised Rachel's limp hand and planted a feather-light kiss on each knuckle, then turned it.

The merest lick at the center, and her knees buckled.

"Stop," she whispered.

No chance of that. Henry nibbled his way up to her wrist, pulling the sleeve of her white nightgown back. Her pulse was rapid. He lowered her to the bench so they both wouldn't fall. His pulse was rapid as well.

Did Walker—if he was indeed her fiancé, the virtuous cur—make her feel like this? Wasn't it a sin for a vicar to kiss a virgin? If not, it should be.

Cradling her in one arm, he slid his fingers into her hair and angled her so that he could kiss her properly. Or improperly, as the case may be. Her lids drifted down, her lips parted, and Henry came home.

The kiss was soft. Sweet. There was no urgency—they had all the time in the world. Until dawn at least, which was a thousand hours away. He explored the inside of a plush cheek and could practically taste pink. She sighed and was boneless in his embrace, all edges blurred, all angles subdued. What would he give for a feather bed right now instead of this hard bench? He'd tip her back and kiss her everywhere.

And she might kiss him everywhere. A shiver ran through him, though the night was mild. To be touched by a woman who truly cared, not one of his actress lovers, who were so professional and precise in their attentions Henry may as well have been a chalked-up haberdasher's dummy. God, she tasted good. Smelled better. She must bathe with lavender soap. Henry had missed such civilized scents in Africa—there, it was all heat and blood and horse. His senses were clouded by Rachel and her surrounding garden. A Garden of Eden, or as close as Henry was ever apt to come to one.

His innocence was lost long ago, but hers wasn't. He wouldn't touch her breasts or the center of her pleasure. Yet. Henry would concentrate on her lips and tongue, the smooth inner cheek, her perfect teeth. She moaned, and he delved deeper.

Moonlight. Lavender. Girl. Well, woman, he supposed. An inexperienced woman, who was not so shy that she wasn't kissing him back in a most profound way. Henry felt his skin dance and the hairs on the back of his neck lift.

And that was his last thought before the shovel came down upon his head.

Chapter 14

If Rachel thought she had been horrified before, it was nothing to what she was feeling now as she looked down at Henry's possibly dead body.

"Dad, I can explain."

"I doubt it. Grab his shoulders."

Rachel did as she was told, as her father took the man's booted feet. Lord Challoner was no lightweight, but he was, praise God, breathing.

"What if he comes to and has us arrested?"

"Who will believe him? He had a bad dream after he tripped and fell. The man can't seem to stand up straight here in Puddling, poor devil." Her father shouldered the gate open and they made their way down the little alley between their house and the neighbor's. The street was illuminated by the moon, but Rachel could have walked the village in pitch blackness.

Of course, she'd never been carrying an inert man before.

"He asked me to marry him," she whispered.

"A lie if I ever heard one. He just wants to get under your skirts, and from the looks of it he was succeeding."

Rachel felt herself blush in the dark. "It was only a kiss."

Pete Everett snorted. They continued in silence. Rachel was rather amazed how strong her father still seemed to be.

"Where will we put him?"

"The graveyard. Where else? He'll get the message."

Rachel wasn't about to argue and wake all of Puddling. The churchyard was much closer than Lord Challoner's house, and she dutifully shuffled down the street.

In her nightgown. Suppose someone was up and saw them? They'd go to prison for sure.

No, Puddlingites stuck together. Pete Everett had a reputation. By the time he was done, the villagers would come after Lord Challoner with pitchforks and brands.

Rachel had had a moment of weakness. A very long lapse. The kiss had been delicious and she'd fallen right into the spirit of things. Of what came before, she resolutely pushed out of her mind.

What would her father think if he knew the cause of Lord Challoner's lust? It was too excruciating to think about.

She had been wicked, and now she was being punished. An accessory, if not to a murder, then to an assault.

Lord Challoner was not safe around the Everetts.

The painted white face of the church tower clock glowed above. Not much further. Just inside the wall of triangular yews were the oldest table tombs. It may have been disrespectful to the dead, but the stones were wide enough to arrange an unconscious man.

Hopefully he wouldn't roll off when he woke up.

If he woke up. He could be so injured...

No, mustn't think the worst. Rachel stepped back from her spurned swain. Even in the dim light, he was so handsome it hurt to look at him.

Her father nudged her. "We'd best be going."

She nodded. This was the end. If he had a brain in his battered head, Captain Lord Henry Challoner would leave her alone for good.

A tear slipped down her cheek and she mopped it away with the sleeve of her gown. Rachel trudged home behind her father, who really was a figure of fun in his nightcap, nightshirt and stockings. Her own feet were bare, and a pebble or two slowed her walk up the street.

It was dreadfully late. How would she be able to rise early and teach school as usual? She couldn't ask Vincent to do it again—he'd had a slightly hunted look about him when he'd come to report yesterday afternoon. He was good with the children, but the days were long and the challenges endless. Though he was a good man—too good for her—not everyone was suited to be cloistered with ten rowdy children all day long.

Oh, dear. What if Henry broke his promise and spoke to Vincent about their "engagement"? She would have to talk to him as soon as possible.

Rachel's father put himself right to bed without any discussion, and Rachel tried to do the same. Her mattress felt as if it were stuffed with the pebbles she'd kicked away walking home. She tossed, turned, worried. What if Henry didn't recover?

He hadn't really been hit that hard, just enough to knock some sense into him, her father said. Was Henry truly unconscious this time, or was he playing possum as he did in the wheelbarrow? There was no hope for sleep. She rose and dressed in the dark. This time she slipped on half-boots. Rachel let herself out, keeping Rufus inside. Getting to the churchyard this time was much easier. An owl's hoot startled her and caused her to stumble. Lord, but she was jumpy, almost waiting for an unknown constable—the village didn't have one—to incarcerate her. The telegraph office was closed, so Henry couldn't have reported the incident—he didn't even know there *was* a telegraph. Any modern communications with the outside world was firmly hidden from the Guests, or who knows what might happen. Music hall girls and gin might arrive by the wagon-load.

Oh, God. He was still there splayed under the stars and moon. She tiptoed to the tomb and bent over.

There was no blood. In fact, he looked like a white marble effigy. Trembling she put two fingers at the pulse of his throat.

"Come back to finish me off?"

"Eep!" She jumped back, heart hammering. "Are you all right?"

"Apparently, despite your every effort. I was just counting the stars before you came. It's quite relaxing lying here in the dark. I never noticed the stars much until Africa; they really are the only good thing about the place, besides the unusual animals. No fog or factory smoke, you know." Henry sat up and swung his legs off the stone. "I hope the fellow under me has not been discomposed by my arrival."

"I—I was w-worried," Rachel stammered. She should have known better. He seemed perfectly fine, jaunty, even. Until his next words.

"I'll bet. It's a capital crime to kill a peer. Death by hanging, I believe."

He wouldn't report them, would he? Her father was much too old to stand trial. "We didn't mean to kill you! My father misunderstood."

"Oh, I think he understood all too well. We'll have to marry now, Rachel Everett. We have been caught practically *en flagrante delicto.* It was only my dubious honor preventing me from pouncing upon you earlier. Does your father know what *you* get up to under the stars?"

Hateful man. "I t-told you. I am promised to V-Vincent Walker."

Henry snapped his fingers. "I don't think the good vicar will mind if I make a large donation to St. Jude's."

"You can't buy me! Vincent l-l-loves me." Rachel always had difficulty lying. Her words sounded hollow even to her.

"I'm sure he'll see reason when he finds out you never said *his* name when you crested to orgasm." Henry hopped down. "You're coming home with me, and we'll finish what you started."

"I will not!" Rachel cried, nearly loud enough to wake the dead.

"You know you want to," the viscount said imperturbably. "And as we're nearly betrothed, why shouldn't we anticipate our vows? Isn't that what country folk do?"

"I wouldn't know," Rachel replied coldly. "You cannot take me against my will."

"I wouldn't dream of it," Henry said, throwing an arm around her shoulder and almost knocking her down. "I may need some assistance getting back down the hill. I seem to have trouble keeping track of my stick, and I must confess, I do have a bit of a headache. Again." He looked down at her, a faint smile curling his lips.

Rachel was guilty. But not *that* guilty. "I will help you get home, and that's all."

"We'll see."

He certainly would. Rachel was not some London lightskirt who would do his bidding for coin and bed him. Up until his arrival in Puddling, she had been a respectable spinster. A teacher. If she engaged in any sort of improper contact with him, she wouldn't be entrusted with the village's children.

Oh, it was all too late. The impropriety was already a matter of fact, and Rachel felt her eyes well up once more. Not only was she ruining her own life, but Puddling's financial security as well. The Marquess of Harland would see her as a temptress. An adventuress who took advantage of his boy in his moment—his month—of weakness.

Henry was not a boy, however, and was quite determined about this marriage business. Rachel hated to admit it, but the man *was* cracked. His wartime experiences must have led to brain fever and he'd lost all judgment. She was not qualified to be a viscountess, as he must surely know. He wanted to teach his father a lesson, and a lowborn schoolteacher was going to be his weapon.

Rachel wanted to be married for love, not revenge. Henry didn't love her; he barely knew her. He was lonely and at loose ends, suffering withdrawal from all his bad habits. And she, idiot that she was, had romanticized and fantasized about him.

Rachel was just as cracked as he was.

Henry touched the stone retaining wall with his free hand as they descended Honeywell Lane. She had a vision of them falling and rolling down to the bottom at Puddling Stream, tumbling arse over teakettle. Maybe she should try to trip him and get away, but he clung to her tighter as if he divined her intention.

The gate to his cottage squeaked as Henry opened it. "Just a few steps more." Rachel wondered whether he was encouraging her or himself. Stone stairs had been built into the incline, and then a narrow high-hedged pathway led up to his front door. Rachel smelled the early roses as she walked under their trellis.

Henry patted his pocket. "No key."

Rachel was almost overwhelmed with relief. "It must have fallen out of your pocket when we…um…"

"No worries. There's another under the flower pot at the door. I bet you know that—you Puddlingites know everything. A Guest can be inspected at any time, correct? Just to make sure we're not dallying with the housekeeper or drinking the drain fluid." He bent over an urn of geraniums. "Ah! Here it is. What luck."

It was not lucky for Rachel. Did she dare bean him on the head again to get away?

No, she would talk her way out of Stonecrop and into her own bed. She just needed to be patient. Cunning. Resourceful.

The trouble was, she felt like none of those things. Her brain was filled with sheep's wool.

Henry lit the lamp in the hallway. It was so bright, she blinked. What a mess she must be after throwing her clothes on in such a panic. She was so sure Henry had been in danger, lying exposed in the night air.

She was the one in danger. And how was she going to get herself out of it?

Chapter 15

Henry should have his head examined.

What was left of it.

An hour or so ago, he was feeling amorous. At the moment, he was anything but, despite his words to the contrary. His ears were ringing, very much like when the damn cannon went off too close to him. He was bone-weary, and if Rachel hadn't come along, he might have spent the night sleeping on top of a grave.

It had been peaceful in the churchyard, with the hoot of a wakeful owl and the occasional chirp of a cricket. As he lay still on the cool stone slab, he swore he could hear the far-off stream rushing. Cloth mills had once been powered by its force, but according to his rival, good old Vincent Walker, there was no industry left hereabouts. They were now in the rehabilitation business, and after tonight, Henry was sure he was not destined to be one of Puddling's successes.

He was not going to ignore his manly urges, and it wouldn't harm him to have a glass of champagne to celebrate that fact, either. He was no true drunkard. Perhaps his father was right—Henry had overindulged when he got back home, but he was steadier now. He'd been foolish. Reckless. Life had seemed random and pointless, and he'd acted accordingly.

Henry knew he was too old for such rebellion. Lucky, too. Instead of dwelling on his infirmities and the death he'd escaped all around him, it was time for him to live. What better way to go forward than with a sensible young woman with sterling values?

Rachel was warm and intelligent. Good with children. Pretty, too. Very pretty. The pater would have to respect his selection, wouldn't he? Henry might be jumping his fences a bit, but life, as he knew, was short.

"You're home safe now. I'll leave you."

Henry reached for her. "Please don't."

"I can't—I won't. Don't you understand anything?"

Henry shook his head. "Enlighten me."

"I've already told you. I—I'm engaged."

He pushed a strand of loose dark hair behind her ear. "Why don't I believe you?"

"I don't know! Because you're insane?"

"Not any more. All those hits to my head have cleared everything up."

"Look, Henry," she said with impatience, "there can never be anything between us. We come from two completely different worlds. Your father would never accept me. And—and—you'll ruin Puddling! We'll never be trusted to take in any more Guests!"

"Ah." So there was the crux of it. Henry frowned. What could be done about that? Rachel was more than likely right. Henry's father would scream bloody murder to all of his friends accusing Rachel of being some sort of Puddling Delilah who took advantage of his addled son.

There went the livelihood of the village.

He hadn't considered that aspect of wooing her. True, he hadn't thought the pater would welcome her with open arms, even knowing that she stood to inherit a considerable sum. Money wasn't everything when it came to marriage. But after what he'd gone through, Henry deserved to marry the woman he wanted, even if he didn't know her favorite color.

"What's your favorite color?"

Rachel stared at him. "You're ill, no matter what you say. I'm going home."

"No, seriously, I'd like to know. I want to get to know you better, Rachel. I'm here for a few more weeks. I'm sure I'll think of something to protect Puddling from my father's wrath. Just give me a chance."

Her eyebrows reminded him of feathery black wings. "You won't stop this nonsense?"

"Don't you want to leave here, charming as it is? Be mistress of a fine house? Have a husband you will treat you well and provide for any children that come along? You can have anything you desire, Rachel."

"Not possible," she muttered.

"Anything is possible with effort," Henry said, almost believing it.

She pulled away. "Look. You are here in Puddling because you made bad choices. How do I know I'm not another one of them?"

Henry opened his mouth, then shut it. She had a point. Henry knew he rushed into trouble. Always had, ever since he was a little boy. His joining the army was just one instance of many. His conduct when he'd returned to London had been deplorable—he saw that now.

But all the resentment he'd felt toward his father had evaporated. If the man hadn't stuck him here, he wouldn't have met Rachel Everett and begun to see the error of his ways.

"I can't fix you, Henry. You have to fix yourself. With Vincent's help, clean living, and your Service, you might. Don't confuse your lust with anything else. That's what brought you here in the first place."

Ouch.

"It's not just lust." He was fairly sure of that.

Again with the eyebrows. Soon they would migrate to her hairline and disappear in the dark thicket of her curly fringe. "Spare me. You are not in a position to make such momentous decisions like marrying. The consequences could be fatal to the village, do you understand? If you like me, you'll leave me alone."

"I don't think I can." He certainly didn't want to. Talking to Rachel— and kissing her—was the most fun he'd had in ages, better than any of the empty diversions he'd tried in the months he'd been home.

"Try. It's vital to my future. Puddling's future. You're not some Prince Charming here with a magical glass slipper to sweep Cinderella away."

Henry gazed down. She was wearing boots now, but he remembered her plump bare feet flexing, toes curling in her garden. He'd never seen anything so erotic in his life as she pleasured herself, and he'd seen a great deal these past few months.

"I can't convince you to come upstairs with me?" He knew the answer.

Mercury. That's what her eyes reminded him of. She gave him a very direct look and shook her head.

"Very well. I'll walk you home." It would kill him to act the gentleman, but he must.

"Don't be ridiculous! I just walked *you* home. I know my way."

"Of course you do, but it's not far. What if you were to encounter some rabid animal, a wolf or something, out there?" Like himself, he supposed.

"There are no wolves left in England."

"Nevertheless." He grabbed a walking stick from a Chinese pot in the vestibule. One last trot up the hill and back down. If he couldn't sleep after that, there was no hope for him.

"We don't have to speak. I'll just feel better if I see you to your door." He extended an elbow, and she, bless her, took it.

"Red."

"I beg your pardon?"

"My favorite color is red."

Henry could picture her in a bare-shouldered red dress with no difficulty at all, her thick hair pinned up. Rubies would be necessary, both for her ears and throat.

He didn't worry about locking the door this time; he'd be home soon enough. The sky was turning gray already. Another day in Puddling, following his routine, being gently chastised by Vincent Walker, eating plain fare.

No frosted gingerbread studded with raisins. No quicksilver eyes. No pillowing lips.

Rachel had given him a challenge. How would his courtship of her proceed without bringing harm to the village? Perhaps it was time to write to the pater. Extol the virtues of Puddling and its inhabitants. Declare he was a new man.

The odd thing—he *was*. He'd had an epiphany today, and his old life did not tempt him in the least. But how to convince everyone, most importantly Rachel?

He had time to figure it all out. That was the beauty of Puddling—the repetition, the certainty, the very boredom of the place. Each day was supposed to be very much like the next, until they blended into a month of enforced monkhood.

Well, Henry had already broken several of the rules, and if he was careful, might break more. But true to his word, he uttered not a one to Miss Rachel Everett as he walked her to her door.

Chapter 16

It had been a miserable day, starting as a drizzle and now a downpour. The first raindrop had hit the back of Rachel's neck as she rushed, hatless, out of the house. She was late, and faced ten pairs of accusatory eyes and wet faces waiting under the overhang when she unlocked the schoolhouse door.

Her damp, dull gray school frock clung to her too-ample curves. Could they somehow tell what their demure teacher had been up to in the wee hours of the night? She could scare credit it herself. It was as if she'd been overtaken by another entity. Had she been truly possessed, or just revealed her own wicked nature?

Twenty-three years of good behavior down the drain.

She blamed Henry. Until his arrival, she had mostly ignored her own body's needs, prizing her common sense and virtue. But somehow out in the dark garden she had touched herself as she never had before in the handful of times she'd sought that elusive relief.

And had been watched as she came apart, which was even worse.

But at least she was successful in drilling into Henry's usually impervious head that anything between them was impossible. He'd been mute on the walk home, and had given her hand the mildest shake goodnight. There had been no attempt to kiss or fondle, for which Rachel was grateful.

Perhaps.

She would still speak to Vincent about their imaginary engagement. Rachel wouldn't ask him to lie—as a clergyman he'd be appalled—but he could skirt any questions Henry might ask with vague answers.

Vague was good. Subject-changing even better. Vincent was dedicated to his role in the redemption of Puddling's Guests, and she had no doubt he was capable of conversational misdirection when the occasion called for it. At the end of the day, she sent Tom out to ring the bell after the longest school day of her life. If she'd ever believed in caning, some of the misbehavior today would have warranted it. It was as if the children knew she was exhausted and vulnerable. It was all she could do to keep her voice modulated and her temper in check as the rain pounded on the roof.

It had been remorseless—there had been no possibility of outdoor recess. All of Rachel's rainy-day creative ideas escaped her, and for the last half hour, the children had fidgeted, their hands folded and heads down on their desks "to rest and rethink." Rachel had wanted to do the same, but knew she had to keep both eyes open to spot any infractions. A third eye might have come in handy.

Her pupils filed out into the storm without the usual cheerful chatter. She was faced with a tall stack of busy work that Vincent had assigned yesterday and dim daylight with which to look through it. She shut her eyes, willing the papers away.

"May I come in?"

Rachel was so startled, she knocked them from her desk. "What are you doing here?"

"I brought an umbrella. Have you noticed it's pouring? April showers bring May flowers, and men with umbrellas. Here, I'll get those." In seconds, Henry had crossed the schoolroom floor and was picking everything up. "Eight plus five isn't twelve, is it?"

"Of course it isn't. You shouldn't be here! You promised." The rain had made his golden hair even curlier.

"As I recall, I only promised not to speak last night. It's today now."

"It was today *then*."

"You are a maths whiz. Your father said you'd left without your hat or umbrella. I thought to escort you home so you wouldn't drown."

Dread spread through her. "You've spoken to my father?"

"Yes, we had a nice chat."

"Even though…" She couldn't finish.

"Even though he tried to kill me. Or at least incapacitate me. He denied the first but admitted to the second. He's quite a character, isn't he?"

Henry sounded so ordinary, as if they were discussing the weather. Which they had been.

"Y-yes."

"I've enlisted his help in getting me out of Puddling's bad books. I don't want to be responsible for wrecking the swindle you've all got going on here."

"It's not a swindle! You make us sound like cheats and frauds. I'll have you know Puddling's methods work. You need only ask Vincent to show you the scrapbooks."

"Ah. Your alleged fiancé. And you know they're confidential. None of us are supposed to know about the other inmates."

Rachel blushed. "I hope you didn't say anything to my father about— about my engagement." The word stuck in her throat.

"Why would I, when I was pressing my own suit? Who do you think the old gentleman will prefer as a son-in-law? A thoroughly reformed viscount, or a dull dog of a parson?"

"Vincent is not dull!" Rachel retorted. He wasn't dull so much as earnest. Very, very earnest.

"Anyhow, I've enlisted his help. Three heads will be better than one."

"His help with what?" Rachel was afraid she already knew the answer.

"Why, *our* betrothal, of course, and the subsequent marriage."

She stamped her foot. She knew it was childish, but couldn't help herself. "Why do you want to marry me? The idea is ridiculous. Absurd. You don't know me!"

"I know your favorite color is red." He pulled an envelope from his pocket. "Sorry, it was the best I could do on short notice considering my limited funds. And Puddling is not exactly a hotbed of shops."

"You cannot give me gifts!"

"It's not much. Don't thank me yet."

"I'm not going to thank you at all," Rachel grumbled. This incorrigible man would drive *her* to drink. She'd never met anyone so pig-headed and annoying. There he stood, holding the envelope out to her, a crooked grin on his face. It deepened the dimple Rachel was training herself not to admire.

She snatched the envelope and tore it open. Inside was a short length of ribbon. Scarlet ribbon, edged in black lace. It summoned up a vision of a very naughty corset trimmed with such frippery. Garters, perhaps. Rachel blinked.

"It's a bookmark. Your father tells me you're a great reader. I would have bought you a red book, but they didn't have any."

A red book? As though one read books for the color of their covers. The man was an imbecile.

A cunning imbecile. His eyes were dancing as if he'd known exactly what she'd thought when she first opened the envelope.

She would bring him back to reality with a crash.

"Do you love me?"

The light left his eyes. "I beg your pardon?"

"I forgot. You're hard of hearing, aren't you?" As well as hard-headed. She raised her voice. "Do you love me?"

Henry shrugged. "I don't believe in romantic love. Never have. I suppose that's the sort of book you read? Castles and knights and rescued maidens?"

It was, but she wasn't going to admit to it. "Then why do you want to marry me?"

Henry leaned on his stick. Rachel noticed it showed signs of Rufus's attentions.

"I'd be a good husband to you."

"That's not what I'm asking. What is it about *me* that makes you so insistent? You've been with a hundred girls."

"Hardly that," Henry murmured. "A gentleman doesn't keep count, or if he does, he wouldn't admit to it to a young lady. Look, may I sit down?"

Rachel realized he was dripping on the floor. He'd probably catch pneumonia and die, and then where would they be? Last night's faux effigy would come true.

Under other circumstances, it would have been amusing to see a man of Henry's size fold himself up onto the school bench. She gave him a practiced look, which usually stopped mischief in its tracks, but held no sway this afternoon. Henry was as deep into mischief as he could get in a teetotal town.

"I—I like you." He looked sheepish.

"That's not enough."

"It's a start. You are intelligent. Very attractive. You, ah, stimulate me."

"Lust wears off." Rachel assumed that was true—she had no first-hand experience. She was still completely in the thrall of lust for Lord Henry Challoner.

But lust wasn't obliterating her good sense. Henry didn't seem to have any to begin with, which was why he was here in Puddling.

"Look, I have to marry someone. Why not you? What have you got against being a viscountess? Eventually, you'll be a marchioness. Only the queen and duchesses will have precedence over you."

"I don't care anything about that." She examined her gray homespun skirt. "Do I look like a viscountess, Henry? Tell me the truth—would I pass muster with your father?"

Henry shifted uneasily on the bench. "We'd have to buy you new clothes, of course."

"You may dress a pig in pearls, but it's still a pig."

"Oh, for heaven's sake, Rachel! You are nothing like a pig. You are... you are a very compelling woman. Beautiful, really. You could do a lot as my wife. Found schools instead of teach in one. Your father could live with us. I've asked him."

Not a word about affection or respect. Henry's proposal was most unprepossessing.

"What does my father think of your suit?" Rachel hoped he wasn't going senile. Forgetful was one thing, but encouraging Henry Challoner in this ridiculous affair was disturbing.

"He has reservations, of course. But I mean to persuade him. And you."

"I would think I was the most important party," Rachel said dryly.

"Of course you are!" Henry said quickly. He cleared his throat. "Do you like *me*?"

"I don't know." To his credit, Henry's face didn't crumple or shoulders sag.

"Quite right. I haven't the best reputation. A sensible girl like you is wise to be wary. See, that's why I want to marry you. You're sensible."

Rachel curbed the urge to throw her inkpot at him. She didn't want to be sensible at the moment! But really, of course Henry didn't love her. She didn't love him either. She hardly knew him, and she wasn't even supposed to know as much as she did. She'd be getting a visit from members of the Puddling Rehabilitation Foundation any second to accuse her of sabotage.

Someone would have noticed him walking down the hill to the school on such a filthy day, and would blame her for being some sort of Circe. Unless he was planning on plunging into the stream and getting even wetter, the school was the final destination.

She stood up. "While I am grateful for both your offer of escort and of marriage, I must decline both. Good day, Lord Challoner."

He rose too, with a blinding smile. "At least take my umbrella."

"Did you hear me?" Rachel cried.

"Yes. I have my good ear turned toward you. And I'm getting better at reading lips. Of course, when I look at yours, I forget what you're saying and just want to kiss you."

Well, that was almost romantic. Rachel tried not to feel a pleased flutter.

"I insist you take the umbrella." Henry propped it against her desk. "I assume you don't wish to be seen with me."

"You assume correctly."

"Very well. Shall I leave first?"

"Don't you have a hat?"

"No, I hate them."

Blast. He would be soaked by the time he climbed back up the hill. He was probably used to marching in the rain. Beneath the scorching sun. Under conditions in countries she couldn't even fathom or find on a map. It wasn't as if it was an Indian monsoon out there—just a heavy warm English rain. Rachel had not been looking forward to it herself, but hadn't been afraid to brave the elements. Why should she worry about a strong, healthy man?

Yet she did. She'd worried last night when she'd left him unconscious in the cool night air. Henry needed someone to take care of him. Care *for* him.

No, Rachel. No. But she picked up the umbrella and took hold of his arm, ignoring the warning voice in her head. Sometimes being sensible was overrated.

Chapter 17

Henry wasn't sure why she'd changed her mind, but was glad of it. To tell the truth, he was rather exhausted, and didn't mind leaning on Rachel a little as they navigated the hill.

It had been an unusual day, and it wasn't over yet. Henry had risen from his bed, as tired when he got out as when he finally fell into it, and made his way to New Street as soon as he'd bolted down breakfast. Mr. Everett had been more than surprised to see him, but Henry had somehow set the man's fears to rest. Rachel's father had returned his ancient gun to the kitchen dresser and they had sat over several pots of tea reaching a rapprochement.

It hadn't been easy. Pete Everett was a wily old devil who loved his only child and was ready to protect her, no matter what the consequences. Henry's charm had proven useless until he began reminiscing about his war. Pete had followed suit. Henry knew much more about the Crimean War now than any history book or military manual had ever taught him.

He knew more about Puddling too, and understood Rachel's reluctance to break the rules. Henry was fully aware of what his own father was capable of—if he set his mind on destroying Puddling's reputation, it would be destroyed. The pater was a bloodless fellow, never emotional unless it involved something Henry did or didn't do.

Henry blamed his mother, not that it was very filial to do so. He had only a cloudy recollection of her, but when she died, the Marquess of Harland died a little too. Henry had difficulty remembering seeing his father smile or laugh, but he had no trouble seeing the man shout when he wasn't freezing everyone around him out.

The Marquess of Harland thought he always knew best. In Henry's case, he grudgingly thanked his father for sending him to Puddling.

The results might not be exactly what his father expected, but life was unpredictable, wasn't it?

Henry could be happy being married to Rachel. He glanced down at her now under his lashes. Her cheeks were flushed from going up the incline, and her wispy fringe was curling enticingly in the damp air. She was robust. Sturdy. Last night demonstrated there was a carnality buried within her that would make her a very satisfying wife. Lying beside her after a bout of lovemaking might make the dreams stop

It was time he married. His father said so. It was, apparently, one of the goals of his rehabilitation. But Henry, by God, was not going to allow his father to pick out his wife.

There was, however, a sticking point. Rachel Everett wanted to be *loved*. Henry had no experience with that sort of thing. He'd gone straight from the barmaids at university to the barmaids near his billets. Going out with actresses and chorines when he got home from Africa had actually been a bit of an upgrade. He didn't know how to woo a proper young lady. They required flowers and poetry, didn't they?

A ridiculous waste. Flowers belonged in the ground. When they were cut for vases, they only died. And poetry? Utter nonsense. Poetry was what drove him out of Oxford and into the arms of the army.

Her mind had been turned by all the silly books she'd read. Her father showed Henry a pile of them on the kitchen dresser, far more of a deterrent to him than any gun would be. Henry was no hero, and knew that to his toes.

Still, if he wanted her, he'd have to make an effort. Suddenly, his mind was blank.

"Are you well, Lord Challoner? You're so quiet."

"Please call me Henry. We've gone past titles and surnames, haven't we?" His hand shook on the umbrella, causing droplets to fall on his face. *Was* he well?

"I suppose. It's not at all proper, though."

To hell with propriety, Henry wanted to say. Instead he concentrated on his feet, watching one shuffling step at a time up the slippery, steep road. His cottage was at the midway point of the rise, he'd discovered. Not too much farther. And then he'd give the umbrella to Rachel, because he really didn't think—

Henry didn't mean to fall, and certainly didn't mean to take Rachel with him. This was getting to be a habit, finding himself on his arse all over Puddling. This time he was cushioned by a soft woman, who was making every attempt to throw him off. How arousing she was. Did he say that out loud? She was frowning in a most ferocious manner.

"Get off me!"

Henry wasn't sure he could. His body felt dreadfully heavy, his limbs leaden. God, he was tired. He could fall asleep right here in the mud if Rachel weren't writhing under him with such vigor. It wasn't restful.

"Henry! Lord Challoner!" She might have been shouting, but her voice sounded so far away. Her lips were right there, though. Moving, pink, her breath soft against his face.

He did what any red-blooded young man would do to his fiancée under such circumstances, and kissed her. Her body stilled beneath him, and after a few fraught seconds, she returned the kiss. The rain pelted his back, but he didn't much care.

Don't look a gift horse in the mouth. Did that have something to do with Troy? Henry had been forced to study the classics, and found them wanting.

The Odyssey. Rosy-fingered dawn, and other rubbish. Though he'd seen red skies for himself, wide sweeps over the plains of South Africa. Skies the color of blood, the ground saturated. Brilliant colors that led to death and defeat.

He was home now. Not home. Puddling. There was something he meant to do, but he was so distracted by Rachel's kiss that he'd forgotten what it was.

He felt awfully hot. Was she hot too? They should get out of this weather.

"Lord Challoner!" The voice came from above. God's voice, or the next best thing in Puddling. Thunderous. A hand wrenched the collar of his coat and pulled him to his feet.

Not quite. Henry slumped back down, knees like jelly. His trousers, he observed, were filthy and soaked through. And, even worse, there was a puddle, and poor Rachel was in it, flailing about.

"Rachel Everett!" The arm reached for her and restored her to a much more secure position. She was now standing over him—looming, actually—her glorious hair tumbled over her shoulders, and her gray dress—well, not so much gray as brown now—soaked. He could see her peach skin and practically hear the beating of her heart.

"What happened? Did he attack you?"

Why was Vincent the vicar being such an idiot? He was supposed to be Henry's friend. Have faith in him. Henry didn't go around attacking girls. Hell, Francie and Lysette had really attacked *him* if one wanted to be perfectly clear.

Henry tried to turn around, but his neck wouldn't cooperate. Damn but his collar was stiff and wet. He really should consider wearing hats more often, but they made his head itch. He'd looked absurd in his pith helmet, but it did keep the sun from baking his brain.

Perhaps not.

"No, of course not. It was an accident. We slipped and fell," Rachel said.

"He was kissing you!"

"You must be mistaken. It may have looked like that, but it—it wasn't."

"I know what I saw, Rachel Everett." The man sounded both shocked and hurt.

Henry wiped his wet hair from his face and managed to swivel his head sideways. The pain was so exquisite he thought he might pass out. He really didn't feel quite the thing.

"Help," he whispered, and then lay back down on the ground. There was some argument over him, but he didn't care. He tucked his arm under his head and closed his eyes. The fabric of his jacket was scratchy on his cheek—in fact all his clothes were a trifle uncomfortable.

"Is the blackguard drunk?" the idiot asked.

Ha. If only. Some hot rum punch would hit the spot about now. Plenty of oranges and lemons. Those little cloves floating about. His bones felt cold, yet his skin was hot.

"No! There's something wrong! Dr. Oakley warned that he might suffer a concussion." He felt Rachel's cool hand on his forehead. Heaven.

"But his injury was two days ago. Wouldn't it have developed sooner?"

"Shovel," Henry said. But no one paid attention. Maybe he hadn't spoken aloud. And anyway, he didn't want to get his future father-in-law in trouble.

"We must get him home, Vincent. Help me, and then go fetch the doctor."

Ah. Vincent the fiancé. His nemesis. Henry would die first before he allowed the man to touch him. He opened his mouth to object, but was quickly overruled as the vicar picked him up and slung him over his shoulder none too gently.

It was clear Vincent was not his friend, no matter how many cups of tea they had shared. Had he divined Henry's interest in his erstwhile fiancée? Maybe that spectacular kiss on the ground gave him a clue. Henry might be concussed, but the kiss had not confused him at all. Rachel was the woman for him, the pater and Puddling be damned.

The road looked diabolically wobbly from this vantage point, so Henry shut his eyes. The blood had rushed to his aching head, and the jiggling about wasn't helpful. He was a little afraid he might vomit down

Vincent's back which, although tempting, would not be at all sporting. The vicar was only trying to help, even though Henry intuited from the rough handling the fellow would like to drop him in a ditch. No doubt he was jealous, finding Rachel in his arms. Or beneath him, to be accurate. Accuracy was important. Close only counted in hand grenades and horseshoes.

Henry heard the squeak of his own front gate, and felt the ecclesiastical brute mount the steps. The crunch of gravel under Walker's feet was deafening. Perhaps Henry's hearing was returning—wouldn't that be a miracle? Almost worth getting hit on the head as many times as he had since he'd arrived. He'd lost count of the total.

Gosh, the very first day he'd hit his head on the beam upstairs and had fallen on his rump. It was an omen. But good could come from bad, no matter what the old wives' tales warned.

Henry had found his bride. Now if only he could find a bucket.

Chapter 18

"I suspect a touch of influenza. His temperature is quite high. I hope this doesn't signal an outbreak in Puddling." Dr. Oakley returned his stethoscope to his bag. "He'll need to be kept quiet. Plenty of fluids. You know the drill, Millie. You've done your share of nursing in your time."

"What about me? Can we continue his lessons?" Vincent asked, his mouth petulant. Rachel didn't think he looked much like a man of God at present. He was wet and muddy and generally grumpy.

"Leave him be for a day or two. He'll be close enough to the angels as is."

Rachel's heart stuttered. "He might die?"

"Now, now. I didn't say that. Just giving Millie here a compliment." The doctor winked at Mrs. Grace and she blushed. Gracious. Was he flirting? Rachel knew they worked closely together at Stonecrop and the other cottages. Romance was in the air everywhere.

And that was a problem.

Vincent took her by the elbow. "I need to talk to you."

"I need to talk to you, too. Mrs. Grace, may we use Lord Challoner's parlor for a minute?"

The housekeeper cocked her head toward her patient. "Look at him. I think you could dance on the roof and he wouldn't notice."

Rachel obliged. Henry was lying still, eyes closed, his face as white as his sheets. She hadn't been present when Vincent had removed his ruined clothing, but had refused to leave until Dr. Oakley's verdict.

"He l-looks awful."

"He'll never know now, will he, sick as he is? Go ahead. I need to ask the good doctor some questions about his care."

I'll bet, thought Rachel. She and Vincent went downstairs. It was extraordinary that she'd been allowed in Henry's bedroom to begin with.

Vincent got right to the point. "What is going on, Rachel Everett?" He'd been using her full name ever since he came upon them wallowing in the mud.

"What do you mean, Vincent?"

"I know what I saw!"

"My father sent him down Honeywell Lane with an umbrella. I was in such a hurry this morning, I forgot mine. My hat, too. He was simply being gentlemanly." Vincent snorted, but she went on. "The weather was so foul, we tripped. You know Lord Challoner is not always steady on his feet."

"Huh. You may have tripped, but you seemed in no hurry to get up. The man was…was…on top of you!"

"Only for a second or two. It was very awkward trying to extricate ourselves."

"You didn't look like you were trying too hard, Rachel," he said stonily. Was he jealous? Oh, dear. Worse and worse. "I assure you I was. Think of a basket of kittens that get all tangled up with one another. Too many paws and tails."

Vincent gave her an incredulous look. No wonder. Kittens? There was no one less like a kitten than Henry Challoner.

A golden lion, perhaps.

"In fact," she continued quickly, "I have done everything in my power to discourage Lord Challoner's inappropriate attentions toward me. I know interacting with him is against the rules. In fact, I m-may have told him a little white l-lie to keep him at arm's length." Drat. Why was her tongue so uncooperative when she told white lies about white lies?

Vincent folded his arms over his chest. It was broad, just not as broad as Henry's. "You were considerably closer than *that*."

"As, I explained, it was just a very unfortunate accident. Anyway…I m-may have said that my affections w-were eng-g-gaged elsewhere."

Vincent lifted a sandy brow. Rachel knew he was attractive. Smart. Good-hearted. But her own heart didn't stir standing in proximity to him in Henry's cozy little parlor.

"And who is the lucky gentleman?"

"Y-you are."

Both of Vincent's eyebrows rose to his somewhat receding hairline. "*What?*"

"So you s-see, I'd like you to p-pretend if he asks you that we have an understanding." Her tongue was as tangled as that basket of kittens.

Vincent more or less fell into a chair. "You want me to lie? Unless, of course, this is a proposal."

"No!" Rachel cried, shocked. "I would never ask any man to marry me. It wouldn't be right." Although, she thought, why wouldn't it be? Why did the men have to do the asking while the women waited around? But she couldn't waste time considering such subjects now.

"Oh for God's sake," Vincent said, who never uttered the word God unless he was in the pulpit. He had very strict ideas. Ideals. "None of this is *right*, Rachel. My dear, as we're apparently engaged." He ran his hands through his light brown hair, making it stand up every which way. Rachel had never seen him so discomposed.

"I'm sorry."

"Sorry? I thought we were friends of a sort. How am I to counsel Lord Challoner if I am being deceitful? I cannot do as you ask."

Rachel sat down on the other chair. She'd known her request was folly from the start. "All right. But if he asks about me, can you just give the slightest impression that we—that I—"

"No," Vincent said, quite firmly. "Not that you won't make some man a fine wife. You know the old biddies here have us matched already. They have been after me since I arrived to court you."

Rachel suspected as much. "But you haven't."

"No. My affections are engaged elsewhere, for all the good it will ever do me. It's nothing personal toward you."

Rachel was both relieved and a tiny bit insulted. "Who is she?" Vincent was a catch, his salary substantial due to his duties for the Puddling Rehabilitation Foundation. Why would a girl turn him down?

Unless she was a Free Thinker or something. It might be hard to be a vicar's wife if one wasn't totally convinced of the Bible's inerrancy.

"Never mind. That is not pertinent to our present dilemma. We can have him sent back if he continues to bother you. Tell his father that he is incorrigible."

"No!" What would the marquess do then? Put Henry in some horrible private "hospital"? It would be like a prison, and Henry's spirit might be broken forever.

Vincent was staring at her. It was a bit unnerving. The probing look would have seemed right at home on a fire-and-brimstone minister's face, where one might confess to anything just to be left alone in one's sinfulness. "Do you have feelings for this man, Rachel?"

Did she?

She did. Very inconvenient, improper ones.

"I hardly know him," she evaded. "He has struck up a friendship with my father, though." If you could call getting whacked with a shovel the beginnings of solidarity. "He wants to do something for veterans who suffer the ill-effects of war."

"Very interesting. I'd thought him a selfish, callow fellow, only interested in juvenile amusements. He doesn't strike me as a serious man. Just stares into his tea and rolls his eyes at everything I say."

Ah, yes. The chorus girls. The drinking, and worse. It was as if Henry was making up for the years he'd spent so far from normal society. "He served honorably," Rachel reminded him. "Was grievously injured in the service of Her Majesty."

"His father told me he went into the army as an act of rebellion. I guess he got his comeuppance."

"What a horrible thing to say!"

Vincent nodded. "You're right. It was most unlike me."

"What have you got against him?"

"For one thing, he was practically rutting with you in the road in broad daylight. It's a good thing I came along when I did. Imagine if it had been Sir Bertram, or one of the other governors of the Foundation. You'd be ruined, Rachel. Lose your position and bring shame to all of Puddling."

Rachel knew he spoke the truth. She had lain on Honeywell Lane in the rain—how poetic!—and didn't stop Henry from kissing her. Didn't want him to stop kissing her.

Oh, what was she to do with herself?

Vincent's next words left her speechless. "He should be forced to marry you, you know."

There would be no force involved—Henry had repeatedly stated his intentions. But Rachel couldn't marry him.

He didn't love her.

"Lord Harland would never allow it."

"Challoner's of age. Has his own fortune. He can't be cut out of the will—his father's properties are entailed. Of course, the marquess could make things miserable for you."

"And for Puddling, Vincent! What if people stopped sending their disappointing relatives here? The village would suffer."

"Hm." He picked up the massive Bible that lay on the table next to him. "Not dusty. That's a good sign, unless we owe that to Mrs. Grace. Do you want to be Lady Challoner?"

Yes. No.

"Don't be silly, Vincent."

"Well, then, I'll try to forget what I saw. It is our duty to see that Lord Challoner is rehabilitated with no further scandal, Rachel. Do not impede the progress. Am I clear?"

"As glass."

"Let me walk you home. I have an umbrella, too."

Two men. Two umbrellas. Rachel had never felt so cossetted or confused.

Chapter 19

She hovered over him like an earthly angel, too sturdy to take flight, thank goodness, for her body brought warmth and solace. Her skin gleamed in the lamplight, a splash of tea in cream. Her hair fell in waves about her shoulders, dark as onyx. And her eyes, those silver-black eyes, were closed as she angled down for a kiss.

Her lips were honey and fire. Henry shuddered in bliss, his tongue meeting hers in gratitude. She knew just where to sweep and suckle, and the kiss deepened.

Such softness. He was falling into the clouds, and she descended with him, her bare body brushing his. Her hands were everywhere, smoothing his scorching skin, making him forget everyone who had come before her.

He had wasted enough time, and would waste no more. He was a new man, perhaps not in body but in soul. No more following foolish orders from deskbound generals and diplomats. No more trying the pater's patience. Henry had been a bit of an idiot, frankly. A rebel with insufficient cause. But Rachel was changing all of that for him. She made him want to be…better. Not someone else, precisely, but a new and improved Henry.

But right now, he remembered how the old unimproved Henry navigated a woman's hills and valleys and plains. He didn't need a map to caress her firm breast and bring it to his mouth. Her nipple peaked between his lips, a mini-mountain of desire. She tasted of clean soap, lavender, if he was not mistaken. He would shower her with sprigs of lavender once they were married, bushel baskets of it. Plant the stuff all over the garden, wild purple blooms marching off in rows as they did in France. He suspected she'd like a garden of her own. Her father might help, too— Henry understood she wouldn't come to him without the old man.

Best not to think of her father now, not when he ached to take her. His hand moved down the satin of her skin. She was wet for him, so wet, as if she'd danced naked beneath the sodden skies.

A torrential rain was falling on the slate roof. Each drop sounded like a gunshot, which was a reminder of times best forgotten. No more thinking. His head and cock hurt too much. It was time. Past time. One quick thrust...

Henry woke on sheets soaked in perspiration. The bed was so wet he may as well have been sleeping outside. Rachel was gone. Had apparently never been there, which was disappointing indeed. He was alone in his bed with a cockstand which needed attention.

He closed his eyes and continued the fantasy. It wasn't near as much fun now that he knew the shabby truth. His mind had played a trick on him, tempting him with what he couldn't have.

Didn't deserve.

But relief was required, and Henry dealt efficiently with the consequences of his erotic dream.

He'd tossed the nightshirt someone had dressed him in hours ago after disgracing himself once again in front of Rachel. She must think him a weakling—no wonder she was reluctant to marry him.

No, that wasn't why. There was the business about his father and him wrecking Puddling's prosperity.

And the love stuff. Rachel wanted hearts and flowers. Like the lavender he'd provided in his dream, he thought ruefully. Henry's father had loved his mother, and where had that gotten him? After all these years, the man had still not recovered from her death. His bitterness had blighted Henry's young life, and was one of the reasons Henry couldn't wait to get away.

Most marriages between those in his class were not love matches, his parents notwithstanding. People married for position, power and money. The women had their domestic sphere and all its petty problems; the men were expected to solve bigger issues in the world. Of course, to Henry's way of thinking, they were mucking it up rather spectacularly. One day he might take a place in the House of Lords, but right now all he'd want to do was lob a grenade into the chamber. Their decisions relating to South Africa and almost everywhere else were ill-considered to say the least.

But forget all that. What was he to do about Rachel Everett? He was awake now, though he wished he was still immersed in false bliss.

He tried to sit up, but swayed back into the pillows. He was so hot, and needed some fresh air. The windows were miles away and shut tight. Henry knew Mrs. Grace was somewhere in the house tonight; she'd been persuaded to stay by that nice old coot Dr. Oakley, though she'd said she couldn't stay all of Saturday. But Henry couldn't muster the energy to call for her.

He would have much preferred Rachel as nurse. Lovely, buxom, all that glossy dark hair bundled-up and businesslike. She would take his temperature and tsk, put a cool palm on his forehead, lean over and brush her lips against his. Kiss him and make it all better.

He rubbed a hand over his face, feeling bristles. Henry disliked facial hair. His own beard made him itch, and worse, it came in bright red. Better than gray, he supposed. There were days he felt like a graybeard.

He'd seen too much. Done too much. But at the moment, he didn't think he could stand long enough to shave.

He could walk to the window, couldn't he? The room was not that expansive, a far cry from his room at Kings Harland. All he had to do was put one foot in front of the other. Speed wasn't required, just determination.

The floor wobbled beneath him. It would not do to have Mrs. Grace find him sprawled naked on the floor, so Henry inched around the bed, grabbing hold of anything he could find. He was proud he maneuvered around the hated nightshirt without tripping and made it to the dresser. Here he clung to the drawer pulls and took several deep breaths, wondering if he was going to vomit again. His stomach felt alarmingly empty, but he'd often seen his soldiers retch with no results.

Steady on, Henry. Slide to the right. The window sill was deep and boasted a toile-covered seat, which Henry took advantage of. Now all he had to do was raise the sash and not fall out the window to his death.

He'd almost welcome death right now. No, that wasn't accurate. He'd escaped that state often enough to know he had no true interest in dying. But he certainly would like to feel less unwell. He had some serious courting to do. Had to finalize this Service business with his dratted rival Vincent Walker. Henry hoped his proposal for some sort of soldiers' retreat would meet the criteria for his rehabilitation. He thought it was rather an ingenious idea himself.

Ah. Fresh air. He gulped a lungful and leaned into the corner. The breeze wafted over his skin, causing him to shiver. He was still so hot and wet; really, this was a ridiculous complication he didn't need right now. He didn't have time to be sick.

He would write to his father at Kings Harland, where the man was probably pruning a bush in the rain waiting to hear how Henry was faring. Explain. Ask for forgiveness. Surely the Marquess of Harland would appreciate Henry settling down with a lovely young woman.

Henry would turn over all the new leaves he could—a veritable tree of them. A forest. He'd purchase a suitable country property and raise... some sort of livestock. Not pigs. The "pearls on the pig" comment from Rachel had seared into his sore brain. She was perfectly fetching, with or without pearls.

It was hard to tell what time it was. The sky outside was leaden with rain, the hills beyond black lumps. But it was a new day, whether the dawn cooperated or not. He'd lounged about in his room long enough. Henry needed to talk to Rachel, no matter what Dr. Oakley said.

Getting washed up and dressed was a tricky thing, but Henry just managed. A necktie was out of the question, however. The mirror told him he had a piratical air, with his black stitches and red stubble and open shirt collar. All he had to do now was get down the stairs. Walk to New Street.

It was Saturday, wasn't it? Rachel would be home, possibly cooking sausages that Henry was too ill to eat. Just thinking about them was nauseating. He'd ask for dry toast instead. Perhaps a cup of tea. He was getting used to tea. It wasn't so awful, as long as it didn't come with the pontificating of Vincent Walker.

But in his hurry, he'd forgotten about that beam. So Mrs. Grace found him on the floor anyway. At least he was dressed.

Chapter 20

He was the last person she expected to see knocking at the back door, but perhaps she should have expected his visit. Rachel removed her apron and invited him to sit at the kitchen table. It was the only available spot. Her father was still sleeping in the parlor, and the noisy downpour outside made the garden bench unavailable. She wiped some of her muffin's wayward crumbs into her lap, hoping he hadn't noticed.

"What brings you out on such a wretched day, Sir Bertram?" Rachel asked in a husky voice, the frog clearly unwilling to jump out of her throat.

"I think you know why I'm here."

She clenched her hands on her lap. "I'm afraid not. My contract is not up for renewal until next year. And," she swallowed, hating herself for groveling, "I have followed the committee's very useful suggestions to the letter. I think you'll be pleased with the progress and deportment of the pupils."

"I haven't come about the school." Sir Bertram Sykes stared at her under bushy black eyebrows. To think that Wallace had had those very same eyebrows, and Rachel had liked him anyway.

"Oh?" *He who speaks first loses.* Or something like that. She didn't know where to attribute the quote, either. Even if she was a teacher, Rachel was aware of the gaps in her own education.

"Our Guest seems to have taken quite a fancy to you."

Rachel looked down at her hands. There were ink stains between her fingers that never came out despite vigorous scrubbing. "I don't know what you mean, Sir Bertram."

He raised an eyebrow. "Really? I gave you more credit than that."

"Oh."

"I see you take my meaning. How on earth did he make your acquaintance in the first place?"

Who had peached on her? Not her father, surely. Vincent? Kindly Dr. Oakley? Anyone with a pair of eyes who saw them rolling around in the road?

"We're not really *acquainted,*" Rachel fibbed. "I mean, I have met him, but do not know him at all. I have seen him…in passing."

In the schoolyard. In the school. In her garden, where he'd seen too much of *her.* In his cottage. In the graveyard. All in all, there had been quite a lot of passing.

"That's not what my sources have told me. Did you not read his treatment plan?" Sir Bertram pounded a fist on the table that made her empty teacup jump. "No women! Absolutely no women! And here you are, sharing umbrellas and practically fornicating on the road like—like a pair of animals!"

Rachel shook, more crumbs dropping to the floor. She had to keep her rage in check; it would do her no good to scream at the man who was in charge of her economic fate. She took a breath to center herself, knowing she must be as white as a corpse. "I beg your pardon, Sir Bertram. I don't know who has told you such scurrilous tales, but they are false. My father himself suggested Lord Challoner escort me home in yesterday's storm. And while performing this—this gallant act, he fell—he's terribly ill, as you must have heard. I was only attempting to help him up. I can see how our actions m-may have been m-misconstrued, but I assure you nothing untoward occurred."

"Hah!"

"It's true! My father and Lord Challoner have struck up a sort of friendship. Two old soldiers, you know. If you don't believe me, you can speak to him when he awakes. If you come back later—"

"I have plans for the day," Sir Bertram snapped. "I'm off to visit friends and must make an early start in all this weather. But I will be home tomorrow to deal with this. Your father is responsible for your conduct, and I must say I am disappointed in the man. He has let you run loose far too long. You do not know your place, Rachel Everett, or your station in life. We have rules here in Puddling, rules that have served us for many decades. You put all of us at risk with your conduct."

Now he had really gone too far, though he only spoke exactly what Rachel had been thinking all along. Well, except for the loose, place and station part.

Oh, dear. Rachel always tried to see the best in everyone, but she was having grave difficulty at the moment. And even though she knew she was slitting her own throat, the frog had abandoned her and her next words were clear as crystal.

"I'm sorry you feel that way, Sir Bertram. I imagine it was just such thinking that made your grandfather send your mother here in 1807. To wean her of her...what did you say? Looseness? To ensure she knew her place. That she be a proper young lady. Obedient. What a trial it must have been for the Sykes family to shelter her. No wonder your opinion of women is...skewed. I understand your mother was never completely broken to bridle."

His own mother had been incarcerated here and married his father, so who was he to speak of correct behavior? Lady Maribel was still a byword in Puddling, though she'd died when Rachel was little more than a baby.

According to rumor, Lady Maribel's ducal father had been overjoyed to hear of the scandalous match between his headstrong daughter and Sir Colin Sykes. Someone else became responsible for the wayward chit, although genial Sir Colin never tried to rein his wife in during the course of their long and happy marriage.

It would have been a hopeless endeavor anyhow.

"That—that's entirely different," Sir Bertram sputtered. "How dare you impugn my family? Some regretted youthful hijinks...why, the Sykes and deWinter families came over with the Conqueror!" And they all were richer than Croesus, though he didn't say *that*.

Rachel was nothing like Lady Maribel, either. She certainly wasn't as beautiful—at the time of Lady Maribel's imprisonment here, three duels had already been fought over her—one resulting in a gruesome death—and she was only nineteen years old. Poems had been written to her eyes, her eyelashes and her nose. A lucky young painter had immortalized her in *all* her charms, and she'd broken two engagements. A portrait of her still hung in the parish hall, but not the nude one, which was reputed to be in the Sykes attic gathering dust. Lady Maribel was renowned for her local charities, if not precisely piety.

Lady Maribel was legendary for speaking up, whether one wanted to hear her opinion or not. Before Henry Challoner had arrived, Rachel wouldn't have thought to talk back to Sir Bertram Sykes or any man, no matter how provoked she was. But the legend of Lady Maribel made her bold.

How disappointed she'd be in her prudish son if she were still alive.

Sir Bertram was still sputtering. Rachel rose. "I'm sure you are too busy to visit here any longer. I will tell my father you stopped by and have charged him with being lax in my upbringing. No doubt he will try to correct my misbehavior at once. I haven't been spanked in ever so long—in fact, I cannot recall a time when my parents ever struck me, but I imagine it's never too late."

His fist fell on the table, this time with less force. "You cannot dismiss me!"

"I'm sorry. Did I misunderstand? You gave me reason to believe you had an important engagement for the day. Certainly if you'd like to wait and castigate me further until my father wakes up, you are more than welcome. May I get you a cup of coffee? Some boiled eggs?" Rachel smiled sweetly.

He glared. If she had half a brain, she would have been scared, but Henry Challoner had pocketed most of hers. "Don't think I don't see what you're trying to do, Rachel Everett. This will not be forgotten."

"I do hope not. I'm not sure about you, but I shall remember this morning for the rest of my life."

"You…you baggage! There is an end-of-term school committee meeting this week, *and* a Foundation meeting. Your ears will be ringing, my girl."

Rachel had gone too far and she knew it. Not precisely Maribel-far, but close enough.

Should she apologize? Sir Bertram probably wouldn't accept it—he'd suspect she was lying. She'd never felt so tall or so livid—or vivid—in her life, and it was a bit sad to take back those rude words and giant steps.

But, needs must. Her father depended on her.

Rachel swallowed. Groveled again, although from her kitchen chair. "*Please*, Sir Bertram. I love my job, and I am good at it. I promise to do better. Be less…me."

"And you'll leave Lord Challoner alone?"

"To the very best of my ability. I can't help it if I see him in church or across the street. But I promise I will not speak to him. Ever." She crossed her fingers in her apron pocket.

"Very well. One more misstep, young woman, and there *will* be consequences."

She lowered her eyes and nodded, hoping she looked sorry enough. Sir Bertram grumbled his way out of the kitchen, and then all the starch leached out of Rachel's spine and she slumped back onto the kitchen chair. She wasn't Maribel deWinter with a face and fortune behind her.

She wasn't an opinionated and obstreperous duke's daughter. Most of her life Rachel had tried to be unobtrusive. Obedient.

And now she'd risked her job and her future. *One more misstep...*

She buried her face in her shaking hands. What would happen to them? Two families had been driven out of Puddling for breaking the Rehabilitation Rules. Were the Everetts about to become one of the cautionary tales?

It was all Henry Challoner's fault, and he would have to fix it, influenza or no.

Rachel peeked into the parlor. Her father was flat on his back snoring, unaware that their life could be ruined at Sir Bertam's whim. He spent so much of his time sleeping now, but she didn't have the heart to wake him.

Instead, she wrote him a note, stuck it under the plate of muffins, and fluffed her fringe—although why she did that was a mystery since she and her hair would be drowned shortly. Her mackintosh hung on a kitchen hook, her hat and the fateful umbrella next to it. If need be, she'd poke Henry with it until he came up with a solution to satisfy Sir Bertram Sykes.

Chapter 21

"Henry! Wake up!"

Henry had no intention of doing so. Why should he abandon this delicious dream? Rachel was splayed beneath him, her black hair waving over his pillow. It was a mix of straight and curly—the hair, not the pillow—with a charming fringe over her fine features. Lots of little tendrils to play with over her well-shaped dark eyebrows. But why should he waste time playing with her hair when there were other parts of her that needed attention?

He rolled away from the poke on his shoulder and smelled lavender. Mrs. Grace must have taken a page out of Rachel's book and bedecked the linen closet with the most delightful scent. Soft, yet with a tang. Henry had seen lavender fields in Provence, acres and acres of purple as far as the eye could see. Sunflowers, too. The vegetation on his deployment to South Africa left a little to be desired, however. Scrub, poor soil. Lots of animals, though. What with the spotty rations the government had provided, his troops had gone hunting often.

No. Banish the army from this Rachel-dream. There was no place for hunger and desolation, just the green Cotswold hills and charming flowerboxes. Gingerbread. Rachel touching herself in her little garden. Ha! A metaphor. Even in his sleep, Henry was a bloody wordsmith.

He was kissing her lavender-scented throat now, nipping her earlobe. She didn't wear earrings, which was convenient. It would not do for him to swallow a diamond and have to wake up. She sighed, and he moved down to her soft, pillowy breast.

"Henry Agamemnon Challoner! Stop kissing that pillow! You look like a fool."

Agamemnon. Who in their right mind blighted their child with such a name? It was exceedingly difficult to make those humps on the m and n without everything running together when writing. Not to mention the rape, murder and incest honeycombed through the House of Atreus. Agamemnon's father fed children to Thyestes. Not cricket at all.

And then poor Agamemnon managed to survive all those years at Troy, only to be killed by his unfaithful wife upon his return. No thanks for his service there, no tobacco tins from a grateful queen. War was hell, and sometimes one's homecoming was even worse.

"Henry, damn you! Wake up!"

No. It really couldn't be. Henry had not heard those stentorian tones for over a week. With the greatest of difficulty, he rolled on his back and tried to open his eyes.

He couldn't do it. They appeared to be glued shut. Now to shut his ears.

"If I had known," Arthur Challoner, the thirteenth the Marquess of Harland, said, "that it would come to this, I never would have sent him here. Look at him! Raging with fever and black and blue all over. What in hell happened to his head?"

"He took a fall, my lord. Several of them. As you can see, Dr. Oakley had to stitch him up. Perhaps he would be better off in a pushchair."

"There is nothing wrong with my son's legs! Just because he had that trifling wound on his foot doesn't make him incapacitated. Henry's not a weakling."

"Of course not, my lord. He's a...he's a very fine young man."

Oh, Mrs. Grace was no kind of liar at all. The pater would see straight through her.

"I suppose you never thought to notify me of these accidents. What if I hadn't decided to drive over on this filthy morning?"

"Now, your lordship. You know part of our procedure is to isolate the Guests from their families. If Lord Challoner had been truly in peril, of course we would have notified you. Dr. Oakley thinks your son has only a mild case of influenza."

"I knew something was wrong! Knew it in my bones! Couldn't sleep a wink all night imagining the pup had fallen into his old ways. At least I was right about the falling part. And now I find my boy out of his head, moaning and flapping his lips on a pillow like a landed flounder. Where is this doctor?"

"He's already been and gone, Lord Harland. He gave your son a very thorough examination after he helped me get him back to bed. There is medicine."

"I want a full-time nurse. Round-the-clock care. No expense is to be spared, do you hear? Henry is my heir. There's no one but my idiot nephew to take over if something should happen to him. I'll not see my title go to that—that deadly dull banker!"

Well, that was interesting. George was making a name for himself in the City. Henry's father had berated him about the perfection of his cousin George for years. How George was so sensible. How George had won the Latin prize at Eton instead of wasting his time playing Fives.

Of course, there wasn't much call for Latin any more unless Cousin George switched careers and decided to become a Catholic priest, and, knowing close-fisted George, he'd never take a vow of poverty. He was too busy counting up piles of money made through shrewd investments to give it all away. He wouldn't even loan Henry a groat when they were boys, not that he needed any help from his cousin now that he'd come into his inheritance from his grandmothers.

Henry would have to ask old Vincent how he felt about having services in English. If he were spouting off in Latin, the poor Puddlingites wouldn't have a clue what he was saying and preparing sermons would be so much easier. How grueling it must be to come up with fresh material every week.

"O-of course, Lord Harland. I'll notify the Puddling Rehabilitation Foundation at once that extra help is needed. I am only one woman after all."

"And I'm sure you've done the best you can. I'm sorry if I was short with you."

What was this—his father apologizing? The pater never apologized. Had he fallen into Mrs. Grace's Venus flytrap along with Dr. Oakley? Henry supposed the woman was not bad-looking for an older woman, although he couldn't see her appeal himself. She wouldn't even let him eat biscuits.

"Of course you are concerned. I understand. You love your son very much, don't you?"

Henry thought he might be sick.

"Love?" He pictured his father frowning, turning the word around in his mouth like a captured spider. "He is my son. Of course I care what happens to him. He may be a disappointment, but life is full of them. One must soldier on."

Ah, Christ. Wouldn't his father have been surprised as to what real soldiering entailed.

"I want to be informed of his progress. As you know, Kings Harland is less than fourteen miles from here. I shall of course fund the expense for any messages or messengers. Are you on the telegraph here in this backwater?"

Henry's ears perked. He listened as Mrs. Grace explained that the telegraph office was in a back room of Stanchfield's Grocery, although he couldn't think of whom he might like to contact.

Henry really didn't want to be sprung from this jail unless Rachel came with him.

The pater continued to deliver orders as Henry feigned sleep, and Mrs. Grace burbled back, sounding for all the world like a woman smitten. Where was Mr. Grace? Henry had never thought to ask.

The chair creaked, and Henry sensed his father was leaning over the bed, probably giving him a gimlet eye. Henry groaned a little and flipped like the landed flounder he was, and heard the snick of the bedroom door. Thank God the man was too impatient to watch the patient sleeping.

Henry refused to acknowledge the rapping at the door downstairs. Oakley again. Or Vicar Vincent, who could pray over him in English. When he cracked his eye open a slit, both his father and Mrs. Grace had disappeared and there was a muffled conversation downstairs. His father's voice rose above the others, but Henry could not hear the specifics.

This faking unconsciousness was proving to be easy as pie. He was getting to be an expert at it. Why had Henry not thought of that strategy earlier in his life? He was prepared to continue as the footsteps up the stairs heralded more interference. He tucked the quilt over his head and smiled.

"Here he is. Mrs. Grace tells me she must attend to a family matter later. Some wedding, I believe, although it's a wretched day for it. Do you feel up to taking the challenge?"

There was silence, but there must have been nodding, for the pater boomed, "Excellent! How fortuitous it is that you stopped by so I could hire you on the spot. You've had some nursing experience, and my son shouldn't give you too much trouble in his present state. According to Mrs. Grace, this Oakley fellow feels Henry will be out of the woods by Monday at the latest. You have no objection to residing here over the weekend? You and Mrs. Grace can spell each other. I want someone with him at all times."

"Yes, my lord."

So his new jail matron had a voice, though she was whispering. Henry was tempted to peek.

But then his father began to explain that he was on his way to a house party, and had just stopped by to see how his son's progress was going. So much for losing sleep over him. Henry wondered if the traveling coach was stuck somewhere on Puddling's narrow streets, the coachman anxious to get back on a proper road that actually went somewhere.

"I shall be at the Entwhistles at Frampton Mansell tonight, and bound for home tomorrow. Please notify me of any change in his condition."

"Yes, my lord."

"Don't let him charm you. Even a simple country woman like you— that is, I am sure once you are dry, you're not so...erm, my son has a reputation, as you must know. Do not let him take liberties. I should hate to think I placed you in harm's way."

"Yes, my lord. I mean, no, my lord."

The door banged shut. The poor thing. Henry had forgotten just how *not* charming his father could be, though the man had no trouble throwing diamond dust in Mrs. Grace's eyes. As far as Henry knew, his father had never looked at a woman since his mother died. Had never taken a mistress.

Aha. That explained the pater's sour disposition. Why, the man only needed to get la—

"Henry!"

A harsh whisper. Henry debated whether he should pull the covers down.

"Henry Challoner! I know you by now. Stop pretending, you possum!"

And Henry knew her as well. With the greatest of pleasure, he untangled himself and looked into the face of his new nurse.

Chapter 22

She was not looking her best. Henry could see why his father thought she might be safe from Henry's predations.

Not that he would predate her. Was that a word? They were predating each other anyway, as he recalled.

"How lovely to see you, Rachel. What happened?" Her fringe, usually so curly and bouncy, hung down almost to her nose. Her face—what he could see of it—was smudged with dirt, and her mackintosh was spattered with mud. She resembled nothing so much as a wet, dirty sheepdog.

"A great big carriage came by. Your father's, I imagine. I tried to get out of the way, and lost my balance on the slippery sidewalk once it passed. I found myself in a—in a puddle."

"Again? Miss Everett, you really are not steady on your feet, are you?"

"Do not tease me, you dreadful man! It's because of you and your father that I'm about to lose my job and get thrown out of Puddling!" With that, she burst into tears.

Henry sat up and handed her an edge of sheet to use as a handkerchief. "What do you mean?"

"S-Sir Bertram Sykes paid me a visit earlier, and I may have lost my temper."

"You have a temper? I hadn't noticed."

Rachel gave him a little shove that did nothing to improve his headache. "Be serious for once! You must help me. Tell Sir Bertram I've done nothing to arouse you. Attract you. Tell him that what's between us is completely innocent."

"I can't do that. I cannot lie."

"Oh! Why do all of the men I ask for help claim they cannot lie? It's infuriating." She blew her nose on the sheet. Henry hoped there were more sheets in the linen closet.

"Who else have you asked for help?"

"It doesn't matter. I am ruined." She smeared a glob of mud across her chin.

"You are not. All right, all right. I'll go talk to this Sykes fellow when I'm allowed to get out of this damned bed. Tell him...whatever you tell me to tell him."

"Thank you." She stood up.

"Wait a second. Where are you going?"

"Home. My father will want something to eat."

Ugh. Food. The very thought made Henry's stomach do a tumblesault. "You can't!"

"Why not?"

"My father hired you to be my nurse, did he not? He expects you to sleep here." Henry couldn't help himself—he patted the bed.

"I have no intention of nursing any part of you!" Rachel said, eyes flashing. "He just took control of the conversation, and Mrs. Grace and I couldn't get a word in edgewise."

"Yes, he does that." Henry's father had never brooked much interruption. It came of being a marquess, he supposed. Henry wondered if that unfortunate trait would be passed down to him as well as the title when the pater went to his reward. "But still, you agreed. I heard you. And I really don't feel all that well."

"I'm sorry about that, but really, Henry—I can't stay. What will people say?"

"That my father hired you. How can they object? You don't cross a marquess, you know. Marquesses are nearly as bad as dukes. This gives us a perfect opportunity to spend more time together without sneaking around. No more shovels and stone walls and puddles."

"But your treatment plan..."

"The grand poobahs will have to make adjustments, won't they? I cannot be left alone—I'm as weak as a kitten. If Mrs. Grace is going off somewhere, I must have assistance."

"But not from me!" Rachel sounded a little desperate.

"I don't see why not. Who else is available? Isn't everyone hereabouts going to that wedding?"

"I doubt it. It's Mrs. Grace's sister over in Sheepscombe. I'm sure we can find someone from the village to take over. Even my father if it comes to it."

"Oh. He can climb these stairs?" Henry asked innocently.

"You couldn't get down?"

Henry imagined he could, with the right incentive. Rachel Everett naked on the sofa below, for example. Or better yet, in *his* garden on the little bench overlooking the koi pond, her legs parted, her hand busy—

But not in this rain. She was wet enough as it was, dripping onto his bedroom carpet, looking entirely miserable.

He wondered if the fish had been fed. It was one of his duties as temporary master of Stonecrop Cottage. Mrs. Grace had passed him a card as soon as he'd moved in with the requirements of residence. Henry thought the items were designed to make him feel like a responsible citizen: feed the fish, take the rubbish to the bin in the garden shed, water the fern in the conservatory. The dratted fern was dying, but he'd managed the other two.

Henry had grown fond of the bright orange-red fish hidden under the green vegetation of the pond. They came right up to the surface now and allowed themselves to be tickled. When he had property of his own, he'd dig a little pond and stock it as a pleasant reminder of his stay.

Hopefully, he'd have another pleasant reminder, the redoubtable Rachel Challoner, née Everett.

"Look, take off that wet coat and get dry. There are clean towels in the bathroom dresser. You shouldn't have allowed yourself to be bullied by my father, you know. But now that you're here…" Henry shrugged.

"But my father! He's alone in our cottage. And he'll never let me stay here with you."

"Doctor's orders."

Rachel huffed off to the bathroom and Henry heard the cry of alarm as she must have caught sight of herself in the mirror, the tap running, the slamming of drawers. She emerged a few minutes later considerably cleaner, her fringe scrunched back up almost where it should be.

"Tell Mrs. Grace to stop at your father's cottage on her way to the wedding. Doesn't she live on New Street too?"

Rachel made a face. "You think of everything."

"I try."

"Would you like a cup of tea or something?"

Henry wasn't sure if he would. But he said yes and Rachel went downstairs to talk to Mrs. Grace.

They returned together, Rachel holding a tray between hands that did not appear to be all that steady.

"I have told Rachel, and now I am telling you," Mrs. Grace began. Henry stopped himself from rolling his eyes. He was tired of his housekeeper treating him like a mischievous ten-year-old boy. Really, if he had known just how much trouble Francie and Lysette were going to be, he would have sewn his pants shut. It had all been a harmless prank, really. He wouldn't be here being lectured, Rachel cowering in the background. He didn't like to see Rachel unhappy—it did something to his insides that were already in an uproar.

"You keep your hands to yourself, do you understand me, Lord Challoner? Self-control at all times. None of that boyish charm, although I do see where you get it. It runs in the family."

Pater? Boyish and charming? Not hardly.

Mrs. Grace opened the curtains with a snap. "We are here to help you mend your ways, not that you seem to understand that. If I did not have to leave, I would not. I know my duty, and you are my responsibility. Why my sister has decided to marry again is beyond me. She's already buried three husbands. I should think that would be enough of a deterrent to any man. I will be back by nightfall, and you can go home, Rachel. There is to be no funny business, or I shall inform Sir Bertram."

Bugger Sir Bertram. The man had already upset Rachel today.

"Yes, Mrs. Grace," Rachel and Henry said in unison.

"This is all most ill-advised," the woman muttered as she left the room. "But how was I to contradict a marquess?"

It was easy. Henry had been doing it all his life.

Chapter 23

"This will work to our advantage."

Henry was sitting up, still pale as death. But there was a sparkle to his blue eyes that Rachel couldn't like. He reminded her of all the little boys she'd ever taught rolled into one.

"You are not in your right mind. As usual." She poured them both a cup of tea and took a sip, burning her tongue.

"Come now. No disparagement or I may have a relapse. This couldn't be simpler. Don't you see?"

Rachel only saw an uncertain future. No job. No cottage. Her elderly father uprooted from his family home.

"I am not hallucinating, my lord."

"None of this my lording business. How can the pater object that I met you when he himself shoved you into my bedroom?"

Rachel had felt shoved; that was true enough. "He asked me to nurse you, not marry you."

Henry waved a hand. "I couldn't help but ask the minute I laid eyes on you. It was a *coup de foudre*. That means struck by lightning, you know."

"I know what it means," Rachel said testily. "I've studied French."

"Better and better. An accomplished wife." Henry grinned and she wanted to slap the smile off his face.

"Your father will only think I've taken advantage of you in your affliction. You pretended to be unconscious, Henry."

"I was merely sleeping. I've always been a heavy sleeper. Until lately." He wasn't smiling anymore.

He was not going to make Rachel feel sorry for him—that would be too easy. "I'm sure if your father had known what was being said about us, he wouldn't have let me anywhere near you."

"He won't find out now, will he? This is just like a *deus ex machina*. That means—"

"I know what that means too! I may just be a 'simple country woman' covered in mud that *that man's* carriage splashed on me, but I am widely read." Rachel didn't know why so was so angry. The House of Harland was very provoking, *pere et fils*.

"Then our marriage is pretty much a *fait accompli*.'

"For heaven's sake, Henry! Why do you want to marry me? We don't love each other!" What she felt for Henry was lust. Desire. Not enough to build any sort of partnership on. He was the heir to a marquess, and her parents had been weavers. Peers might play with unsuitable women, but they didn't marry them.

And he wouldn't be faithful, if his past was anything to go by.

Rachel believed in redemption, she really did. She knew people could change, had seen it for herself. But Henry Challoner would lead any woman he married on a merry dance. He was so…he was so…despite being widely read, her vocabulary failed her.

"We've discussed this already. It's true I don't believe in all the romantic folderol. But we like each other, and I have to marry someone someday."

Rachel wished for her father's shovel. She had never been so unimpressed with a proposal, not that she had many others to compare it to. Only Henry's, and they had all been awful.

"Let's not talk about this anymore. Not today."

Henry nodded. She had thought he might argue, but maybe he *was* too ill.

"What do you propose we talk about then?"

"How are you feeling?"

He sat back on his pillows. "Tolerable. I have a headache that comes and goes. My stitches itch. My stomach is not quite sound at the moment. I don't think you'll have to fix me a seven-course meal this afternoon."

She put a hand on his forehead. He was warm, but not alarmingly so. "Mrs. Grace said I'm to give you this medicine every four hours. I think it's time."

"Will it make me sleep? I don't want to miss a minute with you."

"I don't know what it will do," Rachel said crossly. There was no label on the bottle, and it didn't smell familiar when she took a sniff.

She hadn't lied to the Marquess of Harland—she'd had nursing experience. She'd taken care of her mother for a year before she died, and now was watching over her elderly father. If she had a nickel for every cut and bruise she'd tended at the school, she'd be a rich woman. But dealing with Henry was not the same at all.

She wished he *was* unconscious. When he looked at her with his falsely innocent blue eyes she wanted to—

Kiss him.

"No!"

"I beg your pardon?"

"Never mind." Rachel needed to strangle that annoying little voice in her head that apparently had the nerve to speak out loud too. She filled a glass with water from the bathroom and poured a teaspoon of the medicine into it, stirring with more force than was absolutely necessary.

"Drink this."

"Yes, Mama." Henry dutifully sipped and made a face. "Vile. Why cannot anyone make medicine that tastes good? Something with cherry syrup, for example."

"Speak to an apothecary." She wondered what her father was doing right now. He was self-sufficient, and there was plenty of food in the icebox and cupboard. He was too smart to go out into the garden in this weather.

The rain continued to pelt down, falling on the roof like gunfire. Rachel looked at her wristwatch, counting the hours until she could go back out in it and drown.

Her being here was such a bad idea. She should have spoken up when Henry's father swooped upon her like a long-lost friend in the downstairs hallway. But he was a very forceful man, and despite Mrs. Grace shaking her head and making cut-your-throat motions behind him, Rachel had lost the use of her tongue and her mind.

Henry was looking at her. Just looking. She felt a blush rise. No one had ever looked at her like Henry did, not even Wallace Sykes in the throes of calf love.

Bah. Imagine having Sir Bertram Sykes as a father-in-law.

But the Marquess of Harland would be worse.

"So, swallowed a lemon? What are you thinking?" Henry asked.

"How women are always ordered about by men, who think they know what's best for us."

"Oh, dear. Was it something I said?"

"It's not just you, Henry. Sir Bertram, that pompous prig, annoyed me very much this morning telling me how I should behave. And your father just assuming because I knocked on the cottage door that I'd want to stay all day. Even my father doesn't think I can manage my life without hitting someone with a shovel. It's—it's depressing."

Henry was silent, and then his mouth turned up. "Then we have something in common, although I cannot claim to be a woman. You've met my father. He's overbearing. Knows all, and what he doesn't know he thinks he does anyway. I've lived with that for twenty-five years. Even when I was in the army he managed to pull my strings. My judgment was *always* in question, from the color of my waistcoat to my politics to the girls I chose to nodge. And yes, that word means just what you think it does."

"It's not the same."

"Oh, I know it's not. There are many more opportunities for a man than a woman. But remember, society expects more from us too. To fight and win. To earn. To be right in every conceivable circumstance. It's rather tiring to be in charge all the time."

How did he manage it? Rachel wanted to stay irritated and shake a mental fist at all men, but Henry had diverted her.

"Shouldn't you be napping?"

"You act as a tonic, Rachel. Every inch of me is alert."

Her eyes slid to the blankets below his waist. He had corrupted her entirely.

Chapter 24

Henry had always enjoyed rainy days. There were too damned few of them in Africa. Each footstep there threw up a clot of dust big enough to choke a man. He had yearned then for the green and gray of England, the rolling hills, clouds dappling them with shadows. Fields of daffodils. The scent of lilacs. Church spires and hedgerows.

Just like Puddling.

And pale English ladies, who couldn't imagine any of the horror of war. The lice. The inedible food. The blood—so much of it. More than half his troops had been physically unfit before they ever stepped on the continent, and their conditions had no chance to improve.

Why was he thinking of such things as the English rain pattered down and a beautiful woman was by his side? He really must be ill.

"So, what shall we do?"

"Do?"

She seemed so nervous. Surely she didn't think he was going to leap out of bed and ravish her. As delightful as that sounded, he was not in prime condition at present.

"To while away the hours until the dragon returns."

"I could read to you, I suppose."

"I don't think there are any books here that are not improving tracts. Or the Bible. I'm afraid I didn't think to bring any with me when my father shoved me into our traveling coach. I barely have a change of clothes." His valet had packed in great haste, terrified of the marquess as all the servants were.

What was it about the man? Henry resembled his father down to the last eyelash, and no one was terrified of *him*. Of course, the pater's temples were graying, and there were a few sun lines around his blue eyes. No laugh lines around his lips though. The Marquess of Harland was not a frivolous fellow, and looked to be an authority. He could cut you to the quick with one glance.

What Henry's father needed was a woman to worry about; then maybe he'd leave his son alone to make his mistakes.

"You've looked very smart every time I've seen you."

"Why, thank you, Miss Everett. Likewise." He was fibbing a little. Rachel wore a faded brown printed dress, its hem still wet and muddy. She had tried to get her hair back in order though had not been entirely successful. But her color was fresh and she was simply a pleasure to gaze upon.

Henry liked her very much. He didn't think his mind was playing tricks on him, that he was fooling himself into falling in love. There was no love that lasted. But didn't he deserve a pretty intelligent female companion with some wit? They could make handsome children and build a comfortable life together. Henry would leave his dancers and actresses behind and live like a country gentleman somewhere, maybe within a stone's throw of Kings Harland and Puddling both. What would be the harm? The Cotswolds were very pleasant.

She clapped her hands together. "I know! You can write to Sir Bertram. Explain everything."

"Right now?" That didn't seem like much fun. Rachel was already rummaging through his desk drawers for pen and paper.

"He's gone away, but will be home tomorrow. He can find your letter waiting for him."

"I haven't really thought what I should say."

Henry could see he wouldn't have to think—Rachel was about to dictate everything he'd need to disavow his feelings for her. She shoved a well-thumbed book to lean on in his lap—*Sermons I Have Known and Loved*—and plopped the rest of the materials on the bedcovers.

"Now." She actually rubbed her hands. "'Dear Sir Bertram' comma."

As if he didn't know his punctuation. Henry's handwriting was precariously legible under the best of circumstances, and writing over the pebbled surface of the book was not helpful.

"'It has come to my attention that a misunderstanding has arisen regarding my relationship'—no, make that acquaintance—'with a female person in Puddling, one Miss...hm. Evergreen.'"

"Evergreen?"

"See, you don't even know my true name. It's brilliant. 'I write this to assure you and the other honored governors of the Puddling Rehabilitation Foundation that while I have befriended her father—'"

"Whose name I apparently also do not know," Henry muttered.

"'—I have only met the young woman in passing period I fully intend to adhere to every letter of my treatment program comma and look forward to formulating my Service period.' That's with a capital 's.' You've read the Welcome Packet. New paragraph. 'One's reputation is sacrosanct comma and while I have besmirched mine—'"

"Hold on, hold on. Must I really kowtow like this? I am *not* 'besmirched,' as you put it. And you are talking much too fast." Henry was getting more irritated by the word and hadn't even written them all down. Rachel seemed to think he was some sort of secretarial automaton. He was unacquainted with Pittman shorthand, and even if he was, could never keep up.

"'Besmirched mine comma,'" Rachel repeated, "'Miss Evergreen is entirely innocent of any wrongdoing period It is most unfortunate that the livelihood of an unexceptional school teacher should be threatened by the scurrilous gossip of a few small-minded villagers period I did not go to war to come home to such iniquitous injustice period My father the Marquess of Harland shares my sense of outrage that a person of Miss Everdean's—'"

"Ever*green*," Henry reminded her, scribbling furiously.

"'Evergreen's unblemished integrity has been called into question period. Her father has described her kindness and honor to me at great length comma and I almost feel as if I know her period But I do not period.' New paragraph. 'I trust you will accept the word of an officer and a gentleman that Miss Evergreen remains a sterling citizen of your fine community and should in no way be blamed from my simple misstep on the road when I was near death and she tried to assist me period.'"

Henry rolled his eyes. "You are exaggerating, my dear. A touch of influenza only. And the odd shovel."

"Write it. 'Yours most sincerely comma Captain Lord Henry…' What's your middle name?"

It had come to this, twice in one day. "Agamemnon."

"Really? How extraordinary. 'Captain Lord Henry Agamemnon Challoner.' There! That should do it. Sir Bertram is a dreadful stickler, and a snob, too. Your rank should convince him that there's nothing to the rumors."

"But my besmirched reputation might indicate that I lie on a regular basis. You know how we drunkards and debauchers are." Henry blotted the letter. If Sir Bertram could actually decipher it, it would be a miracle. Rachel gathered up the ink pot and the rest of the things and returned them to the little desk in the corner. She seemed very pleased with herself.

"Piffle. You did nothing no other healthy young man fresh from war would do. Wine, women, and song, etcetera. I believe your father overreacted."

That had been Henry's contention all along. He knew he liked Rachel for a reason.

"What else brings Guests here?"

"Oh, it varies. Usually it's drink and general depravity. But one of our more recent guests had an unusual treatment plan. I can't name names, you know. It goes against the rules. But she was a young woman preparing for her wedding, and her mama wanted her to lose a few stone to fit into a Worth gown from Paris."

"So you kept her here and starved her?" Henry was appalled.

"Of course not! Mrs. Grace fed her plenty of wholesome, nourishing food."

Ugh. Henry could imagine. Lettuce and carrot sticks and celery three times a day, as if the poor girl was a bunny in a hutch. "And did this treatment work?"

Rachel nodded. "It did. Although I don't think Greta—that is the young woman was looking forward to her wedding, though. She was…subdued. Poor Vincent had to lecture her about the seven deadly sins, specifically gluttony, daily, and it bothered him. He's as fond of his food as anyone. And she wasn't a bit sinful, just very, very plump. She was sweet, really."

"Sweets for the sweet. Did she stay here in my house?"

"She did. This is our best cottage."

"The whole thing sounds barbaric. If she was such an eyesore, why did her husband want to marry her in the first place?"

"Money, I believe. Gr—the girl in question is a great heiress, and there was a bankrupt title involved. The marriage was arranged between her mother and the peer."

"Ridiculous in this day and age. People should marry whom they please."

"Don't start."

Henry looked at her with what he hoped was innocence. "What do you mean?"

"You know perfectly well what I mean. You'll start proposing again, and I've told you it is a very bad idea. I am perfectly happy here with, um, Vincent. We are w-well suited."

"Horsesh—I mean, I only have your best interests at heart."

"That's what men always say, and look how that usually turns out."

Henry wasn't up to arguing. Or wasting their few hours together with any lingering unpleasantness. But he didn't think Rachel was ready to snuggle up and kiss him, especially if she was still fibbing about her understanding with Vincent Walker.

He didn't believe it for a minute. Couldn't. Henry could on occasion be as forceful as his father, and by the time this day was over, Rachel would be his.

Chapter 25

Thank God. Henry had finally fallen asleep after fighting yawns for hours. Rachel had kept him at arm's length all day. Which had been somewhat of a challenge. He had...*twinkled.* There was no other word for it. His charm had radiated like shooting stars, and he was nearly irresistible. Nearly.

He had been charming before, of course. Very charming. Rachel had been attracted to him against her will from the very first. And the current quasi-helplessness in his illness appealed to her soft heart.

But that way lay madness.

Henry had even charmed her father, after everything. But even he could not see how Lord Challoner could court her when it would affect Puddling's future.

Rachel had had her first taste of the Marquess of Harland. In five minutes he'd reduced her to imbecilic agreement, and now she was obligated to stay with his son until Mrs. Grace returned. The marquess was quite a force of nature, alternately rude and, well, charming.

Like his son.

He was a handsome man, very like Henry. Or, more accurately, Henry was very like him. The marquess's fair hair was turning from gold to silver, and he exuded the power of his position. He struck Rachel as a man who had rarely heard the word no in his life, and wasn't interested in starting to hear it now.

Like his son.

She needed help, and Vincent had refused to lie for her. Could she make herself so unappealing that Henry would come to his senses?

If he hadn't objected to her horrific mud-splattered self when she arrived, there was no accounting for his taste.

The true problem was basic. Rachel didn't *want* to dissuade Henry. She liked him. Very much. But she just couldn't see how any relationship they might establish would prosper.

She sighed.

"What's wrong?" His voice was thick and rough. Surely she hadn't been that loud, and he was supposed to be partially deaf, too.

"Nothing. I was just breathing. You didn't sleep for very long. Can I get you anything?"

"Some water, I think. No, don't get up. I'm not so weak I can't pour it myself." He sat up and reached for the carafe on the bedside table. His hair was adorably disordered, blond tufts sprouting like a collie's ears.

It was still pouring. What a day for a wedding, though Rachel imagined some of the bride's earlier ones may have boasted sunshine. Would grim Mrs. Grace come home tiddly on the local cider? That would be a sight to see.

"How have you occupied yourself while I was snoring away?"

"You don't snore. I was thinking. Reading a little."

"Which one of my boring books caught your eye?"

"Oh, I have my own with me at all times." Rachel was not going to confess to the romance novel in her skirt pocket.

"Have we heard from our mutual friend Vincent?"

Rachel's face grew warm. "I believe he was officiating at the wedding in the Sheepscombe chapel. He travels the circuit, ministering to three other parishes. The surrounding villages are too small to support a clergyman, so we all club together."

"Excellent. No lecture today. He does go on and on, you know. If I weren't so anxious to get out of here, I'd lock the door against him."

"Nothing can stop Vincent when he is determined."

"Is that how he wooed you? With determination? Like a bulldog? Or like Rufus with my cane, gnawing on it until it drops to the ground in relief and is delighted to be turned into sawdust?"

"I didn't drop down to the ground! Vincent was a perfect gentleman. He's very…he's very sensitive to my feelings."

"Has he kissed you?"

"A thousand t-times," Rachel said, vexed. She hated to lie, and was so bad at it.

"Merely a thousand? He's been here four years." He paused, thinking. "That's one-point-one-one-five kisses per day. The fellow is a slow-top."

Rachel was impressed with Henry's mathematical skills, but wasn't going to tell him so until she had a piece of paper and a pencil to check his work. "Our understanding is of more recent origin. He's been much more attentive than *that*."

"Are his kisses as nice as mine?"

"Henry! A lady doesn't discuss such things." And nice was a vastly inadequate adjective. Henry's kisses were stirring. Sensational. Sinful.

"Where else has the fellow kissed you?"

Rachel blinked. What did he mean? Oh, of course.

"My hand. Sometimes my fingertips. Vincent is very continental."

"That's it?"

"That's plenty, my lord. We certainly will not anticipate our vows," Rachel said firmly. If and when she married, she intended to come to the marriage bed a maid. In the parish women's sewing circle, she'd knitted too many booties for six-month babies. And sometimes the weddings never came off at all, and the poor girls were left with a baby and a bad reputation.

Vincent wasn't the sort who would break rules anyway. Not that she was going to marry him—she'd never even dreamed of kissing him. Briefly she wondered who had captured his heart. Someone unattainable, perhaps a childhood sweetheart who didn't care to be a minister's wife after all. Poor Vincent.

"So he's never..." Henry's lips quirked. "Kissed you where it counts most."

"What do you mean? I have told you he's kissed me!" Rachel felt confused.

"He's never—of course he hasn't. If he had, you wouldn't be trying to find your own pleasure in the dark with such determination."

Oh, damn him. He was a *disgrace*. She had almost forgotten that embarrassing night.

"A gentleman would not bring up such a thing."

"Who said I was a gentleman? If you ask me, old Vincent is too much of one. He could take care of you and you would still be intact. Surely he knows that."

She couldn't believe she was discussing the state of her virginity with Lord Henry Challoner. This was the most improper discussion of her life, if you didn't count almost every other time she'd talked to him.

"I shall go downstairs and fix you some soup or something." Rachel tried to rise, but he caught her elbow.

"I don't want a taste of soup. I want a taste of you."

Rachel tried to wiggle her elbow free. "I will not kiss you!"

"Who asked you to? I'm going to kiss *you*."

The man made no sense. His fever was down, but the numerous blows to his head over the last few days had left their mark.

"I will not kiss you back."

Henry threw his head back and laughed, then winced. "Remind me not to laugh quite yet. Rachel, my poor innocent, you have no idea what I'm talking about, do you?"

She didn't, but did not want to admit her disadvantage. "Whatever it is, I'm sure it's inappropriate and horrible. Let go of my arm!"

"I don't want to. And there's nothing truly…inappropriate or horrible about what I'm proposing. You won't be harmed at all. Old Vincent will never know unless you tell him."

Rachel was tired of hearing her faux fiancé referred to as "old Vincent." He was only a year or two older than Henry, not some shriveled-up pensioner. Before she had a chance to object, somehow Henry had drawn her down into his bed. His arm was around her, cradling her carefully. She felt entirely too comfortable and should be beating him off, but it was rather nice lying next to his warm form. His breath tickled her ear, and goose bumps rose on her scalp.

"We don't know how much time we have, so I'd better be efficient about it all," Henry murmured.

"You need to let me up," Rachel said with much less force than she should have.

"I don't think so. Relax."

The word had an opposite effect. Every sense was on alert now. She smelled Henry's cologne, his tooth powder. The lavender sheets. She saw at close range the red bristles of the beard he'd been too weak to shave off this morning. Without forethought, her hand brushed his cheek. He hissed, and his blue eyes dropped in apparent bliss.

"You cannot touch me," he whispered. "I'll not be responsible." He took her hand away and kissed her palm. He'd done it before, and the same loose feeling shot through her body. *He had the most beautiful mouth for a man*, Rachel thought. Good thing she was lying down—she was a bit dizzy. Was she succumbing to the same malady as Henry?

His lips and one set of fingers concentrated on her hand, stroking, licking, tickling, but his other fingers…oh dear. He was tugging up her skirt and petticoat and she should tell him no. She *would* tell him no, if only she could remember how to say it. Her tongue only needed to go to the roof of her mouth to get the word started.

Instead, she licked her lips. And then it was too late. His hand slipped inside her drawers, caressing her curls. His touch was simply so much better than hers. This was all wrong but felt so right. He was looking straight into her eyes, one wicked eyebrow raised, waiting for the 'no' that would not come.

She shut her own eyes in compliance, and then he dipped a finger inside her. She trembled as he stroked, almost too gently. It was so very... something. A dictionary might be helpful, though she doubted she could see straight to focus on the words.

Rachel tried to lie still, although it was tempting to rise to his touch. And then he carefully extracted his arm from beneath her and moved down the bed. Was he going to examine her like a doctor? She wasn't even sure what she looked like down there herself.

"What—"

"Hush." She felt his breath across her thighs and shivered. She felt him part her folds, then watched as he buried his golden head between her legs.

"Henry!"

This was the kiss he meant, this wicked, wonderful kiss. Rachel bit her lip to keep from crying out again. His mouth was hot against her center, his movements unerring. Lips, tongue, teeth worked in concert to build up her release in what seemed like seconds. Whether it was the idea of what he was doing or what he actually did, Rachel shattered before she had a chance to consider.

It didn't stop him from continuing, ratcheting the pulses up again until no amount of lip-biting could prevent her keening. She knew she was smiling as she did, the widest smile of her life, as if her cheeks would crack. She couldn't help herself—her body was his, her reaction out of her control. The sensation was so intense she wanted it to stop.

Or go on forever. Rachel was past being rational and consistent.

When she was absolutely exhausted from the spasms, Henry finally stopped and returned to her side. His face was flushed, his hair disordered from her pulling at it.

"There. I challenge old Vincent to match *that*. Did you like it?"

Was that the only reason he did such a thing, as a kind of one-upmanship over his supposed rival? Rachel felt a flash of irritation.

"I am not some bone to be fought over."

"Ah, I agree, even if you are tender and juicy and delicious."

Rachel's face was on fire. Perhaps she had the fever now. "You are impossible."

"So I have been frequently told. You didn't answer the question."

Did she like it?
More than breathing.

Chapter 26

Henry was rather proud of himself. He didn't think he'd ever caused such a fulsome response in all the years he'd been pleasuring women. In truth, there had not been all that many women, no matter what his father thought. Zulus and Boers rather interfered with one's ardor and availability, and when Henry had returned home, he was far more interested in getting his own tenuous satisfaction.

He had been selfish. Depressed, too. But he was feeling one thousand percent better now.

It must be the country air. The country girl. Rachel lay beside him, her cheeks rose-stained, her glorious dark hair somehow free of its pins. She was still mostly covered by her clothing, and Henry couldn't wait to see her out of it.

But not today. He reckoned he'd better not press his luck, amazed that he'd gotten this far. The taste and scent of her had made him hard as stone, but this afternoon had been for her. His time would come, God willing.

"You *are* happy, yes?" He couldn't have been mistaken. She had throbbed against his tongue like an electric current and nearly ruptured his good eardrum with her screams.

"I suppose."

Henry swallowed back a laugh. She was embarrassed, but truly, this had been a beautiful thing.

"I take it this was a new experience for you?"

"I think you should shut up now," Rachel said. He could see she wished she had a ruler with which to rap his knuckles. The poor thing was shy about what happened, but she needn't be. Henry didn't believe women should just lie there and submit like an inert china doll. A willing participant was always so much more satisfactory.

"All right. I do want to thank you for the privilege, though. It means a great deal to me that you trusted me." Henry was entirely sincere.

"If I had known what you were going to do, I would have said no." He brushed her damp fringe from her eyes. "Would you have? Then you didn't like it?"

"Oh, for heaven's sake! Are you waiting to be complimented? Fine. It was extraordinary," she huffed. "I had no idea such a thing could be done. Who on earth would think of it?"

"Adam, I imagine. Maybe eating the apple had nothing to do with him getting thrown out of the Garden of Eden."

She gave him a little shove. "Don't blaspheme! You're in enough trouble as it is."

"I daresay you're right. Well, Miss Everett, how are we to spend the rest of the afternoon? I doubt I can top my previous endeavor." He was a smug bastard.

"I wish Mrs. Grace would come home."

"*I* don't," Henry said. There would be no more fun, and he planned on kissing Rachel in a more conventional manner later. He tried to bring her closer but she was already rolling off the bed.

"I must get up."

"No, you mustn't. Aren't we cozy with the rain beating down? There's nothing like the smell of a spring rain." Henry made a show of inhaling. Shouldn't she be checking his temperature? That required propinquity.

Rachel moved to the open window and closed it. "More like a deluge. The curtains are wet."

"They'll dry." He pulled himself up, feeling only slightly light-headed. He put his own hand to his forehead but it was impossible to tell whether he was warm from fever or his ministrations. Rachel remained at the window, staring out at the gray gloom. It really was a filthy day.

"Someone's coming up the path."

Henry sat up straighter. "Who?"

"I can't tell. They're under an umbrella. Oh, God." She'd seen herself in his shaving stand mirror and began frantically twisting up her hair. Rachel was entirely disordered, hair unbound, cheeks flushed, eyes glazed.

"Bloody hell. Why can't people leave me alone?" Henry resolved then and there to pick up the extra key from under the flower pot. A man needed some privacy to make love to his future wife, didn't he? If they had been interrupted just a few minutes ago…

The bell below jangled. Rachel smoothed down her skirt, but could do nothing about the high color of her face without a powder puff, and he didn't have one handy.

"Tell whoever it is to go away," Henry growled. He didn't want their time together invaded in any way.

"It may be Dr. Oakley come to check up on you."

"Tell him I'm dead."

"Henry!"

It was almost true. He was going to die of frustration. Just when things were going his way.

Rachel left him. Henry heard his front door creak open, heard the male voice below. Oh, hell. Double hell.

After an agonizing amount of time, both Rachel and the Right Reverend Vincent Walker entered his bedroom. Walker, despite his umbrella, dripped on the carpet, and Henry was inclined to tell him to go to the devil and dry off in the heat of Hell.

"Miss Everett tells me you are much improved from the last time I saw you, my lord."

Henry coughed, considering his options. Should he pretend to pass out again and be spared his daily lecture? Feigning unconsciousness could become habitual. He might write a treatise on it to help other tortured souls.

"I will fetch some tea and cake," Rachel said, disappearing again.

Henry didn't want any damned tea, although he wouldn't turn down cake. Good luck to Rachel for finding some wherever Mrs. Grace has stashed it. "What brings you out on such a dismal day, Walker? I thought you were busy with a wedding."

"A matter of conscience. I have been enlisted by Mrs. Grace to take over here. Sheepscombe Brook has risen, and the road is washed out. She will be unable to return tonight from her sister's house."

"So?"

"She got a message through to let me know. Some nephew with a leaky punt. I barely got home from the wedding myself. You must see Miss Everett cannot stay here with you unchaperoned."

No, Henry didn't see. That situation sounded absolutely ideal. A night alone with Rachel would be just what the doctor ordered. By morning she would be his and Walker could find someone else to do the altar flowers.

Henry gave the vicar a leveling look. "Do you doubt that I am a gentleman, Walker?"

"Let's not pretend you are here for no reason, Lord Challoner. Your father—"

"Damn my father! He exaggerated everything out of all proportion!"
Walker paled. "I cannot stand by while you break commandments to
my face. 'Honor they father and mother,' don't you know."

Henry did know. He'd tried to honor his father most of his life and
where had that gotten him? Puddling-on-the-Wold.

Well, actually he supposed he should thank the pater. Henry would never
have met Rachel otherwise, never kissed or cuddled her, never licked—

"You look hot. You're still unwell, aren't you? But I'm sure I can
manage any symptoms you still have. You cannot expect Miss Everett to
remain all night. Even someone like you can see that I'm right."

No, even "someone like him" supposed he couldn't expect Rachel to
be alone with him, as much as he wanted her to be. If word got out, it
would be hard to convince Puddling that Rachel was still an innocent.

Although now she was less innocent than she used to be, Henry thought
with well-earned satisfaction.

He would be stuck with old Vincent until the cock crowed or the flood
receded. The fellow might actually be an improvement over Mrs. Grace
in the companionship department.

"You're right. I would never want to compromise Miss Everett's
virtue," Henry lied.

"I knew you would see reason. Do you play chess?"

"Not well. I haven't the patience." Chess was the marquess's game—
the man planned ahead like no one's business. As a boy, Henry became
bored easily and didn't care who took whose bishop.

He'd been the despair of his father even then and hadn't even begun to
flex his rebellious muscles.

"I suppose I could read to you," Walker said doubtfully.

Spare me, Jesus, Henry thought. The drone of old Vincent's voice
reading improving texts would lead him to madness and Hades.

The decision of how to spend the next hours was halted by Rachel's
arrival with the tea tray. Vincent leaped up to help her settle the tray on a
table and Henry couldn't be too jealous. The truth was he was having an
afternoon sinking spell. His headache was returning, no doubt brought on
by the good vicar.

Henry was thwarted, sexually and spiritually.

Rachel had unearthed actual frosted biscuits from a hidden tin—Henry
was sure they were forbidden from his nursery diet and Mrs. Grace would
have five fits. Since he was doomed to kiss Rachel's sweetness no more
today, he took a fistful from the plate and crammed them into his mouth
like a spoiled, defiant child.

Henry did not participate in the genial chitchat between Walker and his supposed intended. If they were truly engaged, Henry was a rosy-arsed baboon. There was no frisson of flirtation between them, no secret smiles or accidental touches over the tea table. The conversation concerning tomorrow's altar flowers sent him into a near-coma. Henry yawned pointedly.

And then, Rachel left to wash the dishes up in the kitchen, and leave for good. Walker retreated to a corner of the bedroom, armed with a pocket Bible. Henry did the only thing he could think of to escape—he willed himself to sleep as he'd learned to do on the savannah and all the uncomfortable billets he'd experienced as a soldier.

In comparison, Puddling-on-the-Wold wasn't so very terrible.

Chapter 27

It was inevitable. Henry had to wake up from his nap sometime. Judging from the gray skies outside, it was still raining but not quite dark. His stomach rumbled, indicating that it was perhaps suppertime and his digestive system was improving. Could old Vincent cook? Henry didn't think he could manage the stairs to the kitchen quite yet.

He hadn't lain abed like this in his life. Even when his foot was almost shot off, the Boers had no interest in coddling him. The pater expected him to be at the breakfast table no later than seven in the morning after a bruising early morning ride. So to lie about like a loafer had been an unusual way for Henry to spend his day.

Of course, there had been an interlude today where he was relatively active. He wondered if the remembrance of it brought a blush to Rachel's cheek. What was she doing now? Fixing dinner for her father? Mending by lamplight? He hoped she'd finished the bloody altar flowers.

Henry didn't intend to see them personally. He figured he could get out of going to church services tomorrow due to his illness. And besides, the vicar had moved in with him for the night. Surely that counted for something towards his immortal soul.

Sainthood by osmosis.

"Ah! You're awake!" Old Vincent sounded disgustingly chipper. He had that voice used by adults to address children and the mentally deficient, all false cheer and bonhomie.

"Just about. What did I miss?" Henry asked, tongue firmly in cheek.

"I've just been reading. Listening to the rain."

"Don't overexcite yourself." Henry stretched and heard a cracking noise in his neck. He really should get out of bed and totter about the room. His daily walks had become almost something to look forward to, especially if seeing Rachel was at the end of the journey. "No chance of that." Puddling's not the place to go if one wants excitement." Walker gave a rueful smile. "Tell me something I'm not aware of. How do you stand it? You're still young, and reasonably intelligent, as far as I can tell. Don't say you find the inmates fascinating. I'm boring myself witless."

"One doesn't enter the ministry for excitement," Walker replied. "In most cases, the work I do here is very gratifying."

Henry stopped himself from snorting. "I suppose you get a cut of the loot. The Puddling Rehabilitation funds that are awarded to the townspeople every year."

Walker's lips thinned. "A clergyman doesn't expect to get rich."

"What, a man of your indubitable talents has no ambition to be a bishop?"

"You are mocking me, Lord Challoner."

Henry supposed he was. Walker had power over him, and he didn't like it. And there was the business of Rachel, who was engaged to both of them although not all of the parties seemed knowledgeable about this fact.

"I imagine you'll want to marry one day," Henry said, working his way toward the truth.

"I haven't given it much thought, actually," Walker said, surprising Henry not in the least.

"Really? I thought marriage was a requirement if one wants to advance in the church."

"You are the one pushing for my advancement. A bishop!" Walker chuckled. "I'm sure my sights are not fixed on so grand a prize."

"Well, a wife would be helpful, wouldn't she? Just in the general way of things. Better to marry than to burn and all that rot."

"I haven't met—" Walker paused. "That isn't quite true. The young lady who once caught my eye proved to be unattainable. We were... doomed, I suppose one might say. She was promised to another."

Henry raised a brow. "Really? I wouldn't let anything stop me if I were in love."

"Wouldn't you? No, I suppose a man like you wouldn't. You'd just charge ahead, no matter the cost."

Henry decided not to be offended. "A man like him" seemed capable of almost anything. "Then you must not have loved her enough."

"That wasn't it!" Walker said with some heat. "There were other circumstances as well."

"There are always circumstances," Henry said, and wondered at the precise state of Walker's.

"Yes, well, it's all very well for you to sit in judgment."

"I'd never judge," Henry said truthfully. "That's my father's specialty. I'm more a live-and-let-live fellow. Was she beautiful?"

Walker's face took on a dreamy cast. "Exquisite. And the sweetest girl imaginable. Her mother treated her abominably, arranging a wretched marriage for her. I hope she's managing."

"You don't know?"

"I cannot interfere. We agreed we couldn't keep in contact. She's a married woman now! It wouldn't be fitting."

"Pah! So you let this poor girl marry some scoundrel? What kind of Christian charity is that?"

Henry knew he'd gone too far when Walker tromped over to the bed and hovered above him, his face mottled in anger. "There is such a thing as honor to the greater cause. I've given my word—I have responsibilities— you don't know the suffering—"

"All right, all right. Calm down. I'm a sick man, remember? You're supposed to be taking care of me, not smashing me to smithereens. So, you and Miss Everett don't have an understanding?"

"Who? Oh, Rachel. No. There's been some village gossip, but I feel nothing for her but friendship. There will never be another woman for me." Walker collapsed in a chair, looking melancholy.

Better and better. Walker was obviously not in any way smitten with Rachel.

The poor bastard.

So, Walker didn't have all the answers. Henry reflected on the man's counsel so far, lecturing Henry on the sanctity of marriage and the perils of the pursuit of excess pleasure. Walker, apparently, would have neither.

"You don't know that. Someone else might come along."

Walker shook his head. "I have a constant heart, Lord Challoner. I view my celibacy as a blessing—now I can devote my total attention to God and the residents of Puddling."

"That sounds awfully grim."

"We all have our crosses to bear. Mine is inconsequential in the grand scheme of things. Are you hungry?"

Henry was, which was a good sign. "I believe I'm over the worst of my indisposition. You don't have to stay the night."

"It's my duty. You are in our care."

"In that case, how about some soup? It shouldn't be too much trouble to heat."

Walker rose. "Shall I bring it upstairs, or are you well enough to dine below?"

"I'll come down." Henry would have to get out of bed sometime. He watched as Walker made to leave the room. "Watch your head!" But Henry's warning was too late. Poor old Vincent fell to the floor. Henry had had a mind to fetch a hatchet and cut the bloody crossbeam down after the first time he'd hit his own head. Of course, the roof might come down with it.

"Damn it all to hell." Henry stumbled out of bed, still a little dizzy. He bent over the vicar, who was out cold in the hallway. "Whoever had designed this house must have had dwarfs in mind. Can you hear me, Walker?"

There was no response. A straight red line ran the length of Walker's forehead, but there was no blood, thank goodness. He went back to the bed, grabbed a pillow and stuffed it under the vicar's head. Now what? Should he try to go for help?

Henry wanted Rachel back. He wished she'd never gone home. He could have been spending his evening in far more satisfactory fashion than sitting next to an unconscious minister.

Henry gave Walker a few light taps on his ruddy cheeks. "Come on, man. Wake up."

Finally, Walker groaned.

"There you are!" Henry said cheerfully. "I knew your head was as hard as mine. You Puddling people really need to do something about this cottage's architecture. You wouldn't want a Guest to decapitate himself, would you? That would ruin the foundation's reputation in one fell swoop. Get it?" Henry laughed at his own inane joke.

"A reputation is nothing to be trifled with," Walker muttered. "'*A good name is rather to be chosen than great riches, and loving favor rather than silver and gold.*' Proverbs 22:1."

"It would be nice to have the money, too, don't you think? Can you get up?"

"Of course I can get up." Walker swayed as he tried to sit, and Henry caught him.

"Look at the pair of us. Tweedle-dee and Tweedle-dum. Stonecrop is strewn with landmines for fellows our size. I'll help you down the stairs."

It was Henry who found the crock of soup in the ice box and heated it. Walker was delegated to cutting up and buttering bread since he was dizzier than Henry at present. The two of them sat at the kitchen table in the waning light enjoying the simple fare, which would have been much enhanced by a slug or three of claret.

"I shall speak to the governors about the lintels and beams," Walker said, wiping up a dribble of soup from his lips. "This place is dangerous. Of course, not all the guests are as tall as you are. The last lady who stayed here had no difficulty."

"What was her sin? Not jumping high enough when her husband told her?"

"It was nothing so trivial."

"I don't know, Walker. I'll bet half the Guests here are no barmier than you or I. This is quite a racket you Puddlingites have, making ordinary high spirits seem evil."

Walker stirred his soup, then dropped the spoon with a clatter. "High spirits? Is that what you call defiling your father's home with prostitutes?"

"They weren't—well, I guess maybe they were. I did a stupid thing." It had seemed amusing to Henry at the time. He hadn't expected his father to discover the girls, but considering all the noise they made, it was inevitable.

"So you've seen the error of your ways."

Henry nodded. "Yes. I'm cured. My father wants me to marry and settle down when I get out of here? Done."

Walker's face lit. "That is good news. I'll report on your progress to the governors."

Henry had to ask. "Is there a chance I can leave before the official time is up?"

"I doubt it. We've yet to settle on your Service."

"But—"

"I'm sorry— it's tradition. Methodology may have changed over the last few decades—we no longer dose the Guests with laudanum or tie them into straitjackets, for example—but the Service is inviolate. You need to do something for the greater good. And it's early days for you. Heaven forfend, but you may backslide."

Henry had no intention of backsliding or frontsliding. He was willing to take on all the labors of Hercules if it meant Rachel would become Lady Challoner.

Chapter 28

Rachel sat through Vincent's service along with the handful of Puddling's other younger women, who had finally been allowed out. Henry's two-week probationary period was up, and it was now assumed he wouldn't attack any of the females simply because they *were* females.

The girls who had come to get a glimpse of the new Guest were disappointed—Henry must still be ill, for he wasn't front and center in the pew reserved for Guests. Mrs. Grace was nowhere to be seen either. The Sheepscombe Brook had not yet receded after yesterday's torrential downpour, so she must still be trapped at her sister's, mucking up the honeymoon. A light drizzle was still falling from the Sunday skies.

Which meant Henry was quite alone in his cottage.

Rachel slipped out the side door, avoiding Vincent greeting his parishioners. Although she was curious as to how they had gotten along yesterday, she'd rather hear it from Henry. He was bound to be far more entertaining.

She hoped Vincent had not denied outright that she was his secret fiancée. She knew he wouldn't lie for her, but perhaps the subject had not come up, or he had tiptoed around it.

What must Henry think of her wantonness yesterday afternoon? If she truly belonged to another man, surely she would not have allowed such—such—whatever it had been.

If she were smart, she'd not be heading for Stonecrop Cottage. But she felt a responsibility—the marquess had hired her to take care of his son, and the least she could do what see if she could get Henry anything before she went home to fix her father's lunch. She knew Vincent was expected at another church service in a nearby village later, so Henry would be on his own.

At least today she wasn't so bedraggled. Her umbrella and hat performed their necessary duties, and her Sunday best dress was spotless except for a scrim of mud at the hem—it couldn't be helped on a day like this. She hurried through the wet churchyard and its impressive table tombs and pyramidal trees before she was hailed by anyone, and practically vaulted down Honeywell Lane. Henry's neighbors were still at church, so Rachel didn't mind the telltale squeak of the gate. She picked up the flower pot, found the spare key, and let herself in.

The house was as quiet as the churchyard. "Henry?" she called in the front hall, somewhat hesitant.

"Right here." She nearly jumped out of her skin as he came up behind her, dropping the key to the flagstones. "You didn't see me in the garden? You walked right by the bench."

Rachel shook her head. She'd only had eyes for the front door. "What are you doing outside? It's still raining! You'll catch your death."

"That can't be true. If wet weather made one sick, the entire British Isles would be depopulated. I was feeding the fish if you must know, and then just sat for a moment thinking." His hair was damp and curling at his collar, and Rachel struggled not to run her fingers through it.

"Why didn't you say something?"

"I was too surprised seeing you marching down the path. For a second I thought I was hallucinating. You were like a dream come true."

Rachel's face warmed. "Stop that. Have you had breakfast? I came to fix you something."

"Old Vincent took care of me before he went to save souls. Or maybe I took care of him—I'm feeling much better. But thank you for the offer."

"I'll just go then."

"You will not. Not after you've gone to the trouble of breaking into my house."

"I didn't break in! I used the key." She bent over to retrieve it, but Henry beat her to it and pocketed it.

"Technicalities. But I'm glad you've dropped by. Did old Vincent make it through his sermon? He had a devil of a headache."

Truthfully, Rachel had not paid that much attention. Vincent was usually fairly eloquent, and she had no reason to believe that he hadn't been this morning. "I hope he's not coming down with what you had."

"Oh, he was down all right. Why don't you fix us some tea now that you're here? I find I'm becoming addicted to the stuff. It's much better than brandy."

"All right." The fire was still going in the stove, and she put the kettle on. A stack of plates sat in a dishpan in the sink, evidence of at least two meals. Men. Did they not have hands to turn on a tap and wash them? She picked up a glass on the drainboard.

And then almost let it slip from her fingers. The smell was self-evident. *Spirits.* Whisky, if she wasn't mistaken.

"Henry Agamemnon Challoner!"

"I knew I shouldn't have told you my full name. You sound just like my old nanny. What have I done now?" Henry grinned and sat down at the pine table.

"Have you been drinking?"

He raised an eyebrow. "Not I."

"Liar! What was in this?"

"Oh. That. You'd have to ask Vincent. He nipped home to get a flask of something last evening for while we talked through the storm. I must say, it doesn't take much to get him tipsy and maudlin. He offered me a sip, but I declined. You should be proud of me instead of calling me names."

Rachel was rather shocked. "Did Vincent get *drunk?*" She'd never seen him have anything alcoholic but a rare glass of cider or the obligatory taste of communion wine.

"I won't peach on him. Brothers-in-arms and all that. We are fast friends now. He's lost his lady-love and was drowning his sorrows, and I can't seem to convince mine that my intentions are honorable. You shouldn't go around calling other people liars, you know. You have prevaricated. Fibbed. Spoken untruths."

Rachel's tongue felt very thick. Damn Vincent. "I don't know what you mean."

"Oh, don't you? You are no more engaged to that man than I am. Though Vincent is a man, isn't he? That would not be at all the thing, though I have no objection to people finding love where they may. I consider myself worldly enough."

"Henry!"

"Don't judge. But it is just as I thought. And I must say I'm relieved. I like old Vincent and wouldn't want to steal his girl."

The kettle started to shriek and Rachel wanted to do the same. "Don't you understand anything?" she asked, shoving a handful of tea leaves in a very pretty china pot. "We have no future. It's impossible."

"You'll forgive me if I don't agree. I've been in impossible situations, and this isn't one of them. We will find a way to keep Puddling in good graces and assuage the pater. I haven't quite worked it out yet, but trust me."

Was Henry at all trustworthy? "You swear you did not share Vincent's flask?"

"Not so much as a drop. I wasn't even tempted. To be frank, I don't think the whisky was of the highest quality. Vincent told me he gives all his money to the poor. Are you going to pour that water into the pot before it gets cold?"

Rachel grabbed a towel and wrapped it around the kettle's handle. Her hand shook so much she was sure she'd scald somebody. It was madness to think she could be a viscount's wife.

Even if Henry was not impaired from liquor, his mental facilities were still suspect.

She clanked the kettle back down on the hob as Henry put a spoonful of sugar into his cup. "We found everything last night, you know," he said. "The sugar. The cakes. A damn good batch of molasses cookies. Mrs. Grace will have to find new hiding spots."

"Henry Agamemnon Challoner," she began.

He raised a hand. "Please don't take that tone and lecture me. You'll spoil our elevenses."

"I must. Why, why, why are you so set on marrying me?"

Chapter 29

What an excellent question.

Well, Rachel was a teacher, after all. She probably spent a good portion of her day ferreting out answers from the little buggers in her classroom. Was that called the Socratic method? Henry had forgotten much of his youthful education. Even if a gun were pointed to his head—

He'd had enough of that in the army, hadn't he? Nothing would help him remember lessons he hadn't been listening to in the first place.

Like literature. This is where he was supposed to wax poetic, quote something fruity and declare undying love, much like that poor sap Vincent did last night over his unnamed inamorata. But Henry had already told Rachel he didn't believe in love.

The bigger question—did love believe in him? Was it possible for him to feel settled and happy and whole?

He cleared his throat. "I wish I had an answer you would like. I just have a feeling about you." He did, too. She was steady and smart and full of natural passion. It would be a long while before he would forget yesterday afternoon. Her taste, her scent, the ripple of her response—all very heady and gratifying.

"Not good enough, Henry." She dropped a lump of sugar in her tea. "Perhaps we can remain friends while you're here."

Friends? Henry didn't want a friend—he wanted a lover. But he was becoming increasingly aware that Rachel Everett was the most stubborn woman he'd ever met. There was no point to fighting. Making a frontal assault. He'd just have to ambush her like a bloody Boer with a rake.

"All right. I'll take what I can get," Henry said. It seemed they were both becoming experts at not telling the truth.

She blinked at the ease to which he acceded to her wishes. Had she wanted him to argue? It seemed he was doomed to disappoint her.

"Good. Fine, then. I'm glad you are being so reasonable." She stirred her tea with such violence that Henry worried about the fragile cup. "Do you still have the letter for Sir Bertram? I should take it to his house."

"Won't that make him suspicious? You might have forged it." She may as well have—it might be in his illegible handwriting, but the letter was pure Rachel. "No, I'll do it. It seems I have nothing better to do today."

"But you're ill! And it's raining!"

"Not much. I don't think I'll melt—I'm not sweet enough. Really, I am feeling nearly normal, whatever that is. Better than the good vicar, certainly."

Henry had had to put Vincent to bed in the spare room last night. This morning, really. The fellow could not hold his liquor at all, and there may even have been some tears and vomit involved over the kitchen table.

Who was nursing and counseling whom here? If that's what love did, Henry wanted no part of it.

"You don't even know where Sykes House is."

"No, but you'll draw me a map, won't you? The village isn't that big. I need to get out into the fresh air. I promise I'll wear a hat this time. Maybe even carry an umbrella." He fetched a pad of paper and pencil from a drawer in the sideboard.

"It's not in the village, but almost a mile out. I'm not sure you're allowed to go that far."

"Rachel, I believe I've already done a few things that are not on my treatment plan. How do I get there?"

"I shouldn't tell you. If anyone asks, just say you were exploring."

Henry snorted. He'd gotten into quite enough trouble exploring Puddling already.

"You need to walk through the churchyard and pick up the other end of Vicarage Lane," Rachel said, knuckling under to his look. "It's very narrow, no more than a grassy sheep track, not even a lane, really. It peters out at the stone wall. The gate should be unlocked. Go through and up the hill. Sykes House is at the crest. It has an unsurpassed view of the valley."

Another hill. Typical. His foot twinged in protest. "How the devil do they get supplies in and out?"

"That's the back way in. There's a road on the other side of the estate. You came into Puddling that way, but you probably weren't paying attention. You—you weren't in very good shape when you arrived."

Very true. Henry had had a roaring headache and had slept and retched between his father's rantings. He'd woken up in the coach in front of the Rifle and Roses only to find his father had tied him to his seat like a common criminal.

Who knew the pater was so good with knots?

It was only two weeks ago. Hard to believe, when so much had happened.

"So, there's an escape route?"

"It's Market Street, actually. You know the stone archway and those studded wooden doors across the road?"

Henry nodded. He'd presumed there was a disused inn courtyard beyond. The wall was much too tall for him to see over.

"That's the main road. You've been locked in, but we all have keys."

"Lovely. How did my father get through yesterday?"

"People take shifts opening the doors. There's never much strange traffic in and out."

Henry supposed he'd stand around every now and then waiting for a carriage to come through himself if he got the Puddling bonus every year. He set the pencil down where it rolled off the table to the flagstone floor. "I guess I can remember the directions. I won't be eaten by Sykes's guard dogs, will I? I suppose I'll be trespassing."

She chewed a lip. "He doesn't have dogs. Well, his oldest son Tristan did but it died. Really, I should go myself."

"Don't deprive me of my outing. After last night, I could use a holiday." He'd been a good scout with Walker, poor idiot. Shown empathy for his fellow man. Could Henry work it into his Service somehow? He'd failed to discuss his soldiers' respite idea, not being able to get a word in edgewise as Walker raved about his thwarted romance.

He put his palms on the table. "I'll just go up to my room and fetch the letter, shall I?"

"No, you sit put. It's the least I can do." She disappeared up the stairs.

Henry nursed his tea, and after a bit he heard the distinct flush of his toilet and the running of the taps. No wonder she was anxious to go up and get the letter.

And then he heard a much more unwelcome commotion at his front door. The knocker came close to being rapped clean off its hinges.

"Henry!"

"Miss Everett!"

What in hell was the pater doing back, and who had he brought with him? Wasn't his father supposed to be at some jolly weekend house party? Henry pulled himself up and limped to the front door.

His father was accompanied by an older gentleman with frightening black eyebrows. Both of them looked choleric in the extreme.

"Father, what a pleasant surprise! I didn't expect to see you again so soon."

"Never mind the blandishments, boy! Where is she?"

"Where is who? Or is it whom? Come in out of the rain. I don't believe I know your companion. May I get you both some tea? We can sit in the conservatory if you like, even if it is a filthy morning."

"I don't have time for tea, my lord," the stranger said. "I am Sir Bertram Sykes."

Bloody hell in a hand basket.

"One of the governors, aren't you? My compliments to the Puddling Rehabilitation Foundation. I feel like a new man and it's only been two weeks."

"Shut up, Henry. I know you're up to your old tricks. What a fool I've been," the marquess said, "practically putting that girl in your lap."

"What girl?" Henry was probably not going to get away with claiming total ignorance, but it was all he could think to do at the moment.

"The dirty wet one! Sir Bertram tells me there has been talk about you two. We met by chance at the Entwhistles. He has told me the trouble she's been making in the village. No better than she should be, and I walked right into her trap. She was here all afternoon and probably all night at my insistence! How you both must have laughed."

Henry straightened. No better than she should be? He knew he shouldn't punch his father and Sir Bertram both, but he was very tempted.

And even wet and dirty, Rachel was divine.

"I beg your pardon. Do you mean Miss Everdean? I mean Miss Evergreen? I sent her away immediately to fetch the vicar yesterday. What were you thinking, Father? You bullied the poor girl and scared her half to death. My understanding is she only came to see Mrs. Grace for a recipe for one of her father's favorites and you dragooned her into staying to nurse me. The old man—he's become a sort of friend—has told me she is an excellent daughter, and a very dedicated teacher, too, but I'm not sure I'd recognize her on the street."

Maybe he wouldn't have to hand the scribbled letter over to Sir Bertram after all. He'd pretty much summarized its contents in one sentence.

"Be that as it may—" his father began, but Henry plowed ahead.

"It was Mr. Walker who spent the night here to take care of me. Ask him."

Sir Bertram's fishlike mouth opened. "Walker was here? All night?"

Henry nodded, praying Rachel would have the sense to stay upstairs and hide in a closet or something. "Yes. All night. I'm afraid we were up very late talking. Past my ten o'clock bedtime. But I do hope you'll forgive him. We were discussing...Proverbs. He's a very sound man, Sir Bertram. Very sound. I was almost well enough to go to church with him, but he bade me stay home. You Puddlingites are to be commended for making such an effort regarding my physical and spiritual health. Father, I hate to say it, but you were right to send me here."

Henry was laying it on thick. He was fairly sure his father was suspicious, but Sir Bertram puffed out his chest in pleasure, crowding the little space even further.

"Come, why are we hanging about in the hallway? Let's go into the parlor. You both drove over all the way from Frampton Mansell? You must have made an early start." The two men trooped after him, looking none too happy.

"Left before breakfast," his father said tersely, arranging himself in the most comfortable chair, as was his wont. Nothing but the best for a marquess. "We were sure there was reason to worry."

Henry practically batted his eyes. "Worry about what? It was only a slight fever, Father. I was never in any real danger. But I thank you for your concern."

"The girl, Henry."

"What g—oh, you mean Miss Evershot. I told you, she fetched Mr. Walker—that is to say, Vincent, as we've become soulmates—post haste. You didn't seriously think—oh, you did, didn't you? I know I've given you reason to doubt me in the past, Father, but I assure you all my hijinks are over. Nothing but respectability ahead, I promise. I might even marry when I meet the right girl."

"I told you there was probably nothing to it, Lord Harland," Sir Bertram said. "Perhaps I've jumped to some conclusions regarding our young schoolteacher myself. Rachel Everett knows which side her bread is buttered on."

Henry had never really understood that phrase, but let it pass. "Who?"

"Don't be obtuse, Henry. There are times when I wondered if you were more injured than the army let on."

"We shall, of course, want to interview Vincent Walker to corroborate your son's story, my lord," Sir Bertram said unctuously.

"My son doesn't lie!" the marquess lied. "But I agree—it will do no harm for me to spend a few days in Puddling to inspect your operations."

Henry's heart sank to his boots. "Will you be staying here at Stonecrop Cottage, Father? It's nice enough, but not at all what you're used to. When Mrs. Grace gets back, I'm sure she'll change the bedding in the guest room." As Henry recalled, there might possibly be some unpleasant Walkerian fluid on the sheets.

"She should be home from church services any minute," Sykes said, looking at his timepiece.

"Oh, she's not in church. She never made it home," Henry said.

"She told me the wedding reception was yesterday afternoon," his father blustered. "She assured me she would be here by the evening to relieve Miss Everett of her duties."

"But there's been a flood so she couldn't. That's why my good friend Vincent was here."

"And he *is* in church, so you are all alone after all." Henry's father looked a trifle guilty.

Good.

"I don't blame you, Father. You couldn't have predicted the weather, and as you can see, I'm almost perfectly fine. I don't know what I can give you for lunch, though."

Was there any arsenic under the sink? Henry might swallow some himself if he couldn't figure out a way to smuggle Rachel out of the house. He hoped she wasn't climbing out a bedroom window right this second and trying to rappel down the Cotswold stone wall.

"Lord Harland, I would be honored if you would be *my* guest for the next few days. Sykes House has every amenity, and we are known throughout Gloucestershire for our gardens. That way both you and your son will have privacy and comfort. We usually encourage complete separation between our Guests and their families, you know, but I have no objection to you visiting for a day or two if it will allay your fears for your son and heir. It seems he has made significant progress."

Was Henry to get gold stars on his chart next? He'd much rather have kisses from the teacher.

Chapter 30

Henry's face appeared under the scalloped edge of the bedspread. "That was too close for comfort."

Rachel could only agree. All those books about hearts beating wildly when faced with danger —she could corroborate the sensation was entirely true now, perhaps not even strong enough. She'd thought her heart would jump right out of her mouth when she dived under Henry's bed, and her squashed bonnet might not ever recover.

If the men had come upstairs and discovered her, there would have been no way for her to appear innocent, even if she was fresh from church and fully dressed, ruined hat and all. Henry might charm the birds out of trees, but Sir Bertram and the Marquess of Harland were a tough audience. Finding a woman in Henry's bedroom would mean only one thing to them.

According to the little chiming clock in Henry's bedchamber, it was now well past noon, and Rachel had thought the men would never leave. It wasn't until Henry offered to heat up yesterday's leftover soup that he drove them out into the mist to Sir Bertram's luncheon table. Henry's bedroom was over the parlor; she had heard every word, her ear being pressed flat against the wood floor. To give Mrs. Grace credit, there wasn't a speck of dust. Rachel had forced back a sneeze anyway in her fright.

Henry snaked a hand under the bed. "Do you need help? I once used to have an old basset hound who crawled under my bed during thunderstorms. Sometimes he got stuck."

"Are you saying I'm fat?"

"Heavens no, you're just right. And you smell much better than Spot ever did. Anyway, I have no objection to an extra pound or two. It's what's inside that counts."

That last sentence didn't sound like any rake that Rachel had ever heard of. Perhaps he *was* telling the truth that he was a new man.

"My knees are numb, Rachel. Do you want to stay under there all day?"

"Of course not." She flattened herself and slid rather like a worm, avoiding Henry's hand. He grabbed her anyway and tugged her out. After an awkward attempt to help both of them up, Henry allowed her to steady him.

That was what he needed—someone at his side to take his side. She'd heard what the marquess had to say below, criticism after criticism. It was a wonder Henry hadn't strangled the man. It was all she could do to not rap on the floorboards to interrupt the conversation. To live under such constant negativity must be a trial. No wonder Henry had wanted a bit of fun.

"Well, now what? I think the letter is superfluous, don't you? I took every opportunity to deny that I knew you. Quite frankly, I felt a bit like Peter."

Rachel stared at him.

"You know. Peter from the Bible."

Henry was a man of many surprises. "I suppose you're right."

"I don't like that Sykes person. And now he wants to ingratiate himself with the pater. Just what we need, more vigilance. How will we be able to meet?"

Rachel realized she *wanted* to see Henry, even if he was thoroughly inappropriate for her. "You could still visit my father."

Henry brightened. "I could, couldn't I? Then maybe I'll find out what his name really is. How can I fix this business with your job? Sykes sounds ready to give you the heave-ho."

Rachel sat down on the bed. "I really don't see how. Sir Bertram has never liked me. He had a younger son, you know, and we—well, it was just a crush. Nothing serious, and wasn't apt to ever be. But Sir Bertram didn't think I was good enough."

"Pah! The man's an idiot! What happened?"

"Wallace died at university. It was…" Rachel swallowed the lump in her throat. "I'm sorry. I'm over it, of course. It was seven years ago, after all. I was little more than a child. And I barely kissed him. But it was a terrible loss for the Sykes family and the community."

Henry put a hand on her shoulder. "Of course it was. One's first love is always special."

"Who was yours?"

"Oh, no one, really. I mean, I had encounters, but there was very little affection involved. It's different for men."

"Is it? That's too bad."

"I can't agree. Why have one's heart broken? Look at old Vincent. The man's a wreck. It's a wonder he can keep his faith."

"Faith is meant to be tested," Rachel said. "Life is not all cakes and ale."

"Now you're quoting Shakespeare. Sir Bertram doesn't know the treasure you are."

Rachel brushed his hand away. "I don't *need* to teach. I enjoy it, and feel useful, but we could get along without my pay. It isn't much anyway."

"Then why don't you resign? Let someone else deal with the little goblins."

She realized she could do just that. Who else would be stupid enough to take her place? The job was not as easy as some might think. Just because most people had gone to school themselves, they assumed they knew how best to teach difficult children. Sir Bertram must have been beaten regularly to think that was the way of it.

"But what would I do?" She had plenty of hobbies, but none would fill her days completely.

"You could marry me, of course."

Of course. It always led back to that. Rachel would have to give Henry some respect—he was not wavering in the face of her relentless refusal.

She fluttered a hand at him. "We have discussed this for days. We are friends only. After listening to your father, I cannot imagine he will approve of anyone you marry but the daughter of a duke."

"He *is* a dreadful snob. My mother was the daughter of a duke."

Typical. Whatever pipe dreams Rachel might have were pointless. She took off her hat and tried to punch it back to life.

"Here, let me."

"What do you know about ladies' hats?"

"You'd be surprised. Isn't that why I'm here?"

For a second she pictured Henry in a feathered bonnet. There had once been a Guest who preferred to wear women's clothing, much to the dismay of his new bride, whose trousseau was immediately appropriated after their wedding day. Rachel was not exactly sure how the situation had been sorted—she had been considered too young at the time to know the particulars.

Henry's capable hands bent the brim back to its original position. "This is a very pretty hat."

"Thank you. I trimmed it myself."

"Did you? Is there anything you can't do?"

Rachel could think of a thousand things. "Stop complimenting me. I'm very ordinary."

"If you say so. Stubborn, too. Care to have some leftover soup with me?"

Rachel shook her head. "My father will be wondering where I am. I'm supposed to roast a chicken for Sunday lunch. It will be more like supper by the time it's done."

"With gravy, I bet." Henry looked pained. And hungry.

"Yes." It was on the tip of her tongue to invite him, but that wouldn't do. With the marquess and Sir Bertram on the loose, she would have to be much more careful.

No touching herself in the garden. No Henry touching her, either.

"I'm sure Mrs. Grace will be back any time now. And you do have your soup."

"Oh, joy. I'll see you to the door."

Somehow, Henry's hand was under her elbow as they descended the steep stairs to the front hallway. He angled the hat on her head, then ducked under the brim for a kiss. Rachel was too startled to turn her face or close her lips. She shut her eyes, and all her good intentions disappeared.

Kissing Henry was just delicious. Better than gravy and her buttery mashed potatoes. The man knew how to kiss. Years of experience, she reminded herself. Years and years, apparently. He was touching nothing but her elbow but she could feel him everywhere.

It was the curse of having a good imagination. Reading too many books. Dreaming too many things. Rachel's spine was disintegrating disc by disc and she could barely stand up. Henry knew, and drew her into the parlor, the recent site of his earlier interrogation.

She should snatch her elbow away and run out the door. But instead, they collapsed on the horsehair sofa together, not even breaking the kiss as they tumbled across the room.

She was soon in his lap, his arms around her. The kiss deepened, settling somewhere inside her soul. Rachel was meant to be kissed in just this quiet way, the firm yet gentle breadth of Henry's hand on her shoulder, anchoring her.

As if she'd ever want to escape.

Henry was deliberate. Calm. The frenzy of getting across the carpet was over, and now they simply reveled in their closeness. Rachel's world stopped even if the clock continued to tick in the distance.

There was nothing but careful fingers. Warm breath. Slowly sweeping tongues. Softness and strength and seduction. Henry seemed unhurried, deliberately in control, yet tender.

He would be gone in two weeks. Rachel had only known him one. Surely this afternoon was ill-advised.

But wonderful just the same. No, the word wonderful was inadequate.

Rachel couldn't think of anything suitable to call it at all without a dictionary handy. She couldn't think, period.

And that was just as well.

Chapter 31

How exactly had this happened? Henry had only intended to kiss her good-bye. Just a quick peck. If she had turned her head, he would have settled for a cheek or an eyelid or a nose. Hell, he'd settled for any piece of Rachel's physical real estate—gently rolling hills and fragrant plains and intriguing valleys. She was just luscious, every bit of her, and Henry was hungry.

But here were her pillowy, pliant lips, kissing him back. She nestled in his lap, still everywhere but for her gorgeous mouth, which met his in seeming delight and generosity. Henry had seen a praxinoscope, where the people in the pictures appeared to be puppets on invisible strings manned by maniacs. If he and Rachel were filmed in the illusion of movement, everything would be slow, as if they were swimming through honey. He had never been so aware of the purpose and power of his body as he was right this minute.

His pleasure was not paramount. Whatever he could do for her was most important. But he was nearly afraid to touch her where he wanted to, to unleash the beast inside him. The sweet, silent synchronicity between them was a revelation. Their breaths mingled and tongues danced. There was no awkwardness or rush.

This was all very, very different from any previous encounter Henry had ever had. A tiny corner of his brain—the convoluted wrinkled inch that was able to think instead of feel—realized he'd been going about life all wrong for so long. He'd sought the loud and the ludicrous to drown out the world and it never worked. His injuries and memories were still present when he sobered up, and more than likely he'd left a trail of idiocy behind him.

Rachel was good for him. Wholesome like…oatmeal with brown sugar and cream. Oh, wouldn't she clout him if he ever said such a thing? It was fortunate his lips were too busy kissing than passing off ridiculous compliments. One didn't compare women to cereal or any other foodstuff aside from ambrosia.

Could he love her? Did he love her already? It seemed rather sudden. They'd know each other what, seven days or so? He'd lost track of the exact day he'd seen her in the schoolyard in that patch of spring sunlight. And he didn't believe in love. *Want* love.

No, that wasn't true. He had no objection to being loved and cosseted. He just wasn't sure he could return the favor. He'd been brave in combat, but in life? Love was a risk he never planned to take.

The best-laid plans…

Rachel pulled away, trembling. "I—I really have to go home."

He tried to bring his eyes and mind into focus. "Do you? I don't want you to."

"I don't want to go. But my father—"

"Your father and the damned chicken can wait. Five minutes. That's all I ask." She deserved hours.

"What do you plan to do in five minutes?" she asked, breathless. She was so beautiful, face flushed, hat askew. He reached up and unpinned it from her hair.

"I think you know."

"What you did yesterday." Rachel's voice was a mere whisper.

"Yes. You did like it."

"I was…startled. I'm not sure I should let you do it again."

Henry was surprised at her hesitance. What woman would deny herself?

"*Let* me?" He would never do anything Rachel wouldn't want, but the natural conclusion to their current kiss was out of reach. Premature, he tried to convince himself. Doing what he did yesterday was a substitute, at least for her. He'd deal with his distress when she left.

Which she was doing. She had pulled his arms away with amazing strength, bounded off his lap and stuck her hat back on her head.

"I'm going home, Henry, before I forget how to behave. You make me…unbalanced."

She was probably right, damn it. He was supposed to be an officer and a gentleman, no matter how far he'd strayed since he got back from Africa.

"Good. I myself feel like I'm on a ship in a hurricane."

He followed her to the front hall, the scene of much of today's turmoil. She straightened her hat in the little mirror, refusing to meet his eye.

"You'll let me know if you need anything." She turned the handle and slipped out the door into the drizzle.

Oh, he needed. He was digging a hole deep into darkest need, and couldn't see a way out. His father was in the village, bound to fight Henry when he discovered what he was up to. But Rachel was refusing to play, as was her right. Henry couldn't connect the dots between his past, his cure and the future he wanted.

But he would. He had to. There were two more weeks left to his imprisonment. Two weeks to woo Rachel, two weeks to convince his jailers and the pater he was healthy and whole. Henry had mastered most of the challenges life had thrown at him, warfare both at home and abroad. Surviving and thriving in Puddling and beyond should be child's play now that he was finally clear-headed.

He wished he had a friend to plot and plan with. Henry had lost touch with his boyhood friends when he entered the army—they had thought him insane to give up his cushy life at the time, as he recalled, and now they had nothing in common. So many of his army pals were in the outreaches of the Empire, bringing the dubious benefits of Britain to the unwilling. Or worse, underground, worm food, all promise wasted. Henry was in a kind of limbo, but he would manage.

He had been feeling much better, but now that Rachel had gone, the effervescence evaporated. There was no point to foraging for lunch when there was no one to share it with him.

Henry trudged back upstairs, suddenly exhausted, not even interested in dealing with his inconvenient erection. But a man could stand only so much frustration, and he dropped his clothes to the floor, pulling his handkerchief from his pocket. Naked, he stood before the window, watching raindrops splatter on the glass. The hills were covered in gray clouds—even the grass looked gray.

He took himself in hand, not bothering with returning to the bed. He could stand on his own two feet for a little while longer, couldn't he? He thought of kissing Rachel's ripe, sweet center again, stroking her white thighs, unlacing her from her corset. He'd only seen the shadow of her breasts in the moonlight the other night, and felt them beneath too many layers of clothing. They were more than a palmful—she was plush and so very perfect.

If she had a fault, it was her stubbornness. Henry looked forward to tempting her of it, convincing her that they would be good for each other. He could make her happy, her life easier, once he figured out how to...

He shuddered and shuttered his practical thoughts. He'd been taking care of his needs for well over a decade, and now had the ideal fantasy to spur him on. The all-too-confining hills blurred beyond the window as a fictional Rachel dropped to her knees in front of him, her dark hair loose, her silver-black eyes opaque with desire. He traced the blush on her velvet cheek with one finger and her lids dropped and mouth opened. *Sweet God.* It was probably profane to drag God into this, but likely Henry was going to Hell anyway. What he was doing was a sin, but he couldn't feel much sorrow. Heat streaked through him, buckling his knees. Rachel remained in place, for he willed her to do so. Her lashes flickered and her imaginary tongue worked its carnal magic until Henry could bear no more.

He clamped the handkerchief down. To spare Mrs. Grace's finer feelings, he would burn it as soon as his legs worked again. Falling into bed, he wondered if his fever had returned. His heart was pounding. Henry couldn't breathe and gulped for air.

He'd never come so hard in his life, and Rachel had not even been real. Surely that meant something.

Perhaps it meant he was just losing his mind in the country. Someone might find it in a hayrick and wonder how it got there.

He'd have to fetch it back himself, for he had need of it. His father had to be got rid of, Sir Bertram soothed, and Rachel wooed. But first, a nap was probably in order. He and old Vincent had practically watched the sunrise together, Henry holding the man's head over a series of bowls. Henry had been proud that he'd washed every one of them himself.

The gentle patter of rain was relaxing, and he soon drifted without too many obstacles into a deep sleep. It was a shock to wake up several hours later to a face he'd never expected to see.

Chapter 32

Guilt. Duty. Which came first, the chicken or the egg?

All afternoon, Rachel had worried about Henry Challoner. He was alone, with his father's recriminations ringing in his ears. Did he have more than old soup to eat? What if his fever returned and he was so weak he couldn't climb the stairs, or worse, fell down them?

Even her father had noticed her anxiety. He sat back in his chair after consuming a gratifying amount of roast chicken and waved his hand.

"Go on," he'd said. "Go to him. I'm fine, and I can clean up as well as you can. I know Millie Grace is still over to Sheepscombe. She won't get back until tomorrow if this rain keeps falling unless she comes by boat."

Rachel hesitated. There would be plenty left over for her father's lunch tomorrow even if she made up a plate for the viscount's supper.

But what if his father and Sir Bertram had returned to bedevil him? She couldn't dive into in the fishpond if they were there; it was too shallow to cover her.

Oh, hell. She'd risk it. Rachel felt honor-bound to take care of Henry, even if his father had been persuaded to change his mind about her.

Wet. Dirty. No better than she should be. It was the marquess's fault she'd arrived in such disarray yesterday. Puddling's streets were not designed for massive traveling coaches—in fact, they weren't designed for wheeled vehicles at all. Four-footed creatures being driven to market by bipeds, yes. The village was ancient, its narrow roads even older, from Roman times.

"I won't be long."

Her father raised a bushy gray eyebrow but said nothing. Could it be Henry had charmed him too?

She parceled up the carrots, potatoes, rolls and chicken and filled a small jug with gravy. Adding wedges of apple pie and cheese, she tucked it all into a covered basket, feeling a bit like Little Red Riding Hood. The wolf had proved too difficult to ignore.

Rufus watched her in anticipation, tongue lolling.

"No. You may not come with me. Don't even think about it."

He wagged his stump of a tail.

"Oh, all right. But you are to behave yourself. He's the heir to a marquess. None of your usual tricks. You are to let him eat his lunch without making a nuisance of yourself, unlikely as that is."

The dog followed her out the kitchen door. It was still raining lightly, and Rachel avoided the puddles where she could. She was not going to turn up on Henry's doorstep in the same condition as yesterday. Rufus was not so particular, dashing about and encrusting himself with as much mud as possible.

If Henry was resting, she didn't want to ring the bell and get him out of bed; she'd leave the food for him in the kitchen. At the last minute, she remembered he had pocketed the key that was always under a flower pot. But the handle turned—he hadn't thought to lock the cottage up when she left in her cowardice.

"You are a filthy disgrace. There's no point in looking at me like that, either. I am impervious to your charms."

Rufus whined, but Rachel was steadfast. "I will be out in a minute. Stay."

He huffed, reluctantly taking shelter under a bush. He gave her one last reproachful look before he turned around in three circles, lay down, and shut his eyes. Rachel was jealous that the dog could sleep virtually anywhere.

The house was silent. Fortunately Henry's lifeless body was not sprawled across the stairs.

"Henry?"

There was no answer. The poor man deserved to rest. Apparently he'd had a trying night and morning. Now that she thought of it, Vincent *had* looked a bit green about the gills in church. She thought it had been a trick of the light through the stained-glass window.

She put the food in the ice chest and left a quick note for Henry on the kitchen table. To be safe, Rachel would just tiptoe upstairs and make sure Henry was comfortable. Place a hand on his brow and check his temperature. Watch him sleep for a minute to make sure his breathing was even. Up the narrow stairs she went, ducking under a belligerent beam.

Oh my. Rachel tripped over her own feet in the doorway. Henry lay on the bed, his clothes on the floor by the window. He was...he was...

Absolutely, gloriously naked.

He was flat on his back, spread out for her visual delectation. His skin was as she remembered, burnished from the hot sun of Africa. Lean and muscled, his was a body that had worked hard and fought hard. There were random white slashes and divots—healed wounds acquired in the army, she supposed. And fresh bruises too that he had acquired in the supposedly safe haven of Puddling.

His poor mangled foot was not a pretty thing. Rachel knew it still gave him great pain, particularly if he was tired. She wished she could do something to help him. Her eyes swept up over his muscled legs. His manhood, partially obscured by his broad brown hand and a nest of golden-brown curls, begged for closer inspection.

Rachel bit a lip, and ventured a few more steps into the room. She might never get another chance to see a nude man again.

Oh, who was she kidding? Henry's beauty stirred something inside her that would no longer be repressed. She might not marry the man, but why couldn't she—

So many reasons not to go any further, either into the room or their relationship. But none of them were of interest to her at the moment.

Goodness, she was a voyeur, taking advantage of a helpless man to examine him in his well-deserved repose. Rachel held her breath as she advanced, promising herself to look but not touch.

The curtain flapped in the breeze from the open window and she nearly jumped out of her own skin. *Leave now, leave now, leave now...*

Henry's eyes fluttered and opened. Rachel was as still as if she were a butterfly pinned to a board. He gave her the laziest, most infuriating grin.

"Like what you see?"

She stepped back but his hand darted out to catch hers. "Don't go." He was lying on the rumpled coverlet—had he made his own bed this morning?—and scooted over and threw half of it over his body.

"There. Better?"

Rachel found she could not speak. She had been caught and had no innocent excuse. From the devilish gleam in his bright blue eyes, Henry knew it, too.

"Sit down, sweetheart. You're listing to the side."

It was a wonder she was standing at all.

She tumbled into the warm spot he'd recently vacated. Now what? What could she possibly say to make this any less embarrassing?

It appeared she didn't have to say anything at all. Henry gently tugged her down on top of him and proceeded to kiss her. This was nothing like the slow, dreamy kiss of a few hours ago. His was a kiss of possession. Purpose. Rachel knew without a question where it would lead.

Where she would follow.

"I dreamed of you," he said raggedly when he broke the kiss. "Please let my dream come true."

She'd be a fool to say yes, and she had never been one of those silly girls whose head was turned by a handsome man. But her heart, not her head, did the talking now.

"Yes. Please."

He shut his eyes. "Thank God. I shall make this right, Rachel."

She hoped so. This would probably be her only chance to experience sexual congress.

"Do it quickly. Rufus is outside."

He raised a sandy eyebrow. "Quickly? I don't think you understand what's involved, my angel. And hang Rufus. He can wait."

And then he showed her with agonizing slowness, brushing his lips across her eyelids, mouth, throat until she wanted that mouth everywhere. He was nimble with the buttons of her Sunday dress, deadly efficient with her corset strings even as his tongue and teeth explored each revealed inch. She was soon as naked as he, and couldn't meet his eyes. She was restless and so hot, even without her clothing.

"Beautiful. Better than the dream. I l—um, I like you so well, Rachel. You are perfect for me."

Had he been about to say something else? She could wish it so and make this easier. Henry said he didn't believe in love, but she did. She knew she loved him—hadn't wanted to, was stupid to, but couldn't seem to help herself. There was nothing possible ahead for them but this grim spring afternoon as the skies opened and rain fell. He was going to be a marquess one day, and she was a teacher—if she could hold onto her job.

He placed her on her back, her generous breasts flopping awkwardly. Hell, all of her felt awkward. Henry sensed it and gave her a look so full of longing she began to believe what he saw. He buried his fair head on her chest and breathed deeply, then took one breast in his mouth, a hand cupping the other. Rachel thought she might just die, and be relatively happy about it. She'd never felt as good or desired in her life.

He was thorough in his kisses. Disciplined. After disarming her defenses, he eased his way down her bare skin to kiss her as he had yesterday. She opened to him like a wanton. No wonder brazen women followed him home—he was a complete genius at this.

Sensation built within her, higher and sharper, and she rose to meet it. In seconds she was crying his name, rolling with each exquisite wave. This time he wouldn't stop at a wicked kiss. This time it wasn't just for her. They would be partners in bliss.

At least Rachel hoped it would be bliss. She knew a woman's first time was often painful. But it would be worth it to return some of the joy to Henry, who so deserved it.

He was bending over her now, his expression questioning, his manhood pressing somewhat insistently into her belly. Rachel nodded.

"You don't have to." His voice was rough. "I can take care of myself."

"I want to."

"You're sure."

"Oh, do stop talking, Henry." She pulled him down to taste him again. With a jolt, she realized she tasted herself as well. She should be horrified, but she wasn't. What was happening to her?

How very, very odd this all was, but the awkwardness had passed. Rachel's body felt alive. Free. The man that she loved was about to change her life forever.

Henry was gentle yet firm. He parted her thighs, centered himself and eased into her, watching her for any sign of refusal. She held her breath at the invasion and he stopped at once.

She squeezed his corded arms. "No. Do it."

"I can't cause you pain, Rachel."

"I don't care, I really don't." She lifted her hips and forced him in deeper.

"Ah." He sounded as if *he* were in pain. "Oh, damn it. You feel incredible." With a thrust, he seated himself fully inside her.

She welcomed him the only way she could, with another blistering kiss. Hands smoothing his rough skin, her own body liquid and flexing. The discomfort was almost forgotten as she responded, driving them both just a bit mad. His halting words blurred amidst his kisses, but when he said her name, she exulted.

She knew what her body expected and needed and reached for it. Her release wasn't very long in coming, but it triggered Henry's immediate withdrawal. She felt a hot spurt of wetness along her thigh and knew from his growl he'd found his satisfaction as well.

They lay tangled in the sheets, too stunned in wonder to speak. Henry pushed her damp fringe from her forehead and kissed her as if she were a little girl. But she was a woman now. The thought of what she had so shamelessly done brought her to the blush. Did she look different? Would people be able to tell?

"Much, much better than my dream," he whispered. "And now, Rachel Elizabeth Everett, you will have to marry me."

Chapter 33

"What?"

Henry winced. She had squealed into his bad ear but he still heard her too loud and clear.

"I am a gentleman, Rachel, and you, no matter how much you deny it, are a lady. Respectable. A gentleman doesn't take his pleasure with a lady unless he has honorable intentions."

She wriggled beneath him, causing his cock to twitch further. "Don't be an ass."

He knew she would fight him on this; she had fought him on everything with the exception of the glorious time they had just spent in his bed. It hadn't been long enough, either. When they married they might spend days in bed. Weeks.

"I proposed to you within minutes of meeting you, didn't I? I might not have meant it then, but I do now."

She opened her mouth and he decided to kiss her again to shut her up. When he'd finished and she was dazed and tingling, he continued, having lost a little of his focus himself.

"I know all your objections. Puddling is important to you and your father, and I swear I'll work a way around our difficulties. When it comes to *my* father, what more can he do to me?"

"He can shut you away!" she said, angry. "I heard him this morning, Henry. He's not a man to be trifled with."

"He wouldn't do that to his heir. He values the Challoner family name too much. How mortifying it would be to have it known that his son is a lunatic. That sort of thing can be inherited, you know. It would reflect badly on him, and the pater's much too full of pride to put up with any scurrilous gossip. I have my own money, you know. I can get us a house in the country somewhere and we can live as we please."

Nothing too grand. Henry had come to appreciate the simpler things in life since he came to Puddling. How many bedrooms might they need? How many children would they have?

Rachel would be good with children, no matter how many they had. If she could corral a classroom full of them, a mere half-dozen would be child's play. But he wouldn't want to wear her out. He was a modern man, and didn't expect his wife to be a drudge.

"What on earth are you thinking of? You have the oddest expression on your face. But then, you *are* odd."

My, she sounded cross. This was not how she should be feeling after such a delightful encounter. More than delightful. Henry thought the top of his head might blow off at the end.

"Right at the moment? Real estate, my dear."

She pushed her hair from her face and tried to slide out from under him. Henry had no intention of letting her loose and gripped her white shoulders, then kissed them. Were shoulders an erogenous zone for her? He threw himself into the inquiry. Rachel squirmed and sighed. Apparently they were.

And then she pinched him. Not too hard, but just enough to get his attention. "Henry, let's be realistic here. As much as I, as we..." She stopped, her eyebrows scrunching. How adorable she was. "I won't deny that this was extraordinary this afternoon. It's left me...breathless. But it cannot happen again, and we will not be needing to buy a house."

"Let's not argue. It might bring on a relapse." He rolled off and curled her toward him, feeling the beat of her erratic heart. He was breathless, too.

"Are you ever serious?"

"Not if I can help it. Really, Rachel, why go through life all doomy and gloomy? Believe me, I've seen my share of unpleasantness. That's what I was trying to forget, only I went about it all the wrong way. The pater was right to send me here, for here you are."

"I'm not your cure, Henry."

"Oh, aren't you?"

Rachel struggled to sit up. "A new person can't change what's wrong inside you. You overindulged for a reason. If there's anything I've learned living in Puddling, it's that change comes from within, and you have to want it for *you*. I'm...superficial to you. What if you hadn't met me?"

"But I did!" Henry objected.

"But if you hadn't, wouldn't you still be asking the shopkeepers to sneak you some alcoholic spirits? Looking for young women to seduce? Chafing at all the restrictions?"

Would he? Very possibly.

"Are you saying I'm weak?" His father had certainly thought so.

"We're all weak, Henry. I can't pretend to know what you went through, or how I would have responded in your place. But what if something awful happens again? Suppose someone you love, God forbid, dies, or you lose your fortune through bad investments? You'll need inner resources—yes, of course you can depend on friends for support, but you must first and foremost rely on yourself. Clouding your senses only dulls and then prolongs the pain."

She sounded very much like old Vincent. They'd all been fed the same Puddling Principles—there was probably a primer somewhere that all local children learned along with their ABCs.

He nodded. "I know you're right. I've tried to change. I think I have." He'd had that idea about a soldiers' retreat, hadn't he? He was prepared to put his own funds into the scheme. And he'd not touched any of the vicar's liquor stash, had not even taken advantage when the man was so deep in his cups he wouldn't have known the difference. That said something about Henry's sobriety, surely.

He could manage his life. Find a purpose. But it would be so much better with Rachel by his side.

He couldn't blame her for doubting. He was only at the midpoint of his Puddling stay.

Which gave him two more weeks to convince her she was not just any port in his storm.

"So you understand then."

"You're not ready for me. I respect your feelings, but I don't like them."

She bit a lip. They were already pink and swollen, and Henry could hardly bear looking at them without acting on his desire.

"I'm not ever going to be ready for you, Henry. When you leave, I'm sure you'll find someone more suitable. You are—you are handsome and rich. The world is your oyster."

Henry had never understood that expression either. What had shellfish got to do with anything? Who wanted to climb into a slimy mollusk?

"So, we're at an impasse. Again. I'm very grateful you gave me this past hour, Rachel. It was the most perfect afternoon of my life so far."

She gave him a sad smile. "So far. See? The best is yet to come."

"One can only hope. Are you all right? Let me fetch some water and a cloth."

"I'll do it." With remarkable grace, she rose from the bed and headed to his bathroom. She walked away as proudly as a queen, as if she marched around in her spectacular nudity all the time.

Henry lay back and stared at the ceiling. He had his work cut out for him on so many fronts. But he'd never shied away from a challenge, no matter how much his challenge shied away from him.

Rachel returned, her dark cloud of hair twisted back up. She gathered up her clothing and began to dress without speaking. She didn't need his help for her corset—of course she didn't. She did for herself every day. It was not long before she looked as respectable as any other church-going miss.

"There is supper for you in the kitchen," she said, her voice strained.

"Thank you. You shouldn't have." Henry wasn't hungry at all, his mind whirring with too many possibilities.

"Mrs. Grace should be back tomorrow. Maybe even tonight."

Oh, joy.

"I'm fine. Much better. You needn't worry. If I need anything, I can summon my father from Sykes House." Henry tried to imagine his father in a kitchen and failed.

And he really was feeling better. Rachel was like a cure, even if she didn't want to be.

"Will I see you again?"

She shook her head. "It wouldn't be wise. Your father—"

"Blast my father! I want to see you. We don't have to do this again if you don't want to."

"Want has nothing to do with it. Of course one would want it."

So, there was a sliver of hope. She wasn't entirely cold to him even if she was trying to guard her heart.

Henry's own heart felt open for the first time in his life. It hurt to feel, he realized. It was worse than when his foot was almost shot off. He had more in common with old Vincent than he realized. The two of them were goners.

From somewhere below, Rufus barked, protecting his mistress. Too late. Henry could only be grateful the dog was not inside chewing off his good foot in retaliation for what he had just done.

Chapter 34

Rachel let herself into the cottage. The walk home had been…peculiar. It was as if her legs had not made the journey before. Her knees felt liquid and there was an ache in the region of her heart.

She was so slow, Rufus had darted ahead. No doubt he was annoyed to have gotten no scraps after actually staying put under the bush, and was hoping for better luck when he got home.

He had been oddly obedient, barking just the once. Could he sense what transpired?

And what was not going to transpire again.

She had done the right thing discouraging Henry. She'd also done the right thing sleeping with him. Technically no sleep had been involved, but she wouldn't take that hour back under any circumstances.

She had no regrets. She might be an idiot for doing what she had, but she'd have been an idiot not to.

Rachel wasn't apt to meet another Henry Challoner in her life, even if she grew into an ancient crone in Puddling. None of the Guests would ever have his allure. It wasn't because he was a viscount and heir to a marquess. It wasn't even because of his disheveled golden curls and sky-blue eyes. His broad brown shoulders and his absolutely magnificent c—

She shivered. Best not to even think about that particular appendage. She would not be seeing it again.

Henry was an odd mix of braggadocio and vulnerability. It was the soft side that interested her, the ruefulness. The loneliness. The emptiness. He'd been in an awful hurry to fill it up before he came here.

Rachel couldn't complete him. Fix him. One sensual encounter was not going to set him on the path of righteousness. If anything, it might hurt him even more.

But Rachel had not really been thinking of Henry's well-being this afternoon. She had been selfishly thinking of herself.

She was not a good person.

But she was wise enough to know she'd make a terrible viscount's wife. He'd be better off with one of his actresses. An actress would know how to wear pretty clothes and address members the peerage. One could imagine one was on a stage every day of the week, only the butlers and housemaids would be real. Rachel couldn't imagine asking anyone to lace her up or dust her knickknacks.

"Rachel, is that you?"

She'd have to face him. Would he somehow know? Rachel didn't want to be a disappointment to her father—he was much too dear to her. He hadn't liked Henry much in the beginning, but had warmed to him since.

But no father would like the young man who deflowered his innocent daughter.

No, be honest. Not innocent. Not innocent at all. Henry had not forced himself upon her. As she recollected, she'd told him to shut up and get on with it.

And oh my, get on with it he did.

She shook her head in an attempt to get Henry and his hands and mouth and…the rest of him out of it. "Yes, Dad. Can I bring you anything from the kitchen?"

It was tidy, as promised. All traces of their roast chicken lunch were packed away and the pine table had been scrubbed.

"Just you. I'm still full."

Rachel brushed her damp skirts down and checked to see if her hairpins were still doing their job. She had washed the best she could and sprinkled on talc in Henry's bathroom before she had gotten dressed. A hot bath would be heavenly to wash away the traces of her insanity, even though she'd had one just last night.

Her father was sitting in a sagging ancient chair in a corner of the front parlor. A precarious stack of books was tipping on a table near his elbow, and Rufus was asleep on one of his slippered feet. The dog thumped his tail once, his eyes still closed. Rachel tried not to take his lack of enthusiasm personally.

"You need more light than this, Dad," Rachel scolded, lighting a lamp.

"Still filthy out there, is it? I didn't even go out in the garden for a sniff today. How do the peonies look? Blown are they, with all this rain?" His peonies were favorites, lush and fragrant, even if they housed a thousand useful ants who didn't decamp once they'd performed their service.

"I didn't really look, but it's not so bad outside now." It was still light out, but gloomy. The rain was but a shadow of its earlier self, and the puddles had been easily skippable.

"How's your patient?"

Rachel's cheeks warmed. "He's not so bad, either."

"Did he enjoy the meal?"

"He—he was sleeping when I got there, and I didn't want to disturb him. I did a little straightening up and then I read a magazine waiting for him to wake up. When he did, I told him there was dinner in the kitchen for him and left."

"Poor girl. Cleaning after two men today."

Rachel kissed him on the cheek. "You don't make much work for me, Dad."

"Aye, your mother trained me well. What are you going to do about him?"

Rachel sat down and picked up her sewing basket. "About who?" The threads were in a hopeless tangle, and since they were damp, she suspected Rufus had been at it again.

"Don't play the fool with me, miss. You're smarter than your mother and me combined. The young lordling, that's who."

"It's not for me to do anything about him, Dad. A—a friendship wouldn't suit. I'd only get into trouble with the governors."

"To hell with the governors. They don't always know best, you know. They're not infallible. I think we've had a few Guests who never should have been here. Challoner's one of them."

Rachel was inclined to agree. What Henry had done was not so very awful considering the horrors of war that he'd lived through. He'd just been larking about in the wrong place.

"It's the money, I expect. The village depends upon it," she said. Families anxious to place their wayward relatives here thought nothing of throwing exorbitant sums at Puddling to solve their problems.

"What's the good of having it if there's nothing to spend it on?"

Rachel chuckled. "Dad, do you want to go shopping? I'll take you to Stroud next weekend for the farmers' market. I'm sure we could get Ham to take us up in his wagon."

"Bah. It's not vegetables I'm after. We could go to London."

"London!" Her surprise was so great she startled the dog, who got up, turned around, and lay back down in his same warm spot once he was sure the house wasn't on fire.

"Why not? School's out for a few weeks soon. The end of the week, right? We could stay in a hotel. See the sights."

"Dad, you don't even *like* London. You've always said it's dirty and filled with degenerates."

"Maybe it's changed. I haven't been in years. Not since before I married your mother. She's the one who didn't like it."

That was not how Rachel remembered things, but she wasn't going to argue with her father.

"Do you truly feel up to such an undertaking?" she asked doubtfully. Her father was fit for his age, but slowing down considerably.

"It's not as though we'd be walking. We'll take the train."

"Let me think about it." Rachel had never been to London. She'd never been *anywhere*. The prospect was both exciting and frightening.

"We could go to museums. I hear there are dinosaur bones somewhere."

Rachel smiled. "You don't have to sweeten the pot any further. I admit, I'm intrigued. What made you think of such a thing?"

"You're buried in the country. It's time you saw a bit of the world. Got some polish."

Rachel threaded her needle. "What do I need polish for, Dad?"

"You never know."

Oh, Rachel knew, and knew what her father was trying to do. A week in London would not make her a fit wife for a viscount. Nothing would come of it, though he meant well.

A trip like that might be a once-in-a-lifetime experience, even if the end result meant she was back in her classroom talking about dinosaurs.

But Rachel was ever practical. "Can we afford it, Dad?"

"Don't you worry about expenses. I have quite a bit put by, you know. Puddling's been good to us, and we've always lived below our means."

What if Puddling stopped being good, and they were drummed out for fraternizing with a Guest? In Rachel's case, it was a good deal more than that. She was a scandal waiting to be revealed, especially after this afternoon.

Her father opened his book, and Rachel began to smock a baby's nightgown for the church guild's charity box. Some poor mite would wear this tiny garment for a few months. She felt a pang, thinking about a warm, soft, powdery baby, then brought herself to reality. Urine-soaked diapers, that odd patch of smelly stuff on the baby's scalp, the inevitable screaming in umbrage as a pin poked or the porridge was too hot.

Best to think of babies in their most unpleasant states.

"What's that sigh for?"

"Nothing. Just thinking. I might need to make a new dress if we're going to London."

"You can buy clothes when you get there."

"Dad!" Rachel had never worn anything either she or her mother had not made, sitting right here in this parlor.

"Why not? You only live once. You can go to one of those new-fangled department stores and buy something off the rack."

Good heavens. He was serious about this Cinderella-plan for her.

"Have you been talking to Lord Challoner about this?"

Her father's bushy eyebrows rose. "Why, should I have? What's wrong with a father wanting a treat for his only daughter?"

Nothing. But something was fishy nonetheless.

Chapter 35

Henry had been sleeping for a change. Really sleeping. He rolled over. A warm waft of fresh air mixed with grass and roses and sheep blew over him like a welcome blanket from his open window. It was too soon to wake up. He hunkered down and tried to get back into his delicious Rachel-dream.

He knew her now, every blessed inch. A rainy Sunday would never, ever be the same for him.

Monday had been sunny and unremarkable and a chore to get through. There had been no Rachel, and Mrs. Grace had turned up full of apologies which Henry waved off. Thank God the woman had not been in the cottage, or else he and Rachel would not have been able to have their interlude.

Their apparently once-in-a-lifetime interlude. Henry would have something to say about that, if he could only think what.

He'd wanted to see her in the worst way yesterday. Send her red flowers or chocolates or a desperate letter. But he had to respect her wish for space, even if it galled him.

He put his mind to his myriad problems, but then he heard the sobbing. What could make Mrs. Grace lose her legendary sangfroid? And what time was it anyhow?

The sound was coming from the garden below. Henry poked his head out the window. There on his iron bench was a woman beneath an enormous hat, her shoulders convulsing with each wail.

It was very early in the day for such crying. Henry checked his watch. Not even six o'clock. Mrs. Grace was not due for at least an hour, and if she had ever owned such a fashionable hat his name wasn't Henry Agamemnon Challoner.

"I say," he said, trying not to shout and alarm her, "are you all right?"

The woman turned and looked up at him. She was a girl really. She couldn't have been much over twenty years of age. She was very blond, blue-eyed, and ruffled. Ruffled everywhere in a misguided attempt to conceal a rather substantial figure. Her eyes and cheeks were pink from crying. Henry hoped she wasn't drowning the koi with her salty tears.

"Oh! Who are you?"

"Henry Challoner." He left out the captain and the lord part. The Agamemnon part, too. This poor thing didn't need to be intimidated any more than she was. "May I offer you assistance?"

"I d-don't see how anyone can," she snuffled. "I am r-ruined."

"Nonsense. Tomorrow is always another day. Hang on a moment. I'll be right down." Henry rejected the idea of just tossing on his dressing gown; he didn't want to alarm her further. He'd never gotten dressed so fast in his life except when ambushed in his tent right before he was shot. Running down the stairs, he managed not to hit his head in the process. A morning miracle, that.

A little breathless when he arrived, he was pleased to see the girl still sitting there, balling up a very wet lace-edged handkerchief. He sat down next to her on the bench and waited while she sniffled and hiccupped.

He patted her ruffled arm. "Take a deep breath, my dear."

"I hoped no one would be here. But the key is missing and I couldn't get in."

"Just as well. As you see, I'm the latest inmate, and I got quite annoyed with people coming in just because they felt like it." He reached into his pocket and drew the flower pot key out. The original was still missing somewhere between New Street and the churchyard after his unconscious midnight ramble at the hands of the bloodthirsty Everetts.

"Why are *you* here?" she asked, her lashes tipped with tears.

"Oh, I was a bit lost. Did some stupid things. Drank too much and fu, uh, fornic—uh, formed an attachment to unsuitable women. I'm completely reformed. A lovely young lady such as yourself has nothing whatsoever to worry about."

"Oh! Don't be so kind to me! You can't understand. *I have left my husband*." She said it with a mix of horror and satisfaction.

"No doubt he deserved to be left. Did he hurt you?"

"N-not the way you think. But he mocked me. Made fun of me all the time. C-criticized my figure."

"He sounds like an absolute cur. What is wrong with your figure?"

"I am f-fat."

"Nonsense. You're a very pretty girl. You're not increasing, are you?"

That made her wail all the more. "See? Merwyn is right. I am as big as a house. He will not even t-touch me, not that I want him to. Ever. He is loathsome." She threw a hand to her pretty pink lips. "Oh! I'm useless. I always say and do the wrong things to perfect strangers."

"I am not perfect," Henry admitted. "Why are you here in my garden?"

"It was once *my* garden. I came back to Puddling hoping something could be done about the mess I'm in. And to see...never mind."

Henry remembered. Greta something. An heiress who was imprisoned here so she could fit into her wedding gown. Instead of the pub being shut down, it had been the bake shop then.

"How did you get here?"

"I took the milk train to Stroud. And then a kindly farmer gave me a lift for most of the way."

Henry glanced down. The girl's feet looked swollen in her boots, and the hem of her dress was dusty. "You walked?"

"I need the exercise. I walked every day the three months I was here. It was p-part of my plan."

"I walk too. Clears the head, doesn't it?"

"Not particularly. It just hurts my feet and I can't catch my breath."

Henry spoke carefully. "I think the more one walks, the healthier one becomes."

"That's all very well for you to say!" She glared at him with red-rimmed eyes. "You are fit."

"Well, I was in the army for six years. It toughens you up a bit."

"Women can't join the army to lose weight. And I shouldn't be trusted with a gun. I might shoot Merwyn."

"Merwyn! He sounds as if he deserves to be shot. How long have you been married?"

"Just two months. And he hasn't once...oh, God." Fresh tears filled her eyes.

Henry put an arm around her. "If he hasn't, as you say, he's an idiot."

"But I'm glad, I assure you!" she shuddered. "He just wanted my money for his amusements. He—he consorts with wicked women. Actresses. And w-worse. And wh-what he makes them do! I have heard things—he told me himself!"

"Sometimes men are very foolish," Henry said. Lord knows, he had been. This girl was an innocent, and not apt to understand men's darker impulses. He'd had some himself when he'd been desperate. Trying to jolt himself with recklessness to feel alive, even if he'd felt very little hope.

But then he'd come to Puddling and seen Rachel in a shaft of sunlight.

"He never cared for me at all. Not like—" She shut her mouth.

Ah. So there had been another swain who lost out in the grand marriage plot. Poor fellow. Greta was a very comfortable armful, and Henry realized, would be quite beautiful when her nose wasn't dripping. If she was a little plusher than was usual, what was the harm, really? Some men would appreciate her with or without her fortune.

"I think you need someone to talk to. I take it your parents are unhelpful?"

"It is only Mama. My father would have known Merwyn for what he was and forbidden the match. He is...he is a *fiend*. I can't even..." Her voice trailed away.

Greta appeared more shaken than would be normal over the average disappointing husband. Was Merwyn some kind of depraved pervert? Henry had never heard of any fiendish Mervyn, but then he hadn't been home very long.

"Let me take you inside and make you a cup of tea."

She blew her nose into the soggy handkerchief. "Thank you. That would be nice. And perhaps some dry toast if that wouldn't be too much trouble."

Dry toast indeed. He'd feed her up better than that if he could find out where his housekeeper hid the jam. Henry led his uninvited guest into the little parlor. He still didn't know her name, but Mrs. Grace would know what to do when she came.

Henry busied himself at the stove. Years of army life had taught him how to hold body and soul together, and in a relatively short time, he had a pot of tea and four perfectly-toasted pieces of bread with lashings of butter and plum jam. The jar had been stuck in the coal scuttle, saved there for old Vincent's tea vigils, no doubt, by his devious housekeeper. No jam or fun was on Henry's plan.

Greta was standing in front of the narrow bookcase, her gloved fingers caressing the spines of the books Henry thought much too boring to read. Her eyes lit when she saw the tray, but then dropped. She was ashamed of her appetite, and for a second Henry wanted to roar at her mother and her wretched husband.

"I'm starving," Henry said brightly. "Please join me."

"I shouldn't."

"You can walk it off with me later. I assume you thought you could stay in this cottage?" He snapped into his toast. The jam was pretty damned good.

"I—I didn't really think. I didn't even bring an overnight bag. But I do have money. Just a little. Merwyn and Mama saw to it I have practically nothing a quarter for pin money," she said with bitterness. She took a delicate bite.

"Well, there are two bedrooms, and I certainly won't charge you, if you can stand the company. You can stay until you figure out what you want to do and see whoever you wanted to see." He'd make sure Mrs. Grace was mollified, no matter how much dosh it took to paper over the impropriety. Greta wouldn't be here forever.

At least Henry thought it was all right if she stayed a little while—she'd come all this way, the poor thing. The cottage was his for the month, wasn't it? The pater was paying top dollar for Henry to be rehabilitated, and helping Greta was one way to prove he was as gallant as the next fellow.

There would, of course, be no funny business, since Sir Bertram and the pater would cut up stiff if they knew the girl was here. Greta was a married woman, and Henry wanted to be a married man. They'd need a chaperone. Ha! Maybe Rachel could be persuaded to come and share Greta's room.

"Have you spoken to a solicitor?"

"I...no. The family lawyer helped to arrange my marriage. He and Mama are thick as thieves."

"Then you'll need someone else." Henry didn't know anyone in the legal profession, but his father had a fleet of solicitors and barristers on retainer. Could Henry ask his father to help? Doubtful. He'd mistake the whole situation, and Henry would wind up in a straitjacket somewhere, even if it ruined the Challoner reputation.

It was damned hard to be helpful.

But if this Merwyn was such a rotter, the pater's finer feelings could be counted on. Henry didn't know anyone who considered himself nobler, more honorable, more *right* than his father. Merwyn would not want to tangle with the morally perfect Marquess of Harland.

They munched in silence. Greta ate three of the pieces of toast and Henry didn't begrudge her one bite.

He looked at the little clock on the mantel. "Mrs. Grace will be coming soon. Can you talk to her about your troubles?"

Greta wiped a crumb from her lip. "She h-hates me."

"Oh, she hates everyone. Shall I go see if our good vicar is awake yet? He counseled you, didn't he?"

Greta turned bright red and nodded. "He—he—oh! He will be so angry with me! I was supposed to forget him and do my duty to my family, but I cannot! I l-l-love him!"

Oh, dear. So that was the way the land lay. Things would be much thornier than Henry imagined. This was the girl Vincent Walker had gotten drunk over, the girl he'd loved and lost to an arranged marriage.

"May I go upstairs and freshen up?" she asked in a small voice.

"Of course. You know where everything is. Don't hit your head."

Henry would just have to walk round to roust old Vincent out of bed and tell him his long-lost love had come back to Puddling.

He grinned. Now *this* was going to be a scandal. And it couldn't come at a better time.

Chapter 36

Once Henry was assured that Lady Bexley—for that was Greta's name now, and she was, of all things, a countess—was not going to run away on a passing farm wagon, he left her to fetch the vicar. He didn't even bring a walking stick; there was a bounce in his step he hadn't felt since his foot was nearly blown off.

So, Sykes and the Foundation's governors were going to have a spot of trouble regarding Puddling's reputation as the premiere place to stash annoying relatives. If rumors had circulated about their schoolteacher and latest Guest, what would they make of their hired clergyman and a married woman?

Who cared if the pater got a little upset when Henry brought home his bride? He would be in excellent company. How could he rage against Puddling when it was going to rage upon itself? The bloody vicar had been in love with one of the Guests and all of Puddling would be in an uproar. It was scandal with a capital S. Old Vincent, the poor devil, earnest, prosy Vincent was about to land in the soup with the charming, chubby Lady Bexley and all hell would break loose.

And then Henry stopped and nearly stumbled over a cobblestone. He should not be taking pleasure in this turn of events. Poor Greta was despondent, and Vincent lovelorn. His woman had been forced to marry another (Henry remembered that conversation and the ensuing vomit all too well), and there would be legal and ecclesiastical difficulties.

The Matrimonial Causes Act had been passed some time ago, but women were still in the soup when it came to divorce. Could Vincent be defrocked? Surely he'd lose his job here as counselor-in-chief. He might be banished to the Outer Hebrides, where his flock would be mostly puffins. Would Greta go with him to live a life of sin and seabird droppings?

Hell, no. Henry would see to it that the poor girl got her divorce from that debauched devil and that Vincent got just what he deserved.

But how?

Damn it, this was the best Service Henry had thought up yet, although he hadn't the faintest idea how to accomplish it. But eventually Sir Bertram Sykes had to be hoisted on his own petard for his callous treatment of Rachel, and Puddling returned to its solicitous solitude without ensuing scandal.

Gah. More alliteration.

He knocked on the vicarage's black-painted door, peering through the pebbled glass. It was just seven, though Henry felt he'd been up for hours.

Vincent came to the door himself, dressed, hair brushed, and a slight coffee mustache on his blandly handsome face.

"Lord Challoner! This is unexpected. Is everything all right?"

Henry looked up and down the street to see if any of the neighbors were peering through their lace curtains. "Not really, Walker. Let me in, will you? We have to talk."

"Have you had breakfast? May I get you something? This is Mrs. Price's day off, but I can make a very decent cup of coffee, if I may take the liberty of saying so." He escorted Henry into his tiny, book-strewn study.

"No time for that. Sit down, Walker. I have something important to say."

"Have you had an epiphany?" the man asked eagerly.

"Oh, yes. And her name is Lady Greta Bexley."

Vincent Walker blanched. Henry had seen men before they fainted, and he caught the vicar before he fell face-down on the threadbare Oriental carpet.

"Gr-Greta?" he gurgled. "My Greta?"

"The very same. She's come back to you, Vincent." It seemed silly to call him Walker when he was cradling the man in his arms.

"B-but she's married!"

"There is that minor detail. We'll have to figure something out. But there's no point in lollygagging here. She's waiting for you at Stonecrop Cottage."

If possible, Vincent paled even further. "I can't go there! You must see I can't!"

"No, I'm afraid I don't see. The girl has walked practically all the way from Stroud when she wasn't carted about like a basket of vegetables on a farm wagon and is emotionally drained. She needs counseling in the worst way."

And kissing, Henry suspected. He sat Vincent down in his desk chair.

"B-but her husband!"

"Not here. Not anywhere, as far as I can tell. Certainly never in her bed."

There was a telling lull. "What?" Vincent croaked.

"She is intact, if that matters to you, old thing. The bastard doesn't love her. Has treated her abominably. Made her feel inferior. Has been cruel."

Vincent's eyes were wide as saucers. "But why? She is the most beautiful, sweetest darling!"

"Precisely," Henry agreed. "Much too good for this Bexley boob. How did you let her get away, Vincent?"

The vicar ran his hand through his hair. Henry thought that was a habit he should soon cease or there wouldn't be that much of it left. "The—the Foundation would have been ruined if I had given in to my feelings. All those years of success, swept away by imprudence. But you've seen her, Challoner. How could I not break my vows to the village and my Lord? I'm only human, but I've brought dishonor to Puddling."

"Forget Puddling. Go to Greta. She's waiting for you. I'll see if I can't head off Mrs. Grace so you two can have some privacy."

Vincent embraced him, nearly knocking Henry off his feet. "I knew there was good in you somewhere! I'll never forget this!"

Henry was a little afraid the vicar was about to kiss him. "Go on. Hurry. You don't want her to change her mind and run off."

Not likely—the poor girl was not much of a walker by her own admission, and running was probably out of the question. But Vincent sprinted out the door and down the hill. Henry made for New Street, resolutely passing Rachel's house. Mrs. Grace's cottage was a few doors down, flanked by colorful pots of daisies and geraniums. He knocked. It took Mrs. Grace some time to answer her door.

"Oh!" She looked very surprised to see him. Her face was flushed, and her hair loose and uncovered. Henry had only ever seen her in a cap, and he had to admit she had beautiful, thick silver-streaked hair to match her silver-gray eyes. She was wearing a very fetching pink peignoir set, which was quite at odds with her usual dull housekeeper's uniform.

Why, she was rather pretty in an ice maiden kind of way. Tall, buxom, proud. And she might actually be under fifty by a few years. She didn't look as supercilious as usual—there had been times when she looked at Henry as if she smelled something funny.

"Sorry to barge in like this, but I want to give you the day off."

She shook her head. "You cannot. It's against the rules. Bad enough I let you down over the weekend. I know I'm running a little late, but I shall be right along."

"But I don't need you today, Mrs. Grace. I've already had breakfast—I fixed it all by myself! The house is spotless, I'm feeling better than I have in ages, and you deserve a day to yourself for all your hard work. I know I've not been easy to do for. But I'm a new man. The pater is going to be proud."

What was that? Henry thought he'd heard a snort somewhere down the dark hall behind his housekeeper. He tried to peer around her but she bobbed to the side, looking suddenly nervous.

And guilty. By Jove, was Dr. Oakley hiding in her kitchen? Henry liked the idea of older people still having a bit of fun. Good for them. But feeling impish, Henry couldn't help but tease her.

"I wouldn't say no to a cup of tea before I leave you though."

"T-t-tea?"

"Yes, you know, that brown stuff. Wet. Goes in a cup."

"I don't think I have any."

No tea in Mrs. Grace's house? Unthinkable. Henry would bet her kitchen was well-stocked and alphabetized.

"Coffee will be fine. I've never been inside your cottage, have I? Would you mind if I came in?"

"Uh, I'm afraid I don't feel very well. And it's not fit for company. It's a—it's a right mess, especially the kitchen."

Also unthinkable. Mrs. Grace could have out-cleaned even the pater's fastidious staff. Stonecrop Cottage was a pristine showplace—Henry was even folding his bath towels properly at her instigation.

"All right then—you won't object to having the day free to recover and tidy up a little when you feel better, will you? I'm so sorry that you are under the weather. If you are no better tomorrow, take another day, won't you? I can shift for myself, I assure you. Toodle-oo."

Her relief was palpable. Something was off. Henry waited a few minutes, then pressed himself against the cottage wall, sidling slowly down the alleyway like a crab. Her cottage was much like Rachel's, so there would be a kitchen window he could peer into and catch her and Dr. Oakley in their middle-aged rhapsody.

Well, that was the idea, anyway. But this was a morning for surprises. Henry forgot to breathe when he saw his father, the Marquess of Harland, sitting at Mrs. Grace's kitchen table in a paisley dressing gown.

What Henry wouldn't give for a camera. Alas, he had only his brain with him, which would have to do.

Chapter 37

Good for the pater. Really. Henry could not recall his father showing an interest in any woman since his marchioness died. Mrs. Grace was an unexpected choice, but she was a handsome woman and Henry could now see her appeal.

By God, would he have to call her step-mama? He supposed anything was possible in this day and age. Puddling was a hotbed of romantic folly. Was there something in the air? The water? Henry needed to make Rachel breathe and drink more.

As far as he knew, the marquess had seen Mrs. Grace exactly twice: the day of Henry's incarceration and the day of the flooded wedding. How on earth had he wound up in her kitchen in a dressing gown? Was Sir Bertram a matchmaker?

Henry needed a place to hide out for a while and gather his thoughts. No doubt Vincent and Lady Bexley would appreciate his extended absence. Since he was in the neighborhood, he rapped on the Everetts' back door. No one came to welcome him inside for coffee and gingerbread. Despite the early hour, Henry thought Rachel was probably at the schoolhouse already; she was all too dedicated. Pete Everett was no doubt sleeping in the front room as a man of his years deserved.

So he sat in the lush little garden, reconsidering the wisdom of leaving his cane home. Unlacing his specially-fitted boot, Henry rubbed his foot and wondered where the hideous canine menace was. Some watchdog— there had been no warning barks or growls from inside heralding his visit. Perhaps the wretched beast recognized him now and knew Henry was no danger to his family and was snoozing with his master.

Henry put his boot back on. He couldn't go home to the love-nest, somewhat afraid of what he'd find. How would Vincent look without his dog-collar?

Henry didn't really want to know.

How could he help Vincent get his happy ending? Perhaps he could purchase a small estate with a cleric's living attached. Install Vincent and Lady Bexley in the rectory—no, she'd have to be un-Lady Bexley.

If a marriage wasn't consummated, could it be annulled? Henry had a suspicion the husband had to be proven incapable, and that boob Bexley was not apt to confess to such a thing, especially if he was cutting a swath through the demi-mondaine and was a renowned cocksman.

What man would admit he was a wilted flower? Henry himself had gone out of his way to stimulate his flagging manhood when he was too depressed to function properly. Thus Francie and Lysette, when all the while not that much had been going on.

Very few swaths had been cut.

He was thoroughly cured now. Sunday proved that, not that he'd ever tell Rachel she was the instrument of his newfound joy. She didn't want to be responsible for his reformation, and she was right. Change did come from within, and change was zipping through Henry like an electric current.

But back to one of his problems. Obviously, the best and most efficient solution would be to murder Bexley. Extreme, to say the least. But Henry had done enough killing, and though he liked Vincent well enough, was not going to put his mortal soul into more jeopardy than it was already.

He chuckled. He was coming unhinged contemplating murder. There had to be an easier way to assist the young lovers.

He was running through various scenarios—all of them sadly insufficient—when he heard Rufus's unearthly howl from inside the cottage.

Henry tried the kitchen door and it swung open. Rufus came barreling down the hallway toward him, whining and tail wagging, an unusual combination.

Glad to see him? No attempt at a bite? Something was definitely wrong.

"Mr. Everett?"

Rufus yipped, turned and raced to the front parlor. Henry followed and found Pete Everett on the floor clutching his chest, his face gray.

Henry was on his knees at his side at once. "Mr. Everett! Pete! Can you hear me?"

Rachel's father nodded. "Hurts."

"Where?"

"Dignity. Heart."

Dear God. Henry had no idea where Dr. Oakley lived, but everyone in the village would.

"Stay here. I'll be right back."

"Of course I'll stay here, you looby. Where will I go?" There was nothing wrong with Everett's wits, even though each word cost him a breath.

Henry grabbed a pillow from the bed and tucked it under the man's head, then tossed a quilt over him. He didn't dare try to pick Rachel's father up, not knowing if he'd broken something in his fall.

Henry dashed up the street and pounded on Mrs. Grace's door. This time she was even longer opening it, and when she did, her annoyance was plain.

"I already told you—"

"Stubble it, Mrs. Grace. Pete Everett has had some kind of attack and needs the doctor. You'll have to let my father stew in his juices while you fetch him. Get someone to tell Rachel to come home as soon as she can, too."

She paled but didn't deny anything.

"Hurry! There's no time to get dressed. I'm going back there right now and see what I can do to help."

Henry left her, not looking back. The damned woman had better shake a leg.

Speaking of legs, his foot was on fire, but that didn't matter. Henry let himself back into the house. Rufus was guarding his owner, but allowed Henry to approach.

"I'm going to loosen your nightshirt, sir."

"Have at it." Everett's words were weak but steady.

"When did this happen?"

"Got out of bed to use the privy. When I came back in, I was dizzy. Fell."

"Are you still in pain?"

Everett shrugged. Which probably meant yes. He must have hit the floor hard.

Henry had performed first aid in the field too many times to count, but there was no blood to stanch and no bone to set or anything to stitch up. He was at a loss.

Rachel loved her father. Henry didn't want to be responsible for the man's death. Where was the damned doctor?

"May I get you water? Do you have pills or anything to take?"

"Healthy as a horse." Everett winked so slowly Henry almost missed it. "Water would be good."

Henry went into the orderly kitchen and filled a mug full of water. It couldn't be bad for someone if they were suffering from a heart attack, could it? Pete Everett was old, but that didn't mean he should die this morning from drinking a glass of water.

"Can you sit up?"

"I can try."

Henry held the glass as Everett took a shaky sip. When he was done, he clutched Henry's hand, spilling a few drops on Henry's sleeve. "You'll take care of my girl, won't you? You'll marry her like you said you wanted."

"If she'll have me. So far, she hasn't said yes and I've asked and asked."

"Damn headstrong chit. Just like her mother. Stubborn as the day is long." Everett coughed and swallowed another mouthful.

Henry tried to smile. "I'll bring her round somehow. I don't want you to worry about anything, Pete. You don't mind if I call you Pete, do you?"

"Best of friends, ain't we? That's what I told that prig Sykes when he came by yesterday with your father. I'm tired, Lord Challoner. Henry, I guess it is now, since we're practically related. Don't let me down, boy—ask her again, and this time make it stick. Let me close my eyes for a little while."

Henry felt a shiver of fear. He cradled Pete's head in the crook of his elbow and touched a withered cheek. It was warm enough, but again Henry didn't know what signs to look for.

They sat on the floor for what seemed like hours. Pete's breathing was regular if rattled. Suddenly, Rufus took off like a shot and ran barking into the kitchen. "We're in here!" Henry called. "Hurry!"

Fuck. It wasn't Dr. Oakley.

The Marquess of Harland gave a quelling order to Rufus and the animal sat and cowered, knowing instinctively he was outmatched. "How is he?"

Every hair was in place, every button buttoned. The pater was a quick-change artist, and made no excuses for his earlier whereabouts.

"I don't know, Father. He's gone to sleep."

"I've sent my coach for the doctor. He should be here shortly—he's at a local sheep farm. There's some sort of hospital in Stroud to which Mr. Everett can be transported."

Henry stared down into Pete's ashen face. "I don't know if he should be moved."

"Well, the man can't lie in your lap forever, Henry. Use your head."

"We'll see what Dr. Oakley has to say. He'll know best."

His father's lip curled. "A country doctor? There must be someone more qualified in Stroud. It's a good-sized market town, from what I understand."

"That country doctor you're so contemptuous of is skilled. A good man. After all, you left me in his care."

"That's entirely different. You are not an elderly pensioner with a heart condition."

"True enough." Henry wanted to be elderly one day though, so he refused to rise to his father's bait. The pater could make Henry's blood sing in his veins and cause his ears to buzz, but not this morning. Some problems were greater than dealing with an annoying parent.

"Is his daughter coming?"

His father shrugged. "I have no idea. I gather there's an issue as to who will take over the school for her. The vicar cannot be found. The village is in quite an uproar. The family is apparently very well thought of."

Henry wasn't going to peach on Vincent. Let him have his fun with Greta while he could. If, God forbid, he was needed here for the Last Rites, Henry would fetch the vicar himself.

"Well, she should close the school down then. It's more important that she come home to be with her father," Henry said.

"I'm sure the people here will work something out. They seem a capable lot." His father picked an invisible speck from his cuff and cleared his throat. "I suppose you'd like to know what I was doing in Mrs. Grace's cottage."

"Not really." Henry certainly didn't want to hear a blow-by-blow description.

"It isn't what you think."

"I don't think anything. It's none of my business, Father. This isn't the time for a family row anyway. We're both adults and should be able to take pleasure where we may. Life is short." Henry hoped Pete didn't hear him and take the wrong meaning.

There were flags of color on his father's usually composed countenance. "Yes. Well. We'll talk about it later."

"Unnecessary. Where the hell is Oakley?'

"He was with some sheep farmer, as I said. He's coming. What can I do to assist?"

The front room was darkish despite the morning sun. "Open the curtains and windows. Some fresh air would be good."

The marquess was as efficient as any upstairs maid. After performing that task, he added some coals to the flagging fire—it was still cool inside the stone cottage despite it being spring.

"Henry—"

Whatever his father planned to say would have to wait. Help had finally arrived.

Chapter 38

Henry. *And* his father. Oh, God. How was this even possible?

Rachel dropped gracelessly to the floor. She'd run all the way up the hill once she'd gotten permission to dismiss the children and could barely catch her breath to ask what happened. She must look a fright—again—but it didn't matter when her father lay lifeless in Henry's arms.

"Miss Ever—um—green! Oh, no, it's Everett, isn't it. How do you do? I—I was just passing by and heard Rufus making a fuss. I knew something was wrong from the sound of him. I let myself in and found your father on the floor. He took a fall. He was conscious and talking a little while ago. I'm sure he'll be all right." Henry's words were brisk for the benefit of his father, but his blue eyes were sympathetic as they searched her face.

Rachel didn't have Henry's confidence. Her father's skin was the color of wallpaper paste and his breathing, while steady, was labored. "He's asleep?"

Henry nodded. Her father was curled up half in Henry's lap like an overgrown child. The viscount didn't seem to mind though; he was absently stroking her father's shoulder while he slept.

"The doctor is on his way. Miss Everett, I believe you met my father briefly the other day. Father, do you know which farm Dr. Oakley was visiting?"

The Marquess of Harland shook his head. "I'm afraid not. I must apologize for my presumption the other day, Miss Everett. I'm afraid I didn't quite understand your situation."

The man was apologizing? Rachel looked up at Henry, who wore a somewhat bemused expression.

"No harm done," she said, trying to keep her voice smooth as if she talked to marquesses all day long instead of ten drippy-nosed children. "I *do* have nursing skills, but I immediately notified Reverend Walker to take my place. It was inappropriate that I remain at Stonecrop Cottage unchaperoned."

"I quite agree. The last thing my son needs is an impediment to his recovery."

An impediment, was she? Not according to Henry. He gave her all the credit for his new lease on life, which was, of course, ridiculous.

Rachel put a hand on her father's clammy brow, and his eyelids fluttered. "I'm here, Dad.'

"He promised."

Her father's words were wheezy but clear.

"Who promised?"

He jerked his chin up in Henry's direction.

Oh, Dad. Not you too.

Rachel straightened up as tall as she could go while sitting on the floor. "I want to thank both of you for being here and helping, but I'm sure you have other things to attend to. I can take care of my father until Dr. Oakley comes."

"Don't be ridiculous, Ra—Miss Everett. I'm not leaving. Father, *you* can go if you wish."

"I'll stay. My coach will be here shortly for your father's convenience, Miss Everett."

"Y-your coach?" She remembered that coach—a behemoth that splashed muddy water all over her.

"To transport him to hospital."

Cold fear washed over her. Surely her father couldn't be *that* ill. He'd fallen, that's all. Old people were not always steady on their feet.

"He might do just as well at home," Henry said reassuringly. "We'll see what Dr. Oakley says."

The marquess gave a little snort but said nothing.

Rachel knew her father would not live forever; he was eighty-four, after all, a great age. She'd watch his abilities diminish, particularly after her mother died. He'd moved downstairs to the front room, and Rachel wondered apart from the steep stairs if he just couldn't bear sleeping in the room he'd shared with his beloved wife.

He'd worked so hard to win her. Proposed at least a dozen times, according to her mother. It wasn't until she was satisfied with his reformation that she accepted his suit. They had been happy together, especially after what they considered to be a miracle—Rachel's birth.

Her father clutched her sleeve. "No hospital. Saw enough of one in the Crimea."

He had been quite an old soldier when he was sent home, returning to the village he'd left when he wasn't much more than a boy. Then, he hadn't wanted to be a weaver, but changed his mind once he was courting one.

"I'm sure medicine has improved since then, Dad." She felt helpless and awkward sitting cross-legged on the floor, but the need to be near him was strong. And Henry was close, too, cradling her father on his lap. She could feel his support, even though he was careful not to touch her, or even look at her much.

"Don't trouble yourself with talking, Pete. We won't do anything you don't like."

Rufus decided he'd obeyed the marquess long enough. He crept over to his master and put his muzzle on her father's thigh. Rachel scratched behind his ears.

"You're a good dog," she said softly.

"He is, you know. If he hadn't made such a racket, I wouldn't have come in."

"I'm grateful you did." Her eyes were filling with useless tears. Rachel needed to pull herself together. It wouldn't help her father any if she lost her self-control. And she had completely forgotten her manners.

"Lord Harland, will you not sit down? The chair in the corner is very comfortable." Patched and boasting of Rufus's shed fur though it was.

"I'm fine." Henry's father was staring at the little tableau on the ancient carpet before him—an ugly dog, a wind-blown woman, his wayward son, and a poor old man. What must he be thinking? It was impossible to tell from his face—he might as well be carved of marble.

The rumble of the traveling coach on the narrow lane heralded that Dr. Oakley was here at last. The marquess himself left the parlor to let him in, and Rachel took the opportunity to lean over and kiss Henry full on the mouth.

Not nearly long enough, either.

"What was that for?"

"For being you, Henry. Thank you."

His eyes were bright. "I would do anything for you, you know."

"I'm beginning to realize that. But I still don't see how—never mind." This wasn't the right moment to talk about the future.

If there was one.

Dr. Oakley entered the room, shooing her out with a few kind words. He must know how worried she was, but it probably was best. If she stayed, her father might try to be brave and pretend everyone was just making too much of a fuss. Rachel reluctantly rose to her feet and put a kettle on in the kitchen. The marquess had disappeared into the garden. She could see him through the window examining one of her father's prize peony bushes with considerable interest.

Henry had remained to help get her father back into bed once the doctor had deemed there were no bones broken. Fingers crossed—she had seen many elderly people take too long to heal—sometimes never heal. She could hear the low male voices, her father's included. That was an encouraging sign, wasn't it?

Rachel carried a tray outside. It wasn't fancy, certainly not what the Marquess of Harland was accustomed to. No sterling silver tea service on New Street. But she had used her mother's best flower-sprigged teapot and matching cups, china that was meant for "special occasions."

This probably was not what her mother had in mind.

"Will you have a cup of tea, my lord?"

The marquess turned and quickly took the dented toleware tray away from her, looked around in vain for a table and then set it on the weathered barrel.

"You shouldn't have gone to the trouble, Miss Everett."

"I needed something to do. It's hard to wait."

The marquess took a seat on the bench, and Rachel busied herself fixing the two cups of tea. There was a spare cup for Henry when he came out.

The marquess took a sip, then cleared his throat. "You are an only child?"

"Yes. The heiress to all this." Rachel smiled at her cheek. The Marquess of Harland probably thought their cottage was a hovel.

"And you teach."

"Since my mother died. Before that, I took care of her and my father."

"A dutiful daughter."

"I've tried to be." She'd even delivered an unconscious viscount to the graveyard at her father's direction.

The marquess set his cup next to him on the bench. "Explain to me why my son calls you Rachel and then claims he cannot remember your surname."

Oh dear.

Chapter 39

"Miss Everett, Dr. Oakley wants to see you now."

Perfect timing, Henry old boy. A few seconds later, and Rachel would have been forced to deal with his father's inquisition. Henry knew from experience his father was a skilled interrogator. One dismissed him at one's peril. Nothing much got by him. And here Henry thought he had been so careful Miss Everett-ing. He must have Racheled at least once.

Rachel stood up quickly. "Is my father…"

"In his bed, resting comfortably. No hospitalization required. Oakley feels the carriage is unnecessary at present, Father. Shall I go tell your coachman to expect you shortly?"

"It's a fine morning. I'll walk back to Sir Bertram's in a bit. First I think I shall finish my tea and catch up with Henry for a few minutes if you don't mind, Miss Everett. My best wishes for your father's recovery."

So much for hint-taking. Henry resigned himself to his father's displeasure. It was the usual state of affairs, wasn't it? At least Rachel had got out of the line of fire, rushing through the kitchen door.

"Pour yourself some tea. Miss Everett brought an extra cup."

"No, thank you." After a busy morning like this, what Henry wanted was whiskey. But that would be falling back into bad old habits, and wouldn't do at all.

He was a new man, or so he kept saying to anyone who'd hold still to listen.

His father looked extraordinarily comfortable on the bench, as if the garden and all its gardeners, birds and butterflies belonged to him. Henry recollected the man preferred country living, and was happier at his Cotswold estate than anywhere. But duty called, and the man had never missed a vote in Parliament.

He must be missing some now. Henry had not expected the pater to stick around to monitor his recovery.

Henry took Pete Everett's usual seat. "What did you want to talk about?"

"I had a productive day yesterday with Sykes. We interviewed the villagers about your progress."

Henry had had very little to do with anyone aside from Dr. Oakley, Vincent and the Everetts.

And Mrs. Grace, of course.

What could anyone have said? Yes, I saw your son stumbling along the lanes. Poor crippled fellow. Yes, he came in for forbidden gingerbread. He's got a sweet tooth, hasn't he, poor lamb. Yes, I heard him sing in church.

Off-key.

"And the verdict?"

"You've settled in nicely, apart from your unfortunate tendency for injury and illness. It's a wonder you survived South Africa."

Wasn't it just? "I'm too stubborn to succumb."

"Apparently so. But it wouldn't hurt to bolster your good behavior once your stay is up. There will be temptations, even at Kings Harland, not to mention Harland House in Town. I've hired Mrs. Grace to assist you."

It must have been an interesting job interview in their dressing gowns. Henry's throat closed. When it opened, he was very much afraid he was going to leap across the grass and throttle his father, possibly to death.

But he wasn't about to duplicate a Greek tragedy, and took a calming breath. "I don't need a nursemaid, Father. I'm twenty-five years old. Perhaps my wife can see to my health and happiness."

"Your wife? What is this nonsense?"

"I understood from my treatment plan you want me to marry as soon as possible. I am willing."

His father's golden eyebrows met in a frown. "But you haven't even met Miss Clark yet. Her father and I have not quite come to terms."

"Father, this is the nineteenth century. Arranged marriages are passé, don't you think?" Whoever this Miss Clark was, Henry had no interest in her, her father, or any terms the pater was trying to hammer out.

"As my only son, you have a duty to the family name to marry a suitable girl. Miss Clark is entirely unexceptional. She's handsome enough, and a niece to her godfather, the Duke of Welford, who has taken an interest in her education. She knows what's what, and will make an excellent marchioness when the time comes. Between her and Mrs. Grace, your household will be well managed."

Managed. Henry was not some child to be denied pudding or told where to sit. When to wake up or when to go to bed. What to read. What to think.

And he'd hire Mrs. Grace over his father's dead body.

Was there something Henry didn't know? He gave his father a thorough look. The man could have stepped out of a gentleman's fashion plate. His silver-gilt hair was gleaming, his color healthy—even his fingernails were shiny.

"Father, you aren't dying or anything, are you?"

His father's cheeks reddened. "Of course not. But one must think to the future. Anything could happen. We never expected your mother to pass at such an early age, did we? I'd like to see you settled."

"I don't mind settling, but I'll pick a bride of my own, thank you very much."

"You haven't had time to meet anyone proper since you've come home."

Henry snapped off a bloom and tucked it into his lapel. "Oh, but I might have."

It was best to get this godforsaken conversation over with. Puddling was about to be rocked by scandal, and the sooner Henry and Rachel could skate through it, the better.

Henry's father rose unsteadily. "You don't mean to make some actress your viscountess! I'll not have it, Henry! I'll see you institutionalized before you bring further shame to me."

Henry stood too. "Relax, Father. You'll have an apoplexy, and then it won't matter whom I marry. You won't know from inside your silk-lined coffin, will you? My unsuitable wife and I might be doing the cancan on your grave."

Although it would be difficult for Henry to find his balance, not to mention he'd look damned silly in a skirt.

"Don't be disrespectful!"

His father was angry. It never took much for the marquess to go off like a rocket, especially if he was thwarted. Henry attempted to rein in his own temper. "Father, you're making it far too easy for me. I am of age. I served the queen for six very long and eventful years and have seen a bit of the world. I'm sorry if it threw me off kilter temporarily. I'm lame. I'm a quarter deaf. Perhaps I felt sorry for myself for too long. But I doubt any qualified physician would declare me incompetent, so kindly refrain from threatening me with further incarceration. Unless, of course, you mean to bribe someone to lock me up. That would be very much beneath you."

If Henry had to, he'd flee Britain, preferably with Rachel Everett.

But it all depended on Pete Everett's condition. Henry knew he hadn't a chance of wooing Rachel when she was so worried about her father. Henry didn't want true harm to befall *his* father, but he wouldn't mind at all if the man returned to Town and began to mind his own and the queen's business.

"Who is she?"

"I beg your pardon?"

"This girl you want to marry. Don't tell me it's Miss Everett." The marquess blasted the little cottage beyond with a disdainful pale blue glare.

"All right. I won't tell you then."

His father sat back down on the bench. "God damn it, Henry. To fall for the lures of a plain country bumpkin—after the recent dazzling company you've kept, I would have thought you'd have different taste."

Was the pater blind? If Henry had his druthers, he'd darken his father's daylights for all the good his eyes did him now. Rachel was beautiful, her hair an ebony fall, her skin delicious as double cream. Granted, her wardrobe was deficient, but that could be easily mended.

"Rachel is not plain. She's from, as you said earlier, a well-respected Puddling family. Her father was a war hero. And she'll inherit a small fortune when the time comes."

His father's lip curled. "Don't gammon me, boy! Look where they live. A tumbledown weaver's cottage in the middle of nowhere. She's a spinster schoolteacher, and not a very good one according to Sir Bertram."

"Because she's soft-hearted and doesn't beat her students! Sir Bertram's a snobbish idiot. You should know that after staying with him a few days. I love her, Father, and that's all I care about."

Well, so much for remaining discreet. But once Henry had started, he hadn't been able to dam up his words. Rachel would lecture him, if she was still speaking to him after all this was done.

"Love! Pah! People like us don't marry for love."

"You did."

"I was lucky. And your mother was a duke's daughter. It's not the same at all."

"I should like you to give Miss Everett a chance, Father. And anyway, you may be surprised—she doesn't want to marry me."

The marquess laughed, an entirely unpleasant sound. "And you believe her? What better way to get her hooks into you, Henry? All the more reason for you to pursue her! The thrill of the chase—it's what you've always lived for. She's a clever puss, I grant you that."

This was going just about as badly as Henry had expected. "She has no hooks, Father. She's worried about Puddling and its reputation. And I imagine she has second thoughts about becoming a viscount's wife. I don't have much to recommend me for the kind of sacrifice she'd be making."

"What the devil are you talking about? You are a Challoner! We came over with the Conqueror! She is a little nobody who—"

Whatever else Henry's father was about to say was interrupted by the little nobody herself. Henry swallowed hard, wondering how much she'd heard.

"I would thank you both to take your argument somewhere else, my lords. My father is resting." Rachel's eyes resembled the kind of clouds one saw right before a violent thunderstorm.

Her ears worked perfectly well, then.

"And furthermore, Lord Harland, you needn't worry. I wouldn't marry your son if he was the last man on earth. Not because there is a single thing lacking in him. He is—he is an extraordinary man, worthy of any woman's regard. But I cannot imagine having you for a father-in-law."

Chapter 40

Well, that pretty much burned all her bridges. Those flames would never be doused. Poor Henry looked shell-shocked and the marquess gave her a look that would have withered her right into the ground if she cared at all about his good opinion of her.

Rachel didn't wait around to see if they left, but returned to her father's side. His color was a little better, his snores gentle.

Dr. Oakley was returning his instruments to his leather case. "Is everything all right out there?" he asked quietly.

Rachel shook her head. "I may have done something irretrievably stupid."

She loved Henry, but what was the point? It was best to put whatever was between them to rest.

Dr. Oakley put a warm hand on her shoulder. "I heard. You're under a great deal of stress and worry. I'll speak to them. I'm sure they'll understand you were provoked."

Rachel sat down next to her sleeping father. "I doubt it. I'm just a nobody who's aimed too high."

"Have you? Is it true? Has young Lord Challoner proposed marriage?"

Rachel's mouth trembled to a near-smile. "Almost from the first minute he saw me. I didn't take him seriously—he was funning then. But now—" She squeezed her idle hands in her lap. "Things have become serious, if that's the right word."

She had, after all, lost her virginity, which was serious indeed. "But I cannot see anything coming of it. We're from different worlds, and Henry's father would never approve. Especially now."

But even if she could call back her words, she wouldn't. Henry's father was awful in his own untouchable-marquess way. No wonder his son had rebelled.

"He seems a nice lad. When he's not dragging prostitutes to his ancestral home."

Rachel's face grew hot. "He—he was a little wild, I grant you. But he *is* changed. He wants to do something for injured soldiers, not just ones missing limbs, but men who—who cannot sleep. Who think too much. Drink too much." Peace treaties may have been signed, but many soldiers' demons were winning their war.

"Very admirable. Was that to be his Service? What do Vincent and the other governors think? I haven't heard of it yet."

"I don't know. I don't think it's gotten that far, and probably can't be done in the two weeks he has left here. But Henry feels strongly about it. He's discussed it with my father." She brushed a tuft of sparse white hair off her father's damp forehead.

"Hm. Well, I approve of the scheme at any rate. But I have an easier Service in mind for him before we let him leave if the governors agree to it. And I think they will. We take care of our own first. Needs must and all that."

"Oh?"

"Yes. You'll be required here, Rachel. I know even if we have a nurse or neighbors come spell you, you'll want to be with your father while he recovers. I'm going to ask Lord Challoner if he'll teach for you."

"*What?*" Rachel could think of nothing less likely. Gorgeous Henry Challoner in her dusty classroom? Ridiculous!

"The spring term is over at the end of the week, is it not? I believe the man can hold his own against eight or ten children for a few days. He was an army officer, after all. Accustomed to commanding rough men. A handful of children should be...child's play." Dr. Oakley chuckled.

Little did he know. The man had no children of his own. "But—"

"No buts. I know Vincent usually takes your place, but it's not his favorite task. He has enough on his plate watching out for our immortal souls, don't you think? I cannot imagine anyone else in the village with the patience you have, but you'll be needed here. Your father will not be an easy man to take care of if I know him."

Rachel would probably have to tie her father to the bed before all was said and done. He'd want to get up and weed and water his precious garden at the very least.

"I'll try to keep him quiet."

Dr. Oakley shook some pills into a paper sleeve and twisted it up. "Good luck with that. Give him one every morning at breakfast—a sensible breakfast, mind you. No fry-ups. Just toast and tea and oatmeal.

He won't live forever, Rachel, but I see no reason for any immediate danger. His heart isn't what it was, and he may get lightheaded if he moves about too quickly. We don't want him falling again—he was lucky this time, no bones broken. You need to watch out for that. A man his age doesn't mend well."

She thought of several of her father's contemporaries, who'd gone downhill rapidly after such an injury. "I shall lecture him."

"Ha! That I should like to witness. I'll be back later this afternoon to check on him. Before supper for certain. Chin up, my dear. All will be well."

If only. Rachel couldn't see it just at present. She and her father were to be trapped in the little cottage for the foreseeable future.

And she had alienated a powerful lord and hurt another. Henry would get over her. But would she get over Henry? Could she forget Sunday afternoon and all it entailed? To never have him touch her again—

She delved into a basket of sewing while she waited for her father to wake, keeping her mind on her uneven stitches and not her problems. Eventually, her eyes filled with tears, making her task impossible. What a fool she was!

"How is he?" His voice was soft against the back of her neck, causing goose bumps down to her toes.

Rachel dropped the shirt button to the floor, where it rolled under her father's bed.

"How did you get in?"

He held a finger to her lips, then spoke quietly. "You neglected to lock the door after your magnificent set-down of my father. I don't think I've ever seen him quite that color before, not even in the worst of my mischief. Well done, you. And Rufus and I are old friends at this point. He didn't even bark once."

"Oh, Henry." She covered her face in shame. He was a good man, and now she'd made his life—and her own—more difficult.

"Now, now, no more tears. I spoke to Dr. Oakley. Your father will be all right, and so will we."

"But *your* father!"

"It's time the pater learned where the lines of demarcation are. He can't hurt us, Rachel. And he can't hurt Puddling. I have an ace up my sleeve." He gave her a cocky wink.

Trust Henry to see the silver lining when there was nothing but tarnish. The very fact he was here in her cottage proved he was still not yet in his right mind.

Oh, God. How she loved him, no matter how hard she'd tried to convince herself otherwise. But she didn't really know him! They had nothing whatsoever in common besides the fact that they breathed the same Cotswold air.

And had been perfect in bed.

He bundled up the shirt on her lap and tossed it back in the basket. "Come outside for a minute so we can talk properly. I want you to hear everything I have to say, and I don't want to disturb your father."

She rose, hesitant. What if her father woke up and was confused? Tried to get out of bed again against Dr. Oakley's order?

"Just for a minute. We'll leave the door open."

Henry went to the front door that opened to the street. Rachel hadn't used it since her father made his bedroom in the parlor, and the hinges creaked like a crypt being opened.

"People will see us!" she hissed.

"Good. I want them to. Let them gossip their heads off. I have a plan, Rachel, and you can help me with it."

Rachel doubted she could help anyone with anything. Sir Bertram was bound to come round shortly to fire her after the marquess told him of her effrontery.

What would she do if something happened to her father? Puddling was her home, the cottage humble but cozy. She'd managed to fill her days and nights with activity, but the truth was she wanted *more.*

She wanted Captain Lord Henry Agamemnon Challoner.

And there it was. An impossible desire. Unsuitable in every way. Poor Henry was not even recovered from what had brought him here—he was still impulsive. Still willful. He may not have imbibed any alcohol, but he was fizzy nonetheless.

"Rachel."

She looked up into his bright blue eyes. "Yes?"

And then he dropped to his knees on the cobblestones.

"What are you doing?"

"Proposing. Again." He craned his neck. "Are people looking out their windows?"

Rachel's panic welled up into her throat. "Get up!"

"Not until you've said yes. I'm obeying the wishes of your father, Rachel. We discussed this before the doctor came."

"He's off his head!"

Henry clasped her hands. "That's as may be, but a gentleman doesn't ignore what might possibly be the last request of a dying man. Everyone will understand why I must offer for you."

"You *cannot*."

"Oh, but I am. I have—I forget how many times. It's as if your father planned his indisposition."

"What?"

"Oh, I'm not accusing the old bird per se. But he's a smart man and has taken advantage of the opportunity. It's a good thing I came along to find him rather than old Vincent. Vincent wouldn't do for you at all. Pete's asked me to take care of you. Marry you. I gave him my word to do so."

Rachel didn't know whether to laugh or cry. "That's no reason to get married! No one would really hold you to it."

"I quite agree. It helps that I think I've fallen in love with you. Notice I said 'think.' A man like me has very little experience with love, poor idiot that I am. But I'm fairly sure you are the only woman for me. I shall do my best, and I don't believe it will be especially difficult to fall head over heels in no time. But do say yes, Rachel. The cobblestones are killing my knees."

Chapter 41

Her resolve was cracking; he could feel it. Henry wished she'd hurry up and say yes, for he wanted to get practical and talk to her about the school once his knees stopped aching. He'd accepted Oakley's Service suggestion immediately, for here was a need to be filled, and it would help Rachel the most not to worry about her children. How hard could it be, as long as little Mary Ann didn't decide to scream her head off again? His deafness might actually come in handy if she did.

Rachel was so organized she probably had lessons planned for the rest of the week, which Henry would follow more or less faithfully. He had some diversionary ideas about children's education as well, having driven his tutors to distraction over the years.

And there was Greta Bexley to settle. It was not precisely a propitious time for a houseguest at the Everett cottage, but perhaps Greta could help Rachel nurse Pete. It could be put about that she might have returned here for that very task, having formed a friendship with Rachel during her pre-wedding stay in Puddling.

Then came Vincent. He would be ideal to manage Henry's soldiers' sanctuary. Puddling could find itself a new padre, and eventually the legalities of Greta's marriage could be managed. In the meantime, Vincent and Greta could live in sin in some quiet country location. Not in the Cotswolds, obviously. Henry would have to look for property farther afield of potential gossip.

Yes, there was a great deal to do, if only Rachel would accept his proposal and he could stand up. He needed to speak with his father, too, and for some odd reason he looked forward to it.

"Henry—"

"Yes, my love. Say it. You know you want to."

"But—"

"No reasonable or unreasonable objections. Nothing is certain. You'll probably always question one thing or another, but we'll deal with the answers together. Now, do the right thing."

"It cannot be right! We are...unequal."

"Yes, yes. You are so much better than I. I promise to improve as fast as I can. You've seen my father—look what an improvement over him I am already! The Challoner line will only be enriched by an injection of Everett blood. You have nothing to worry over. We'll get you new clothes. A companion to tutor you to navigate the ways of the beau monde, although you are perfect as you are. We'll have our own establishment far from Kings Harland and can do just as we please. Please, Rachel. I am in agony, and I spy a donkey cart coming down the road."

"For God's sake," came a bellow from inside her cottage. "Say yes! I want my lunch!"

Well, her father must be feeling better. Rachel looked down, her face pale. "You are both bullying me."

"There will be plenty of time for you to bully us back. Your father will live with us, of course. That's all right with you, Pete, isn't it?" Henry shouted.

"Aye, I suppose."

Rachel licked her lips. "You are impossible."

"All the more reason to take me in hand. Say yes. That donkey does not look friendly."

"Yes, oh, yes! Now get up."

"I thought you'd never let me." Henry lurched up, his legs full of pins and needles. "There, that one syllable wasn't so difficult, was it?" He took her in his arms, hoping they would both not fall down in the gutter.

By God, he was going to be happy. He was happy *now*. In a couple of weeks he and Rachel could begin a new life together. It would all work out somehow.

She shook like a leaf in his arms, but her mouth opened to him shyly. She tasted just as sweet—perhaps sweeter—than she had on Sunday, because now she was his absolutely. He'd known her a week, but he felt as if they were very old and dear friends.

He'd just make sure she never encountered any garden implements wherever they wound up living.

Rufus snuffled around their ankles. Henry had best end his kiss before his trouser cuff was devoured by the little beast once again. But it was difficult to stop when she fit so neatly against him, her tongue sliding, her sighs so soothing. The driver of the cart had stopped to watch and there was a distinct aroma of donkey clouding all around them. In his peripheral vision, Henry could see a few Puddlingites in their doorways, their arms folded, their faces void of smiles.

"We have an audience, my dear," he whispered against her lips. "Follow my lead."

Rachel blinked, as if returning to the surface of a deep lake.

"Good people of Puddling!" Henry began, having no idea where this greeting might take him, but he plowed on, buoyed by the fact that Rachel was by his side. "Miss Everett has agreed to make me the happiest of men."

There was an audible intake of breath up and down New Street.

"J-just like Lady Maribel and Sir Colin Sykes," his fiancée said.

"Who?" Henry asked.

"I'll tell you all the details later," Rachel whispered. She spoke louder, her teacher's voice carrying to the end of the lane. "Puddling survived then, and it will survive now. There's no reason to be afraid."

The donkey-cart man sniffed. "Lady Maribel's pa was happy to get her off his hands. 'Course he didn't object to her carrying on with the Sykes heir while she was locked up here. She was a wild piece and no mistake. But that marquess fellow—"

"Don't worry about my father. I hardly ever do," said Henry, stretching the truth.

There was a shuffling sound behind them, and Henry was appalled to see Pete Everett clinging to the door frame.

"They have my blessing. In fact, the young lord is following my deathbed wish. Word of one soldier to another."

There was a cry of dismay from the neighbors.

"Dad! Get back into bed!" Rachel extricated herself from Henry's arms and rushed to her father.

"Not until they all understand. Someone's got to take care of my Rachel when I go."

"You are not going anywhere," Rachel said. "And I can take care of myself."

"Very true," Henry said. "But won't it being a sight more fun taking care of yourself as a viscountess than a teacher? Let me help you back inside, Pete. We don't want Dr. Oakley to read us all the Riot Act."

They left the cart, the donkey, the man and the neighbors to discuss this latest event. Pete went back inside with his future son-in-law's assistance, collapsing into the bed with a chuckle.

"There. Showed them. Let anyone object before the governors. Can't contradict a dying man."

"You are not dying!" Rachel wailed.

"Nonsense. We all are, every minute. Nothing to fear. Cycle of life," Pete said with ancient wisdom. "I'm awfully hungry. I thought you'd never say yes."

"Neither did I," Henry said.

Rachel threw up her hands. "Men!"

"Hungry men. Some cheese toast would be nice. Do you care to join me, Lord Challoner?"

"I thought we'd settled on Henry. I'd love to, but I really must ferret out my father and Sir Bertram. There are some points we must go over before we send a notice into the Times. Rachel, could you explain a little more about this Maribel and Sir Colin?"

In three minutes, Henry had more ammunition for his case. Apparently Puddling had been a hotbed of intrigue almost from the get-go. Duke's daughters, clergymen, somewhat deaf and crippled soldiers—they were all vulnerable to the Cotswold Cupid's arrow.

With a promise to return and discuss his Service at the school, he indulged himself by kissing Rachel good-bye as Pete grinned. First stop was his own house to pick up a walking stick, maybe two. He was not as steady on his feet as he would like. Henry had the good sense to knock first. After waiting a decent interval—were they deaf too?—Henry opened the door and waited in the hall.

"Vincent? Lady Bexley?"

There were rustles and whispers from the parlor. At least Henry wouldn't be embarrassed by flushing the lovebirds out of the upstairs spare bedroom.

"L-lord Challoner?" Greta sounded frightened out of her wits.

"It is I, and I'm alone. May I come in?"

"It's your house after all." This from Vincent, who sounded equally nervous. Henry strode into the room. Greta sat, only slightly more mussed than before, upon the sofa. The vicar was a thousand miles away in a corner, making himself as invisible as possible. It was difficult since his dog collar had come undone and his thinning hair was on end.

"Good news. Rachel and I are getting married."

Vincent's kiss-chapped lips dropped open. "What?"

"Her father's dying wish. Don't worry, your services will not be needed for his funeral for ages, I hope. It's a scandal, isn't it? A Guest falling in love with a Puddlingite. Imagine."

"I don't appreciate your levity, Lord Challoner. This has serious implications for us all." It was very difficult to take Vincent's disapproval to heart when Lady Bexley looked so obviously kissed. Her cheeks were pink, her lips swollen and moist. Good for them. Henry was in a sterling mood, and wanted to share his happiness with everyone.

"Can't be helped. I admit your situation is a bit more dire than mine—there is Greta's annoying husband to deal with."

Greta's cheeks lost all their color. "I w-won't go back to him. I won't!"

Vincent emerged from his corner and took her hand. "And I swear you won't have to, my darling."

"So, we're in agreement. Love conquers all, or something like that. I have a plan, my children, and each of you has a part to play. Now, are you listening?"

Chapter 42

It was a lovely day, with nary a cloud in the sky. The sun was directly above him, and Henry was amazed that so much had happened since Greta Bexley's blubbering woke him up a mere few hours ago. He remembered Rachel's directions to Sir Bertram Sykes's estate, and the grassy track and gate were just as she had described it. The backs of Henry's legs protested just a little as he climbed the inevitable hill. His body, not to mention his wits, was certainly getting excellent exercise in Puddling.

There were a number of neat Cotswold stone outbuildings, and a rather magnificent manor house at the top of the rise. Below was a vast formal garden with several charming garden follies and every conceivable spring bloom scenting the air. Henry took a deep breath and went around the stable block to the front door, escaping the notice of an elderly groom who was busy with buckets of mash. Henry's father's coach was in its gleaming splendor on the paving stones, but there was no trace of the Harland team, coachman or outriders.

A proper butler opened the door before Henry had a chance to rap upon it. He informed the man of his identity and asked to see his father.

"Won't you come this way? The marquess and Sir Bertram are at luncheon. It will be no trouble to set another place."

Henry *was* peckish, and causing indigestion to both men had some promise. He followed the butler to a large yellow-papered dining room and plastered on a smile as he was announced.

"Captain Lord Henry Challoner."

Not for long. The captain part would go the way of Henry's bad habits. The army wouldn't have him anymore, but had yet to cut him loose. Henry was rather anxious to leave his captaincy behind.

"Sir Bertram, Father. I hope I'm not intruding."

Both men exchanged guilty glances.

"Talking about me, are you?" Henry asked, sliding into a seat a footman proffered. Glasses, plates and silverware were laid out in a trice. Sir Bertram's staff was well-trained.

"*Pas devant les domestiques*," the marquess muttered, as if Henry had to be told not to speak of anything significant.

"Anstruther, Kinsey, that will be all. We'll serve ourselves," Sir Bertram said hastily. Why, the baronet seemed a little frightened of Henry, which was fine by him. "Lord Challoner, would you care for a croquette?"

"I haven't really come for lunch, you know," Henry said conversationally, pushing the place setting to the side.

"Henry, this is neither the time nor the place," his father warned.

"I don't intend to embarrass you in front of your host."

"Embarrass me! Pray tell, how?"

"Your local liaison, Father," Henry said softly.

His father's face turned puce. "I told you that you misinterpreted what you saw."

"Perhaps it's now *comme il faut* to interview servants in their nightgowns. I've been out of the country too long to be sure."

"Don't be impertinent!"

"Forgive me, Father, but impertinence comes so easily for me. It's difficult to break the habit of a lifetime. But that's neither here nor there. Sir Bertram, I thought I should inform you that my Service has been chosen."

"What? Already? But the governors are meeting tomorrow—"

"There really is no time to meet over it. Dr. Oakley will no doubt be getting in touch with you and the rest of them. I am to take Miss Everett's place at the school while her father recovers. *If* he recovers."

Sir Bertram set down his fork. "If? Your father told me he's resting at home. There was no need to transport him to hospital."

"How would you rather spend your last days, sir? Amongst strange faces and smells and medical devices, or in the comfort of your own home in the bosom of your family? Of course, Sykes House is a good deal more comfortable than a tumble-down weaver's cottage in the middle of nowhere."

Henry's father flashed him a look but said nothing.

"I had not thought his condition was so serious. Dear me. Poor Miss Everett."

"You needn't concern yourself over her. She has agreed to accept my hand in marriage."

Both men visibly jumped in their seats and spoke in unison. "*What?*"

"It is her father's deathbed wish. I could do nothing but agree." Henry examined his reflection in the silver knife blade waiting for his father to erupt. He barely got to check one eyebrow.

"You can't do this, Henry. I forbid it. She's not—"

"I warn you to go no further," Henry said, his voice icy. "Father, would you have me break my word to a dying man?"

It wasn't a lie. *We're all dying, as Pete said. Cycle of life*, Henry reminded himself. "A man's promise and his honor are sacred. You taught me that."

"This is ridiculous! I never meant—"

"And *you* can surely have no objection, Sir Bertram. It's not unheard of for a Guest to become attached to a Puddlingite. Your own mother was, I believe, a Guest prior to her marriage to your father. They fell in love right within these very walls."

"That's completely different!" Sir Bertram sputtered.

"Well, it's all ancient history, isn't it? I won't stir up old rumors. Your and the town's reputation is safe. Puddling can go on for the next hundred years reforming wayward individuals with no one the wiser. And I doubt my father will want to reveal the conditions under which I met my wife."

Both men looked faintly green. Henry was counting on the double blackmail—triple if you counted throwing Mrs. Grace in his father's face—to keep them quiet for at least a little while.

"There was another matter I wished to speak to you about," Henry continued. "It's come to my attention that Puddling recently played a part in forcing a young woman into an unsuitable marriage."

Sir Bertram stood up. "Never!"

"Calm yourself, sir. Sit down, sit down."

"I can't imagine where you heard such a thing," Sir Bertram huffed. "The circumstances surrounding our Guests are completely confidential. If I find out who's been bearing tales—"

"Likely it's Miss Everett," the marquess interjected.

"No, Father. It was not my fiancée who told me of this travesty, but rather the young lady herself."

"How do you know Gr—I mean, the young woman in question?"

"We Puddling prisoners have to stick together. As I understand it, she was kept here until her will was broken and then was married off to a disreputable fortune hunter. In my opinion, that's coercion, and Puddling was complicit in torturing the poor girl. I wonder what the Archbishop of Canterbury might have to say about such a thing."

Henry was pretty sure his father was on a first-name basis with the archbishop. What had happened to Greta would touch even the hardest of hearts. Henry was counting on his father's sense of propriety and chivalry.

"Torture! Now see here! No one laid a finger on the girl. If you mean she was deprived of bread and cakes and candies, that's something else."

"She was starved?" the marquess asked, suddenly interested. Through trim in figure, the marquess had a very healthy appetite.

"No such thing! She was given wholesome food, just as your son has been! We have never maltreated a Guest in three-quarters of a century!"

"There might be a difference of opinion on that. I wonder how many other Guests were placed here to satisfy their families' wishes rather than their own needs."

Henry's father lifted an eyebrow at the oblique insult. "Are you accusing me?'

"Not at all, sir. I know you've always had my best interests at heart, even if I have tested your patience time and time again, for which I apologize. I like to think I've grown up a little, and I have Puddling and her people to thank for that. This isn't about my case at all. The young lady's mother and solicitor have benefitted by the marriage, but she herself has not."

"Preposterous! The girl's an heiress!" Sir Bertram's high color was really quite alarming.

"And the settlements included a very healthy return to those who arranged this loveless match, with very little allowance left for her. They bought a bankrupt titled bridegroom for their own consequence. He's been unfaithful already—repeatedly—and cruel. She's trapped. Miserable."

And still a virgin, although how long that might last with Vincent in the vicinity was anyone's guess.

"You can't blame us…"

"Oh, I think I can. In your greed, you overlooked the injustice of keeping a young woman against her will for no legitimate reason. Did you not question her mother?"

"She was worried over her daughter's health!"

"Balderdash. The woman wanted to be mother-in-law to an earl, no matter how depraved he was."

"Good God," Henry's father said. "You're not talking about Merwyn Bexley, are you? I heard he had married some poor innocent. Miss Holmes-Hamilton, wasn't it?"

Sir Bertram shook his head. "We name no names, my lord."

"I had a passing acquaintance with the girl's late father. He must be rolling in his grave. I should hate to have any daughter of mine married to that Bexley wretch. If he doesn't have the pox yet, he will have."

Henry looked at his father. The man had a righteous streak a mile wide, and had never, as far as Henry knew, ever broken his marriage vows when his wife was alive or consorted with the kind of woman one shouldn't when she wasn't. The pater was proving to be remarkably sympathetic to Greta's cause, and Henry was pleased with his strategy.

And the fact that he'd known Mr. Holmes-Hamilton was an unexpected bonus.

"We had no idea—you can't think we are responsible for an unsuccessful marriage. The bride's mother was most persuasive that she had only her daughter's future in mind. Her h-happiness."

"Would you swear to that in a court of law?"

"A court! You don't mean to pursue this. Why, it's none of your business!"

"I think standing idly by when a fine young woman's life is ruined is everyone's business. She was isolated here and, if not starved, put on short rations. Forced into a marriage that was abhorrent to her. This wasn't about her fitting into a wedding dress, Sir Bertram."

The baronet was very pale now. "I don't see what you want me to do."

"Just tell the truth. That Puddling received an even more exorbitant amount than usual to punish an innocent girl. You were an unwitting accomplice to her avaricious mother, I grant you." Henry cleared his throat. "I understand the marriage has not been consummated, which is the only piece of luck in this whole sorry affair."

The marquess steepled his fingers. "You seem to be very well-informed, Henry."

"I've seen enough misery, Father. If I can stop it where I may, I will. I hope with all your connections you can help me."

"I might," the marquess said. "If you give up this foolish idea of marrying Rachel Everett."

Chapter 43

Rachel had spoken regularly with Greta Holmes-Hamilton. The girl had participated fully in Puddling's minimal social life for the three months she had resided here, meeting with the sewing circle and taking her turn reading and shopping for blind Mrs. Flint. When she had the time, Rachel had accompanied her on some of her thrice-daily walks in the company of the prune-faced maid who had been an extra set of eyes to ferret out any signs of dietary backsliding.

Usually Guests weren't permitted to bring personal servants—they had often been enablers of the very problems that were supposed to be solved by the Guest's stay in Puddling. Greta's maid was much like a prison guard and had gotten on like a house on fire with Mrs. Grace. The woman had made free conversation with Greta difficult, though Rachel was smart enough to hear what wasn't said.

But she hadn't really thought of Greta precisely as a friend, and never expected to find the young woman at her back door, accompanied by a pink-cheeked Vincent.

Rachel wiped her hands on her apron. Her father had eaten a substantial lunch, making Rachel feel much more optimistic about his recovery. She was now preparing his dinner, and not really in the mood for company. "Miss Holmes-Hamilton! No, I'm sorry—it's Lady Bexley now, isn't it?"

"Please just call me Greta."

"May we come in, Rachel?"

"Of course! You know my father took a bad turn today—I expect you want to see him, but he's sleeping. Dr. Oakley will be here again soon."

"No, it's you we want to see."

Puzzled, Rachel bade them sit down at the kitchen table. "May I get you a cup of tea?"

Greta's cheeks were pink too. "No, thank you. I'm about to impose upon you for far more than that."

She looked very different from when Rachel had last seen her. She was plumper and didn't have the pale, haunted aspect that she'd left Puddling with. For a girl who had been placed in the village for her health, her eyes had been deeply shadowed, her smile wan as she'd been driven away that last morning.

"I'll help you any way I can," Rachel said, not having the faintest idea what she could possibly do for a countess.

"I know this is an inopportune time, Rachel, with your father being ill, but Gr—Lady Bexley needs a place to stay for tonight."

"Stay? *Here?*" She knew she sounded rude, but Rachel's cottage was nothing like what Greta must be used to. She was an heiress, for heaven's sake, and now a countess!

"You have an extra room," Vincent reminded her.

She did, and there was no bed in it. It had been carried downstairs to the parlor for her father's use.

"I could help you take care of your father," Greta said quickly.

"Oh, I couldn't ask you to do that," Rachel said. "My father can be difficult."

"My husband can be difficult," Greta said quietly. "I've left him."

"Oh! I...I see." Although she didn't.

"If you agree, I won't be any trouble. I spoke with the Marquess of Harland this afternoon, and he's pledged to help me. I'll return with him to Kings Harland when he leaves tomorrow."

The Marquess of Harland? Rachel swallowed. "He thinks it's a good idea that you stay with *me*?"

"I cannot stay at Sir Bertram's. He has his position as chairman of the governors to consider. And since we might be suing the Puddling Rehabilitation Foundation—"

"*What?*"

"I don't think it will come to that, but it never hurts to threaten. Lord Challoner thinks we have a case for collusion and fraud and coercion between Mama and her lawyer and the governors, and has convinced his father to be my champion. I plan to get an annulment of my marriage in any case. We have never, thank goodness, consummated it."

The Greta before her was full of confidence and was very matter of fact, a far cry from the unhappy girl who'd spent three months drooping about Puddling.

"You would have been amused to see Sir Bertram wriggle," Vincent said. "The Marquess is none too pleased with Puddling's methods at the moment. Who would have thought he'd have such a soft heart for Gr—Lady Bexley?"

"It's all due to Lord Challoner," Greta said. "He's a lovely young man, and explained everything so well. B-but not as lovely as you, Vincent."

Rachel looked from one of her uninvited guests to the other. Vincent was the color of raspberry fool.

Oh, Lord.

"Of course you can stay," Rachel said.

"I'm afraid I don't even have a change of clothing with me," Greta said, blushing more. "Could I borrow a nightgown?"

"Certainly," Rachel said faintly. She turned to Vincent. "Do they know about you two?"

"No! That is to say, Henry does. Lord Challoner, I mean. But he's been sworn to secrecy. It wouldn't do for there to be any question of Greta's innocence."

"And I *am* innocent," Greta said, sounding exasperated and giving poor Vincent a look that said she wished he'd change that status as soon as possible.

"All in good time, my love. Henry has promised his assistance."

Henry! The man who until two weeks ago couldn't keep his own trousers buttoned. Suddenly he was a magician.

"Oh, and I have a message from him," Vincent remembered. "I'm to take your plan book and deliver it to him. I'll introduce him to the children tomorrow morning and smooth his way."

Rachel had hoped Henry would come by himself so she could explain her routine. Warn him what to watch out for. She swallowed her disappointment and pushed the canvas bag that she'd thrown on the table in her rush to see her father toward Vincent.

"Everything he'll need is in there. Seating chart. Lesson plans. I wanted to give them a picnic on the last day."

"Excellent. And you'll be pleased to know the Marquess of Harland is terminating his son's stay here. Henry will teach for the next three days as a favor, but then it's back to civilization for him. He won't bother you anymore." Vincent smiled at her benignly, and Rachel wanted to punch him.

Rachel schooled her face to hide the terrible shock. What about their engagement? Henry had proclaimed it in front of all the neighbors!

"He told me to tell you not to worry. He has everything in hand."

Did he now? Rachel was glad someone did.

What would she tell her father? He was so set on her marrying Henry and living a new life. How could Henry have changed his mind between lunch and supper?

The Marquess of Harland had probably changed it for him.

Rachel's bitterness threatened to choke her. She rose and stirred the pot of boiling potatoes just for something to do. The wooden spoon slipped from her shaking hand and fell to the flagstones.

"I'll get it!" Greta said, leaping up and rinsing it under the pump handle. "I would so like to be useful tonight. Can I read to your father? I did enjoy doing that for Mrs. Flint. Even though it was my Service, it was very enjoyable. She's a remarkable old lady, isn't she, living all by herself even if she is blind."

Would that be Rachel's fate here in this cottage in fifty years? She might become someone's Service project in the future. *Poor Miss Everett, who used to teach school before she lost her five-hour fiancé and her marbles.*

She was perilously close to losing them now.

Vincent left them after giving Greta a discreet kiss on her cheek. Rachel had no time to feel sorry for herself. She needed to mash potatoes and slice ham and make up a clean bed for a temporary countess. She would give her bed to Greta and sleep in the weaving room on some old blankets. It wasn't as if she was going to sleep much anyway. Dr. Oakley would be here any minute and she'd ask him to stay for supper. He was a kind man who could carry the conversation with his former patient while Rachel's mind lay in tatters.

Chapter 44

Henry's respect for Rachel had reached new heights. He'd only had three days with the little blighters, and he was almost ready to commit himself to an asylum.

He'd survived the early obstacles—one being the mischievous rearrangement of the children from their seating charts. If he'd not recognized shrieking Mary Ann, he might have called her Helen for the duration. But Rachel, bless her, had a diagram of who sat where, and once Henry reshuffled the children with a stern stare, they mulishly sat through their lessons until they discovered this old crippled soldier wasn't so bad after all.

Vincent, who was supposed to have been assisting to prevent such pranks that first day, had not arrived until nearly lunch time. Farewells to his beloved had taken longer than expected, but at least Greta was now safely at Kings Harland, meeting already with the marquess's legal and spiritual advisors. There had been a scrawled missive from Henry's father yesterday relating the progress, with a reminder to give up Rachel Everett, or he'd withdraw his hospitality and his help from Lady Bexley.

Henry was a man of honor. He'd made promises to quite a lot of people lately, some more obvious than others. A public proposal and a pledge to an elderly man was one thing, a brief silent twitch of acceptance with his fingers crossed behind his back was something else altogether.

A childish trick, true, but the latter had achieved the desired result. His father thought Henry had given up Rachel. He had not. But how to let her know that fact was a bit of a conundrum.

Mrs. Grace was at his elbow night and day, even deciding to sleep in, as though she expected him to make a run for it. By the time he came home from school at the end of the session, he could barely walk, much less run.

If it was in his power, he'd flatten every hill in Puddling. Patrolling desks all day, supervising lunch and recess and then climbing that damned cliff to his house would be his undoing. He might be ready for a Bath chair before all this was over.

He looked at his watch. One hour. There was the picnic to get through, and then he'd be a free man, free from Mrs. Grace at least.

Ostensibly she was in Stonecrop Cottage to assist him through his abbreviated stay and Service, but Henry knew better. She was in the pater's employ, a paid spy in Henry's household. There was no possibility of a midnight stroll with the house locked up tight from inside, no chance of dropping a letter at the post office.

Vincent had told him all Guests' mail was opened, and usually destroyed. Henry wasn't supposed to know there was a telegraph room in the back of the store, and that wouldn't have served anyway. A message to Rachel would only have telegraphed their situation all through Puddling.

Henry couldn't even say he was paying Pete a visit—Dr. Oakley had mandated absolute bedrest for the old gentleman, no company allowed. So he'd repeatedly reminded Vincent to tell Rachel he had everything in hand.

He hoped. One more hour. Then his father's coach was coming for him.

He rang the small brass bell on his desk. He'd become quite proprietary about it, discovering an organizational bent he'd never known he'd possessed. Graded papers were stacked neatly for Rachel's perusal. A cache of shiny apples, and one confiscated slingshot, was on top of them. He was, apparently, a popular fellow. It had been touch and go at the beginning, but he took more pride in the children's capitulation than he'd ever done with his troops.

"Attention!"

Pencils dropped, books slammed shut. His little crew sat up, hands folded, eyes fixed on him in expectation.

"Catch!" Nine pairs of hands raised, one of the children being absent, having a putrid sore throat. Henry pitched an apple, aiming at the littlest children in the front row. His nemesis Mary Ann was the victor.

"Mary Ann, how can you make one apple feed two children?"

"Cut it in 'alf, Captain C." It had been easier to dispense with the "Lord" altogether. The class was bloodthirsty and Henry had spent a good portion of time discussing various battles in their geography and history lessons.

"Very good. Come on up." The little girl handed him her prize, which Henry used his knife to slice into two pieces. "Now then, Mary Ann, I expect you have more than one friend."

She nodded solemnly.

"What shall we do?"

"Cut each piece in half again."

"Very well. How many friends will that feed?"

"Four!" Charlie Motley cried out.

Henry remembered getting rapped in the knuckles every time he gave a wrong answer. He didn't believe in that—it wouldn't teach anyone anything but to damage their hands and develop a hatred for schools and teachers. And why punish the boy for speaking out and trying?

"You are partly right, Charlie. There will indeed be four pieces, but if you give them all away to friends, what will be left for you?"

"None."

"What's the mathematical word for none?"

"Zero!" A whole host of voices called out.

"So, Charlie, how much of the apple are you willing to give away? Remember, you're a hungry lad."

Charlie grinned. "Three of them, sir. Three-fourths of the apple."

"Excellent," said Henry. He cut the apple up. "But I see nine children here, and only four apple slices. What should I do?"

The children discussed dividing up the apple nine ways. Henry invited one of the older girls he trusted with his knife to come up and try to turn four pieces into nine.

After making a juicy mess and just eight slices, she licked her fingers and grinned up at him. "What about the other apples on your desk?"

"Yes, we'll start again. How can three friends share an apple?"

It was trickier to cut the fruit into thirds, trickier still to cut each third in three even pieces. While his student was cutting, some of the other children came to the chalk board to draw apples and show the problem with numbers. The littler ones just looked hungry.

"Knowing how to multiply and divide will help you with cooking, you know."

"You mean we'll make applesauce?" Charlie asked.

Tommy snorted. "Boys don't cook!"

"I beg to differ," Henry said. "It's a useful skill to know your way around a kitchen or a campfire. Think of an army cook, who, Tommy, is most certainly a man. A very important one. His unit depends on him—an army travels on its stomach. He could feed a hundred soldiers if he knows how to take a recipe that feeds four and multiply the ingredients." He passed out the unsanitary apple slices and wiped his hands on his handkerchief.

"Now then. It is our last day of the term, and you are to have three whole weeks of holiday. Miss Everett suggested we have our lunch, and the rest of these apples, out of doors, and perhaps have some races. Charlie, you may ring the dismissal bell, since you were willing to take a guess on an answer. Risk should be rewarded."

The children spread out under the biggest tree in the schoolyard, the very same one Henry had had to climb on his first day to disentangle naughty Holly Smith from its branches. There was no tree-climbing today, just eating and a few relay races. The maths lesson continued as they figured out how to divide themselves into even teams. Henry sat in the shade, proud he'd survived.

Charlie rang the bell when the time came, and Henry shook each child's hand as they went through the gate. He hoped they wouldn't forget everything they'd learned—three weeks was a long time in a child's life.

His, too. He'd been in Puddling for three weeks and everything had changed.

He returned to the schoolroom and sat down at the desk. Pulling a piece of lined paper from Rachel's drawer, he began to write. He poured his heart—he had one!—out on the page, and slipped the letter to Rachel between worksheets. He wished he could be there to watch her face as she read it.

And hoped she could read his handwriting.

***

School would reopen in a few weeks for the summer term, and adjourn again in July. Rachel was responsible for tidying the school building as well as teaching, and she trudged down the hill to see what sort of mess the building had been left in.

Despite everything, for some reason Sir Bertram had taken pity upon her and she still had her job. Things were very unsettled at present in Puddling, and her tenure was one less thing for the governors and school committee to worry about.

Thank goodness, for she was not getting married after all.

There had been no word from Henry. His father's traveling coach had rolled into town the last day of classes and he'd climbed in with no objection. Stonecrop Cottage was now being readied for its next inhabitant, who was due any day.

There was worry that several Guests on the waiting list might not be sent here after all. The Marquess of Harland had great influence, but at least it wasn't Rachel's fault that Puddling had fallen into some disrepute.

She was impervious to the scents and sounds of the perfect cloud-free day. It may as well have been raining all around her, her spirits were so low. Who knew what chaos she'd find in her classroom? She'd seen a few of her students in church the past two Sundays, and they had been full of Henry's wild war stories, wondering if he would come back and help her teach.

Not bloody likely. He was now in training to be a marquess, much too exalted for the likes of Puddling.

Drat. She was crying again, for all the good it would do. Even "old Vincent" had given her a sympathetic look from the pulpit. Rachel was certain his Prodigal Son sermon referenced Henry.

Rachel was trying to trust in the Lord as Vincent suggested after the service, but just now she felt unequal to the task.

The classroom was, surprisingly, orderly, except for a sticky spot on the demonstration table next to her desk. She scrubbed at it ineffectually, her tears adding to the soapy water of the bucket.

With the windows shut, the aroma of apples permeated the air. Odd. The scent was more than pleasant, but the room was too hot and stuffy to work in. Rachel put her rags down and threw the windows open. A fresh breeze stirred the children's papers on her desk, and she caught them before they fell to the floor.

When she saw the children next, their mistakes would be three weeks old. Rachel was a big believer in fresh beginnings, and she tossed the old schoolwork into the trashcan. She'd have to start fresh too.

Chapter 45

"What's that you've got there, Dad?" She knew perfectly well what it was, but had yet to get a straight answer from her father.

Pete Everett folded up the paper and stuck it in a book. It was unusual for him to get mail, and he'd been fiddling with that letter ever since he got it the other day.

"Just something from a friend."

"Oh? Who?" She'd asked him before, and hoped he'd forgotten she had.

"An old army chum." He plucked the plaid blanket off his legs and tossed it over a bush. "I'm hotter than hell."

It *was* warm. The garden was wild without her father's careful daily tending and heavily perfumed. "I bet you're glad you got permission to get out of bed," Rachel said, smiling fondly at him. He'd been a bear for days, complaining that Dr. Oakley was an old woman, far too conservative in his diagnosis and treatment.

"That's not all I've got permission for. How would you feel about that trip to London?"

Rachel's first inclination was to say no, not only because she worried such a journey would be too much for her father. She was...in a mood.

It was very hard to be positive. Here she had free time, yet she couldn't settle onto anything. And every time she stepped foot onto New Street she knew her neighbors were talking about her. Feeling sorry for her.

She really couldn't abide that.

"Dr. Oakley thinks it's a good idea. Says it will cheer us up."

"Really?" Rachel asked doubtfully. She didn't believe anything would cheer her up, at least not in the immediate future. Ten years from now, who knew?

"Aye. And Vincent's to come with us."

She plucked a daisy and pulled off its petals. He loves me not. "I'm not interested in your matchmaking, Dad. You know Vincent is spoken for, even if it's a secret."

Eventually Greta would be free. Someone would have their happily ever after.

Pete chuckled. "I wouldn't want a parson in the family. Never did, despite what the local gossipmongers have tried to promote between you two. Why, I'd have to be on my best behavior all the time, never say bloody or fuck, and that would get tiring pretty fast. But Vincent has some business in the city, and wondered if we'd like to come with him for a day or three. He can help out if either one of us decides to faint at the excitement of it all."

"Are you sure Dr. Oakley approves?"

"Would I lie to my only daughter?"

He very well might.

"I don't know, Dad." She'd talk to the doctor herself.

"Vincent's leaving the day after tomorrow. We need to let him know."

Her holiday was more than half over. She'd done nothing but mope and mend so far.

She *should* go. If it was safe for her father's health. Maybe she'd see something she could use in her lessons.

"I'll think about it."

Her father clapped his hands. That woke Rufus up from his sleep.

"Oh, dear. What about the dog?"

"Ham will take him. It's all settled."

"You're really set on going, aren't you?"

"It will do us both good, Rachel. It's time you saw the sights." Her father stood and reached for the cane that was now to accompany him everywhere. "Nature calls, my dear."

She watched as he made his way on the slate path to the privy. His step was sure, even jaunty.

In a trice she snatched up the book and unfolded the letter. The handwriting on it was practically illegible, and from what she could read had nothing but a list of famous battles and commanders on it. It made no sense, and was unlike any sort of letter she'd ever seen. She stuffed it back into Gibbon's *The History of the Decline and Fall of the Roman Empire,* regretting she's been so nosy. The two old soldiers were probably playing at codes.

***

Two days later, she was on the train to London—in a first class carriage! Her father had insisted on splurging, and Rachel worried if he had in fact hit his head when he fell. She was to have a new dress from Harrods, a department store he'd read about, once they got there, and they were staying at Claridge's Hotel. Claridge's! Rachel was afraid they'd be laughed out of the lobby in their country clothes. But her father had shown her the wire confirming their reservation. The telegram was safely in her handbag in case a snooty concierge attempted to turn them away,

Vincent would not be staying with them, but with a friend. He was in alarmingly good spirits, and Rachel wondered if perhaps he was going to have an assignation with Greta.

It was none of her business. It might be spring, the birds and the bees busy, but there was no lover in London for Rachel Everett.

They were met at the station by a liveried driver in a magnificent carriage belonging to the hotel. Rachel dropped her handbag right onto the pavement in shock. The man bent elegantly to pick it up.

"You don't want to misplace your purse, Miss. Hang on tight to it—there are thieves and pickpockets about."

Precisely why coming to London was such a bad idea. The Everetts were honest folk—usually, unless it came to shovels and fibbing—and didn't belong here.

"Dad, I can't do this," she whispered.

"'Course you can! You've nothing to be ashamed of. Prettiest girl on the train, you were."

"No, I mean the…carriage! I—I—I'm afraid!" It was much too plush, shiny and…*new*. Cinderella would have been right at home in it.

"Pooh. We haven't that far to go, and if it wasn't safe, the hotel wouldn't offer its services to their guests. Don't want to kill us, do they, before we pay the shot? Get in. The chap's holding the door for you."

Their battered baggage, pitiful as it was, had already been stowed in the back of the carriage. There was nothing to be done but put her foot on the step, sit down in the smooth leather seat and hold onto her hat.

Her father seemed to enjoy the brief ride very much, poking her with his cane to make her open her eyes and see the buildings fly by. She'd have to take his word for it. The sounds of London were enough to stimulate her—the frightened whinnies of horses, the bleating of carriage horns, the multitudes who were embroiled in a conversation where all the words were shouted.

And the smell! Horse droppings. Humanity. Rachel was a country girl, but she felt queasy.

Fortunately they arrived at the stately hotel in jig time, its brick façade bright in the sunlight. It was the highest building Rachel had ever seen. She tried not to gawk and strain her neck as the doorman summoned a porter to retrieve their suitcases from the carriage.

"Sergeant Everett? We have been expecting you. I hope you had a pleasant journey. Your guest is waiting for you, and your suite is ready."

She tugged her father's tweed-covered arm. "Guest? What does he mean, Dad? And suite? What on earth are you thinking of? Have you gone completely mad?" They'd be broke before tomorrow's breakfast. She was already making plans for them to check into a much less expensive hotel once she talked some sense into him.

"Don't worry about a thing, Rachel. Be a good girl and let me go. You're causing a scene. Go sit down somewhere and be comfortable."

Comfortable! Most unlikely. She found a squashy chair in the lobby and reluctantly dropped into it while her father checked them into the hotel. He spoke too softly for her to hear anything useful, but she was becoming very uneasy. How could they afford such luxury? Claridge's was absolutely stunning, with every amenity, according to the brochures on the marble table in front of her. If she'd felt gauche before, she was positively stupid now.

Her father returned, leaning on his cane. "I'm going to wet my whistle in the bar, my girl. You go on up with the porter and get yourself settled." He dropped a key in her lap.

"You're meeting your friend?"

"Just so. Run along, and try to relax."

Relax! As if she could. The very word was an irritant. But she did need freshening up, and her good shoes pinched her toes. It would be heaven to kick them off and loosen her corset.

She followed the porter and the baggage cart to a bank of elevators, where another young man in the Claridge's livery operated the lift. The close of the door made her feel trapped, and the rapid ascent made her heart drop to her sore feet. This day had too many firsts altogether. But at least she wasn't climbing up the stairs. She handed the key to the porter and he unlocked the door of their rooms.

And then she took one look inside and slid to the floor in a faint.

Chapter 46

"Rachel. Darling." He waved the smelling salts under her nose and she shuddered.

There were too many people in the room—the porter, the hotel doctor, someone from the front desk. Pete Everett, too, who was supposed to stay out of the way while Henry surprised Rachel.

Well, he guessed she was plenty surprised.

"Wh-what are you doing here?" She was parchment white, except for the blue lips. It would have been a fascinating medical study except he wanted his fiancée well.

Henry patted his pocket. "I have a special license. Vincent will marry us tomorrow if it's all right with you."

She tried to get off his lap but he was having none of it. "I say, Pete, can you get these fellows out of here? Drinks are on me."

"You heard the viscount," Pete said in a voice he once must have used in battle. "Out!"

Pete failed to follow his own edict. Leaning over the couple, he said "You two better not disappoint me. That's an order."

Henry gave him a left-handed salute since his right hand was busy keeping Rachel from escaping. "Yes, sir."

Rachel waited till the door closed. "I don't understand. You left me. You *left* me!" She gave him a little shove. Ah, there was his Rachel, feeling more the thing.

"You never got my note? I explained the plan in complete detail." Or as much detail as he'd managed to come up with at the end of the school day.

"What note?"

"I put it on your desk with the children's papers."

Rachel blinked. "I—I threw all the papers away. I could barely see for the tears."

He wiped away the ones that coursed down her cheeks now. Days had passed, and she hadn't known he loved her. She must have wished him to the devil every waking minute.

"Didn't that idiot Vincent tell you I had everything in hand?"

Rachel sniffed. "I thought he meant about the school. Or Greta. Sir Bertram told everybody your father made you change his mind about marrying me."

"As if he could! I can't believe you didn't have faith in me!"

"How was I to know? You never even tried to see me those last three days, and then you disappeared. I didn't know about any note."

"I am sorry for that. But I wanted no word to get back to my father. Mrs. Grace is his spy, you know. And maybe his mistress, although I could be wrong about that. Apparently he had an encounter with a bull in a field when he went walking early one morning and he—oh, never mind."

Rachel frowned in confusion, but he wasn't going to waste precious time talking about the pater.

"Anyway, I wanted nothing to interfere with my father helping Greta. He's quite chivalrous, you know, but if he thought he was being defied, he would have refused to speak to the archbishop. And the attorneys— there's a whole hive of them on Greta's team. It's all in train now, and nothing can stop it. Briefs filed, court dates appointed. It's amazing what a powerful man can do in a very short amount of time if he wants to. She should be free by the end of the year. Poorer, too. Her hideous husband is still making things difficult, but he'll be bought off in the end if someone doesn't shoot him first. No one messes with the Marquess of Harland."

"Or Viscount Challoner." She nestled into his shoulder. "I thought I'd never see you again."

"Poor lamb. I couldn't write to you—the damned post office is run by those Stanchfield people and Vincent told me they steam open suspicious letters on orders from the Foundation. But I did contact your father."

"That was *your* letter! But it was gibberish! How could you know he'd understand?"

"Your dad studies history. I knew he'd figure it out, and Vincent got one too. Only his had Bible verses." Henry thought he'd been pretty damned clever.

Rachel almost smiled, but then she shook her head. "You're going back on your word to your father if you marry me."

"I never gave it. Oh, I may have inclined my head when he made his ridiculous demand, but that was his interpretation of acceptance. Who can say? I might have just had a crick in my neck. Or was avoiding a bumblebee."

"In Sir Bertram's dining room? Oh, Henry! He'll be so angry!"

"Will he? I wonder. I think he knows I've changed, and for the better. And however he shows it, he wants me to be happy. You make me happy, Rachel."

The tears were flooding now, and he kissed them as they slid down her pale cheeks. He would pink her up again. Everywhere. The past few weeks had been hell for both of them.

"School starts in a week."

"Hand in your notice. You're going to be Lady Challoner, and we might be in…Switzerland? Would you like that?"

"I hardly know. I've never been anywhere," Rachel said, smiling through her tears.

"I'd like to show you the world." Not the sad, difficult parts, though if he knew Rachel, she'd want to fix them. She'd never be satisfied unless she was taking care of someone.

Soon she would be taking care of *him,* and Henry swore by all that was holy, he'd take the very best care of her too.

***

Henry's first opportunity to do so arrived the next morning. He had taken a risk, but risk had its reward, did it not? He'd said so to Charlie Motley anyhow.

He wanted to make things right. Proper. Henry had turned over a new leaf—hell, he was a whole new tree.

The Marquess of Harland was admitted to the suite by Henry's valet, who was relieved that he still had a job and a young gentleman to do for. The man had had fussed so around Henry since he'd come back from Puddling that he almost longed for Mrs. Grace.

"What's this about, Henry?" He held the telegram out, as if Henry might have forgotten he wrote it.

"I'm glad you came, sir. I didn't want to have the most important day of my life without you."

The pater's eyes narrowed. "What nonsense are you up to now?"

"No nonsense, just sense. I am marrying Rachel Everett today." Henry waved his arm at the baskets of white roses that decorated his suite. Pete had already been in, and didn't think much of London florists.

His father sat down on a brocade sofa. "I see."

This was not the reaction Henry expected. "You do?"

"I had a rather eloquent letter the other day from the young lady's father. Peter, I believe?"

"Y-yes." Henry sat down too.

"I may have misjudged her. Greta sang her praises too. She was very kind to her during that difficult time in Puddling."

The pater had fatherly feelings for Greta, and was casting about ways to help old Vincent too. Greta had confessed all, but the pater was *not* going to steal the vicar from Henry's soldiers' retreat.

"So I have your blessing?"

"You don't need it. As you've pointed out often enough, you're of age, you have your own funds, and certainly your own ideas. Your scheme for your troubled soldiers shows great merit. I'm proud of you, Henry."

"Thank you," Henry said, when he'd finally found his voice.

"I think Miss Everett will keep you in line. If she can put a marquess in his place, dealing with a mere viscount should be easy."

"She doesn't think she's suitable, Father, although I'm pretty sure she loves me," Henry blurted out. He didn't want his father to make Rachel feel inadequate on this day of all days.

"Pretty sure, eh? Still pressing your luck."

"But I *am* lucky. Undeservedly so. Rachel is…well, she's Rachel. I'd like for you to get to know her."

His father nodded. "She shan't hear any criticism from me. She may not be a typical Challoner bride, but perhaps that's a good thing. None of them were as sweet as your mother." The marquess reached into his pocket and brought out a velvet box. "I expect you've already bought a ring, but your wife should have this necklace. My grandmother wore it on her wedding day. Awful woman, but the diamonds can't be sneezed at."

Henry walked across the room, his heart much lighter. Even his foot felt better. "Thank you. I hope to make her as happy as you made Mama."

His father rose and, by the gods, hugged him. "Do better, my boy. There's always room for improvement."

Epilogue

June 1881

They'd been to Paris. Rome. Florence. And now Venice, the most beautiful city Henry had ever seen. His wife sat straight up in the gondola, looking worried that if she breathed too deeply—or breathed at all—they'd tip over.

If Henry had planned this as a romantic interlude—and he had—he'd failed miserably. Rachel was tense and pale, and no half-baked singing from the gondolier made headway to squelch her terror.

And she'd been ill this morning—too much wine and pasta the night before, poor girl. The foreign food had not agreed with her the last few days.

"Relax, my love."

"Henry, you're an intelligent man. Don't you know when you ask someone to relax, you only drive them deeper into distress?" she hissed.

"We are not going to fall into the Grand Canal. Or if we do, we wouldn't be the first. I'm sure the gondolier would save us. Stick out a paddle at least," Henry teased.

"No fall, no fall, no drown," their gondolier said, tipping his hat. He was not fluent in English, but probably had had enough anxious passengers so these words were in his vocabulary.

Rachel's face lost the little color it had. "I can't swim."

"I'll teach you when we get home. When we have a home. Someplace with a pond, or maybe by a river, where the children can sail an armada of wooden boats."

"That will be dangerous! What if they fall in?"

"I'll teach *them* to swim. Their nanny too. Here, lean on me." He slipped his arm around her and felt her shiver.

"A nanny. I cannot imagine it."

"You'll want the help. We're going to have a lot of children if we are so blessed, Rachel—a whole classroom full," he teased. Pray God their children would be nothing like the little Puddling people. He was *not* climbing up a tree to retrieve someone again, especially when Holly bit him when he was trying to be heroic.

Rachel grew very still beside him. "About that."

"About what? Never tell me you miss teaching school."

"No, how can I? You've kept me much too busy on our honeymoon. But I think, that is I'm almost certain, that...that..."

Henry grew equally still. "Rachel, what on earth are you trying to say?"

"That Sunday, the first time we made love...I think we made a baby, too."

Henry gaped at her. He'd been careful then, hadn't he?

Maybe not careful enough.

But he couldn't be sorry. He had a beautiful wife, and hopefully a child on the way. His father had forgiven him and probably liked Rachel more than he liked his own son. His life could not possibly improve more even if he spent his entire life following the Puddling Rehabilitation Rules, whatever they were.

"You clever, gorgeous girl!" Henry held her close and kissed her.

Much relieved, the gondolier resumed his song. He had a fine tenor voice, if he did say so himself. There would be no more talk of drowning while those crazy *Inglese* fell under the spell of *Venezia.*

Be sure not to miss the next book in Maggie
Robinson's Costwold Confidental series

SEDUCING MR. SYKES

Keeping reading for a special sneak peek.

A Lyrical e-book on sale soon!

Chapter 1

"It's Lady Maribel all over again," the grocer Frank Stanchfield muttered to his wife, checking the lock to his back room. "How the girl discovered the telegraph machine is a mystery."

Except it wasn't such a mystery, really. Lady Sarah Marchmain—"Sadie" to her late mama and very few friends—had eyes, after all, and there it was behind an open alley window, gleaming on a worn oak desk. She had climbed in, her tartan trousers very convenient for hoisting oneself into the building. After being caught trying to send a message to who knows who, she was now unrepentantly inspecting the jars of candy on the shop counter.

She might try to steal some of it, if only the shopkeepers would stop hovering over her.

"Bite your tongue!" Mrs. Stanchfield whispered, looking over nervously at Sadie. Apparently no one wanted another Lady Maribel de Winter in Puddling. The first had been bad enough. Sadie had heard of her in snatches from the villagers, and the woman's portrait hung in the parish hall. Her wicked reputation had outlived her, even if her decades of good works once she married had mitigated some of it. She had been a wild young thing who would have made Napoleon quake in his boots.

Or take her to bed. Lady Maribel had been, according to gossip, irresistible to men. Fortunately her husband, a local baronet called Sir Colin Sykes, had taken her in hand as best he could once they were married.

Sadie was determined never to be taken in hand.

Puddling was known as a famous reputation-restorer, a place to rusticate and recalibrate. Prominent British families had sent their difficult relatives here for almost eighty years, Lady Maribel among the first to be gently incarcerated within its limits in 1807, according to the elderly vicar's wife, who seemed to know everything about everyone dating back to William the Conqueror.

Now it was Sadie's turn to be gently incarcerated, and she didn't like it one bit.

The village had a spotless reputation. It was a last resort before a harsher hospital, or worse, killing one's own offspring. Or parent. Lady Sarah Marchmain had angered her father so thoroughly that they'd come to blows. When the Duke of Islesford dropped her off, he had been sporting a significant black eye.

Well-deserved, in her opinion.

Sadie's own eyes were unbruised and light green, the color of beryl, or so her numerous suitors had said. Occasionally they threw in jade or jasper—it was all so much nonsense. Right now she was examining the penny candy in a glass jar, lots of shiny, jewel-like drops that looked so very tempting. Sweet, edible rubies and citrine, emeralds and onyx. Frank Stanchfield hustled over to the counter and screwed the lid on tighter.

She licked her lips. Unfortunately, she didn't have a penny to her name. She was entirely dependent on her housekeeper Mrs. Grace to dole out a pitiful allowance every Friday, and Friday was millions of days away. Sadie had spent the last of her money on a cinnamon bun earlier and had reveled in every bite.

Her father's draconian restrictions were designed to sting. Or so he thought. Sadie didn't really mind being impoverished and hungry in Puddling-on-the-Wold. It meant she was not about to be auctioned off to Lord Roderick Charlton, or any other idiot her idiot father owed money to.

The Duke of Islesford's taste in men and luck at cards was, to put it bluntly, execrable.

So far Sadie had overstayed her visit by one week. Originally consigned to her cottage for twenty-eight days, she had somehow not managed to be "cured" in that time.

Rehabilitated.

Restored.

Brought to reason.

Knuckle under was more like it. She was *not* getting married.

In fact, she'd like to stay in Puddling forever. It was very restful. Quiet. The little lending library was surprisingly well-stocked, and she'd gotten a lot of reading done between lectures from the prosy ancient vicar who instructed her daily. She also helped Mrs. Grace keep the cottage up to a ducal daughter's snuff.

Despite the fact that Sadie had no interest in becoming a wife, she was remarkably domestic. It came of hanging about the kitchens of Marchmain Castle, she supposed. The servants had been her only friends when she was a little girl and she'd been eager to help them.

All that had changed after she was presented to the Queen at seventeen, wearing those ridiculous hoops and feathers that threatened to put out someone's eye. Suddenly, Sadie became a commodity, a bargaining chip to improve her father's ailing finances. A surprising number of gentlemen—if you could call them that, since most men were absolute, avaricious, thoughtless pigs—were interested in acquiring a tall, red-headed, blue-blooded, sharp-tongued and two-fisted duke's daughter as wife. For the past five years, she'd avoided them with alacrity, aplomb, and those aforementioned fists.

Needless to say, her reputation was cemented in ruination.

It amused Sadie that her father was using the last of his funds to lock her away here in this very expensive Puddling prison, hoping that she would change her mind, acquiesce and marry the one man who remained steadfastly interested.

Not bloody likely.

She touched the glass jar with longing.

"What may we help you with, Lady Sarah?"

The poor grocer sounded scared to death. His wife hid behind him.

Sadie batted her lashes. Sometimes this feminine trick worked, although these Puddling people seemed remarkably impervious to charm. They were hardened souls, harboring the odd, uncooperative and unwanted scions of society for a hefty fee, believing that being cruel to be kind was the only way.

"Do forgive my transgression, Mr. Stanchfield. I so longed to communicate with my old governess, Miss Mackenzie. Miss Mac, as I so affectionately call her. I found a book on telegraphy in the library and wondered if I had any aptitude for it," she lied. Science in all its forms confounded her. In truth, she'd read nothing but gothic romances since her arrival, very much enjoying the fraying sixty-year-old books written by an anonymous baroness.

Moreover, Sadie's old governess had been dead for six years and had been an absolute Tartar in life. There had been little affection on her part,

Sadie thought ruefully. The woman was at this moment no doubt giving the Devil a lesson on evil and grading him harshly.

"You know that's forbidden, miss. No telegrams, no letters. Perhaps when you are r-r-released, you may visit with the lady. A r-reason for your good behavior, what?"

Goodness, she was causing the poor fellow to stutter. She stilled her lashes.

"Ah." Sadie gave a dramatic sigh. "But I just can't seem to get the hang of it. Being Puddling-perfect, that is. Every time I get close, something seems to happen."

Like stealing Ham Ross's wheelbarrow full of pumpkins. It had been very difficult to push her loot uphill, and so many of the bloody orange things chose to roll out and smash along the road.

Or turning up in church in her tartan trousers...her *stolen* tartan trousers. Some poor Puddlingite was foolish enough to hang them on a clothesline to tempt her. After some tailoring—Sadie was handy with a needle—they fit her slender waist and long legs as if they were made for her.

Her father had always wanted a son. Instead her horrible cousin George would be the next duke, and Sadie would lose the only home—well, castle—she'd ever known.

It wasn't fair. She sighed again.

"Here, now, Lady Sarah. I don't suppose I'll miss a few boiled sweets." Mr. Stanchfield relented and unscrewed the jar, his wife looking disapproving behind him. He filled a paper twist with not nearly enough, and passed them to her.

Sadie saw her opportunity for well-deserved drama. Any chance to appear happily unhinged, so she might stay here in Puddling just a little longer. Dropping to the floor on her tartan-covered knees, she howled.

She had been practicing howling at night once her housekeeper Mrs. Grace went home. Her neighbors were under the impression a stray dog was in heat in the village, perhaps even a pack of them.

"Oh! You are too good to me! I shall remember this always!" She snuffled and snorted, slipping a red candy into her mouth. Red always tasted best.

"A polite thank you would do just as well."

The voice was chilly. Sadie looked up from her self-inflicted chest-pounding and the candy fell out of her open mouth.

Good heavens. She had never seen this man before in all the walking she was made to do up and down the hills for her daily exercise. Where had he been hiding? He was *beautiful.*

No, not beautiful exactly. His haughty expression was too harsh for beauty. Compelling, perhaps. Arresting.

But, she reminded herself, he was a man, and therefore wanting. Lacking. Probably annoying. Not probably—certainly. Lady Sarah Jane Marchmain was twenty-one years old and had more than enough experience with men in her short lifetime.

The man was reaching a gloveless hand to her to help her up, but it didn't look quite clean. Something green was under his fingernails—paint? Plant material? Sadie made a leap of faith and gripped it anyway, crunching her candy underfoot when he lifted her to her full height.

He was still taller than she was.

Not lacking there. Not lacking physically anywhere that she could see.

His hair was brown, curly and unruly, his eyebrows darker and formidable. His nose was strong and straight, his lips full, his face bronzed from the sun. His eyes—oh, his eyes. Blue was an inadequate adjective. Cerulean? Sapphire? Aquamarine? She'd have to consult a thesaurus.

But they weren't kind.

She found herself curtseying, her hand still firmly in his.

"Thank you, sir, for coming to my rescue." She fluttered her eyelashes again.

"You were in no danger on the floor. Mrs. Stanchfield sweeps it thrice a day. One could eat off it, it's so immaculate." He dropped Sadie's hand and kicked the crushed candy aside.

The grocer's wife pinked. "Thank you, Mr. Sykes."

Sykes. That was the name of the family the infamous Lady Maribel married into. Interesting.

"I only speak the truth, madam."

Sadie considered whether she should fall to the floor again. It would be fun to gauge this Mr. Sykes's strength if she pretended to swoon. Would he pick her up and hold her to his manly chest? Whisper assurances in her ear? Smooth loose tendrils of hair behind her pins?

But perhaps he'd just leave her there to rot. He wasn't even looking at her anymore.

Sadie was used to being looked at. For one thing, she was hard to miss. At nearly six feet, she towered over most men. Her flaming hair was another beacon, her skin pearlescent, her ample bosom startling on such a slender frame.

She had been chased by men mercilessly, even after she had made it crystal clear she had no interest. These past years had tested her wits and firmed her resolve. She was mistress of her own heart, body, and mind, and determined to remain so.

Mr. Sykes probably knew that—apparently everyone in Puddling had received a dossier on her. She'd come across a grease-stained one at the bakeshop tucked under a tray of Bakewell tarts, and had tucked it into her pocket for quiet perusal, along with one delicious raspberry pastry. Theft was apparently in her blood.

It had been most informative. The dossier, not the tart. Sadie had been gleeful reading an account of her past recalcitrance. She rather admired the clever ways she'd gone about subverting her father's plans for her— she'd forgotten half of them.

It had meant, however, that she had to exercise creativity in Puddling and not repeat her previous pranks. No sheep in the dining room. No bladder filled with beet juice tossed out the window. No punching fiancés or fathers.

There was only the one father, but Sadie had endured several fiancés. The latest, Lord Roderick Charlton, was getting impatient. He'd given her father quite a lot of money to secure her hand. To be fair, he'd tried to woo Sadie with credible effort.

There wasn't anything really wrong with Roderick, she supposed. But there wasn't anything right about him either.

If Sadie could just resist the pressure to marry, she'd come into a substantial fortune when she turned twenty-five. She wouldn't have to turn it over to some man, and her father wouldn't be able to touch it. She could live her life just as she liked. She might even buy herself a small castle, if one could be found. One that wouldn't fall down around her ears. One that had working fireplaces and no rats.

However—and this was a *huge* however— the Duke of Islesford was threatening to have her declared incompetent, seize her funds and lock her away in a most unpleasant private hospital. Sadie did not think it was an idle threat, and to some, it might look as if she deserved to be there.

She was much too old now for the tricks she'd played, and four years was a very, very long time to stall. Sadie was beginning to realize she hadn't done herself any favors with the pumpkins or the trousers or the howling.

But she couldn't succumb—she just couldn't. No matter how many times Mr. Fitzmartin, the elderly vicar, reminded her of a proper woman's place—as helper to her husband, silent in church, subordinate, obedient— she felt her fingers close into a fist.

About the Author

Maggie Robinson didn't know she wanted to write until she woke up in the middle of the night once really annoyed with her husband. Instead of smothering him with a pillow, she decided to get up and write—to create the perfect man—at least on a computer screen. Only to discover that fictional males can be just as resistant to direction as her husband. The upside is that she's finally using her English degree and is still married to her original, imperfect hero. Since she's imperfect, too, that makes them a perfect match. Until her midnight keyboarding, she had been a teacher, librarian, newspaper reporter, administrative assistant to two non-profits, community volunteer, and mother of four in seven different states. Now Maggie can call herself a romance writer in Maine. There's nothing she likes better than writing about people who make mistakes, but don't let the mistakes make them.

Visit her on the web at maggierobinson.net.

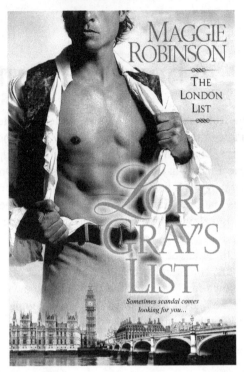

From duchesses to chamber maids, everybody's reading it. Each Tuesday, *The London List* appears, filled with gossip and scandal, offering job postings and matches for the lovelorn—and most enticing of all, telling the tales and selling the wares a more modest publication wouldn't touch…

The creation of Evangeline Ramsey, The London List saved her and her ailing father from destitution. But the paper has given Evie more than financial relief. As its publisher, she lives as a man, dressed in masculine garb, free to pursue and report whatever she likes—especially the latest disgraces besmirching Lord Benton Gray. It's only fair that she hang his dirty laundry, given that it was his youthful ardor that put her off marriage for good…

Lord Gray—Ben—isn't about to stand by while all of London laughs at his peccadilloes week after week. But once he discovers that the publisher is none other than pretty Evie Ramsey with her curls lopped short, his worries turn to desires—and not a one of them fit to print…

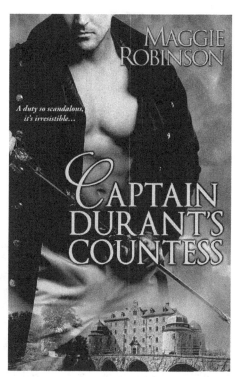

Tucked amid the pages of The London List, *a newspaper that touts the city's scandals, is a vaguely-worded ad for an intriguing job—one that requires a most wickedly uncommon candidate…*

Maris has always been grateful that her marriage to the aging Earl of Kelby saved her from spinsterhood. Though their union has been more peaceful than passionate, she and the earl have spent ten happy years together. But his health is quickly failing, and unless Maris produces an heir, Kelby's conniving nephew will inherit his estate. And if the earl can't get the job done himself, he'll find another man who can…

Captain Reynold Durant is known for both his loyalty to the Crown and an infamous record of ribaldry. Yet despite a financial worry of his own, even he is reluctant to accept Kelby's lascivious assignment—until he meets the beautiful, beguiling Maris. Incited by duty and desire, the captain may be just the man they are looking for. But while he skillfully takes Maris to the heights of ecstasy she has longed for, she teaches him something even more valuable and unexpected…

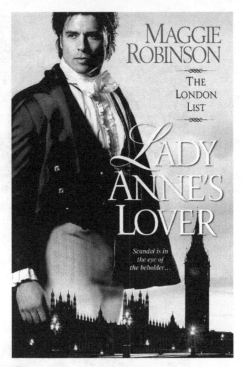

Lady Imaculata Anne Egremont has appeared in the scandalous pages of the London List often enough. The reading public is so bored with her nonsense, she couldn't make news now unless she took a vow of chastity. But behind her naughty hijinks is a terrible fear. It's time the List helped her. With a quick scan through its job postings and a few whacks at her ridiculous name, she's off to keep house for a bachelor veteran as plain Anne Mont.

Major Gareth Ripton-Jones is dangerously young and handsome on the face of it, but after losing his love and his arm in short order, he is also too deep in his cups to notice that his suspiciously young housekeeper is suspiciously terrible at keeping house. Until, that is, her sharp tongue and her burnt coffee penetrate even his misery--and the charm underneath surprises them both. Trust the worst cook in Wales to propose a most unexpected solution to his troubles. . .

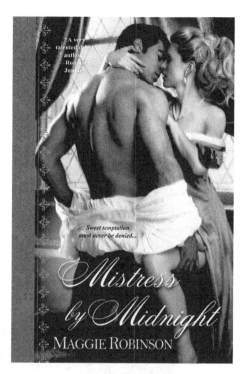

First comes seduction...

As children, Desmond Ryland, Marquess of Conover, and Laurette Vincent were inseparable. As young adults, their friendship blossomed into love. But then fate intervened, sending them down different paths. Years later, Con still can't forget his beautiful Laurette. Now he's determined to make her his forever. There's just one problem. Laurette keeps refusing his marriage proposals. Throwing honor to the wind, Con decides that the only way Laurette will wed him is if he thoroughly seduces her...

Then comes marriage...

Laurette's pulse still quickens every time she thinks of Con and the scorching passion they once shared. She aches to taste the pleasure Con offers her. But she knows she can't. For so much has happened since they were last lovers. But how long can she resist the consuming desire that demands to be obeyed...?

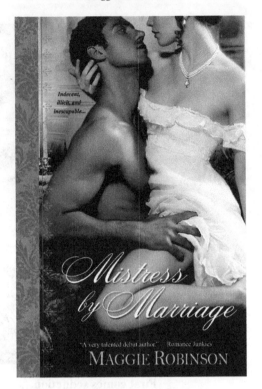

Too late for cold feet

Baron Edward Christie prided himself on his reputation for even temper-
ament and reserve. That was before he met Caroline Parker. Wedding a
scandalous beauty by special license days after they met did not inspire
respect for his sangfroid. Moving her to a notorious lovebirds' nest
as punishment for her flighty nature was perhaps also a blow. And of
course talk has gotten out of his irresistible clandestine visits. Christie
must put his wife aside—if only he can get her out of his blood first.

Too hot to refuse...

Caroline Parker was prepared to hear the worst: that her husband had
determined to divorce her, spare them both the torture of passion they
can neither tame nor escape. But his plan is wickeder than any she's ever
heard. Life as his wife is suffocating. But she cannot resist becoming her
own husband's mistress...

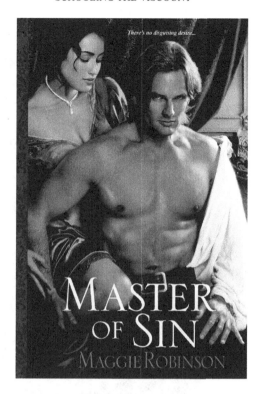

Flying from sin…

Andrew Rossiter has used his gorgeous body and angelic face for all they're worth—shocking the proper, seducing the willing, and pleasuring the wealthy. But with a tiny son depending on him for rescue, suddenly discretion is far more important than desire. He'll have to bury his past and quench his desires—fast. And he'll have to find somewhere his deliciously filthy reputation hasn't yet reached…

…into seduction

Miss Gemma Peartree seems like a plain, virginal governess. True, she has a sharp wit and a sharper tongue, but handsome Mr. Ross wouldn't notice Gemma herself. Or so she hopes. No matter how many sparks fly between them, she has too much to hide to catch his eye. But with the storms of a Scottish winter driving them together, it will be hard enough to keep her secrets. Keeping her hands to herself might prove entirely impossible…

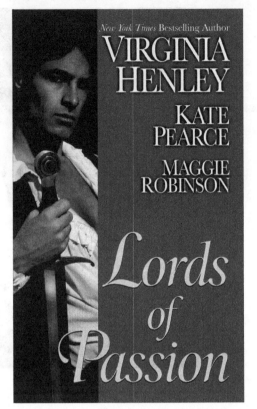

New York Times Bestselling Author
VIRGINIA HENLEY
KATE PEARCE
MAGGIE ROBINSON
Lords of Passion

"Beauty and the Brute" by Virginia Henley

It's been three years since Lady Sarah Caversham set eyes on arrogant Charles Lennox—the husband her father chose for her to settle a gambling debt. Now Charles has returned, unaware that the innocent ingénue he wed is determined to turn their marriage of convenience into a passionate affair...

"How to Seduce a Wife" by Kate Pearce

Louisa March's new husband, Nicholas, is a perfect gentleman in bed—much to her disappointment. She longs for the kind of fevered passion found in romance novels. But when she dares him to seduce her properly, she discovers Nicholas is more than ready to meet her challenge...

"Not Quite a Courtesan" by Maggie Robinson

Sensible bluestocking Prudence Thorn has been too busy keeping her cousin Sophy out of trouble to experience any adventures of her own. But when Sophy begs Prudence's help in saving her marriage, Pru encounters handsome, worldly Darius Shaw. Under Darius's skilled tutelage, Pru learns just how delightful a little scandal can be...

Printed in the United States
by Baker & Taylor Publisher Services